Mountain Peril

Also by Tom Eslick

Deadly Kin
Tracked in the Whites
Snowkill

Mountain Peril

A White Mountains Mystery

Tom Eslick

Viking

VIKING

Published by the Penguin Group

Penguin Group (USA) Inc., 375 Hudson Street, New York, New York 10014, U.S.A.
Penguin Group (Canada), 10 Alcorn Avenue, Toronto, Ontario, Canada M4V 3B2
(a division of Pearson Penguin Canada Inc.)
Penguin Books Ltd, 80 Strand, London WC2R 0RL, England
Penguin Ireland, 25 St. Stephen's Green, Dublin 2, Ireland (a division of Penguin Books Ltd)
Penguin Books Australia Ltd, 250 Camberwell Road, Camberwell, Victoria 3124, Australia
(a division of Pearson Australia Group Pty Ltd)
Penguin Books India Pvt Ltd, 11 Community Centre, Panchsheel Park,
New Delhi – 110 017, India
Penguin Group (NZ), Cnr Airborne and Rosedale Roads,
Albany, Auckland 1310, New Zealand (a division of Pearson New Zealand Ltd)
Penguin Books (South Africa) (Pty) Ltd, 24 Sturdee Avenue, Rosebank,
Johannesburg 2196, South Africa

Penguin Books Ltd, Registered Offices: 80 Strand, London WC2R 0RL, England

First published in 2005 by Viking Penguin, a member of Penguin Group (USA) Inc.

10   9   8   7   6   5   4   3   2   1

LIBRARY OF CONGRESS CATALOGING IN PUBLICATION DATA
Eslick, Tom.
Mountain peril: a White Mountains mystery / Tom Eslick.
      p.   cm.
ISBN 0-670-03386-3
      1. Search and rescue operations—Fiction. 2. White Mountains (N.H. and Me.)—
Fiction. 3. New Hampshire—Fiction.
PS3605.S57 M68 2005
813'.6—dc22   2004043133

This book is printed on acid-free paper.

Printed in the United States of America • Designed by Nancy Resnick

This book is dedicated to
all those involved with search and rescue,
for their caring, expertise, and service.

Acknowledgments

In doing research for this novel, I had the help of three individuals who deserve special mention: Rick Wilcox, of International Mountain Equipment, Rick Estes, retired New Hampshire Fish and Game officer, and Brooks Bicknell, fellow teacher and mountaineer. Without their aid with the details of mountain rescue, this book would not have come into being. While I have been careful in getting the facts straight, it is human nature to err; any mistakes are truly my own.

Thanks also to my editor, Lucia Watson, and my agent, Alison Picard. Their informed suggestions during the drafting process were invaluable and greatly appreciated.

Author's Note

While this is a work of fiction, it is set in a locale with actual names of mountains and trails, and for the most part, the reader should be able to follow along with a guidebook. The town of Saxton Mills, however, would be a little more difficult to find, except in the pages of this book.

Murder is uncommon in the White Mountains, but it does occur. In November of 2001, a woman named Louise Chaput, an experienced hiker from Sherbrooke, Quebec, was found stabbed to death at Pinkham Notch. This still-unsolved murder stirred the author's imagination, but the novel draws on no other association with that tragedy and is based on pure invention.

Mountain Peril

Prologue

I t was a little after three o'clock on a hot August afternoon when the woman descended from Slide Peak and took the Glen Boulder Trail back to Pinkham Notch. There hadn't been much of a view off Boot Spur because of a gauzy haze caused by high humidity.

Heading down the Glen Boulder Trail was relatively easy, and she made good time catching up to the Direttissima Trail, which runs parallel to the highway and directly to Pinkham. She kicked it into high gear over the rolling terrain when her attention was drawn to rustling at the side of the trail.

She heard a muffled scream. Then she saw him. He stepped out onto the trail holding a long knife, his shirt covered with blood. She gasped. His head snapped up.

They both looked at each other. Then he shot a glance back up trail. She knew what he was doing. He was checking to see if anyone was coming.

She bolted away and sprinted up a small rise, tripped on a root, and fell. She picked herself up and stumbled as she tried to get her legs moving. He was coming fast. She screamed. Surely someone would hear her. His footfalls pounded in her ears, the sound getting increasingly louder. Suddenly he tackled her and she crashed to the ground.

He sat on her and placed a hand over her mouth. She fought and kicked, brought a knee to his groin. His eyes popped. She heard him groan. She squirmed from underneath him and took off again. Her arm felt hot. She looked down and saw blood. He had sliced her.

She ran, one hand holding her injured arm, and looked for anything—a rock, a stick, something to hit him with—but the trail was clean. Then he was on her again. She sensed him at her heels and suddenly dropped and rolled. She clipped him at the knees and he catapulted over her. The knife flew out of his hand and landed near her on the trail.

He was momentarily stunned. She grabbed the knife. Her first impulse was to stab him, but he was already crawling toward her. She sailed the knife in a high arc off the side of the trail.

She heard him curse as he went to retrieve the knife. She rushed off again in the direction of Pinkham. All she had to do was outrun him. But she felt her strength ebbing.

She came to a bend in the trail and caught her breath. For a few moments, she felt she had outfoxed him, but then she picked up the faint, dull plod of his footfalls again. She wanted to run, but her legs wouldn't move. She spied some deadfall and broke off a branch. She pressed her back against a tree on the side of the trail, held the branch cocked, and waited.

The clumping steps grew louder. She wound up, swung, and caught him in the jaw as he passed the tree. The blow knocked him flat. She batted wildly at him again but missed. He rose slowly, shaking his head. She pulled the branch back to take another swing, but he came after her, slashing with the knife.

She dropped the branch and fended off his knife thrusts with her arms. Her skin was on fire. He was in close now. There was a faint yeast smell to his breath. She pummeled his chest with her fists.

Then she heard a dull thud and the air shot out of her lungs. She grabbed on to him to keep from falling and heard another terrible chunk, like the sound of ax to log. The blade ripped into her stomach. He gripped the hilt and jerked the blade harder. She slumped into him.

He pulled the knife out slowly and let her slide to the ground. He stood over her, breathing heavily. He had not counted on this. He quickly looked around to see if anyone was on the trail. Empty.

He stared down at her one last time. She had put up quite a fight. He admired that. But he didn't have time to deal with her. He had unfinished business.

Chapter 1

A nine-year-old boy had been missing for over four hours when Will Buchanan stopped to check his pack at the Direttissima trailhead at Pinkham Notch. He glanced up and caught his rookie partner, Toby Winston, staring at him. "What's the matter?"

Toby started. "Oh, I'm sorry, Mr. Buchanan. I was just looking at your pin."

Will self-consciously fingered the enamel pin he had fastened on a leather patch that hung from a lanyard he wore around his neck. It was circular, a gold compass rose with the heavy points of a Red Cross sticking out behind. In the center was the profile of the Old Man of the Mountain, and in the foreground, a raised hand holding an ice ax.

The pin identified Will as a member of an elite volunteer search and rescue team. "And I guess you want one of these," Will said.

"Yes, sir. That's what I'm working for."

Toby, a part-time carpenter from Colorado and the new kid on the block, was an inveterate backcountry skier and rescuer-in-training, reputed to be an expert in avalanche work.

Will hooked his thumbs through his pack straps. The wind suddenly picked up, the air heavy with moisture. "Looks like we're going to get some weather."

"Thunderstorms. Sometime this afternoon."

"Then I guess we better get going to find this kid. Ever been on this trail?"

"No, sir."

"Look, Toby. Before we get started, you have to stop calling me 'sir.' Call me 'Will.' "

Toby looked askance at Will, like he wasn't sure. "Okay."

"The Direttissima is kind of rolling." Will moved his arm, simulating a ripple effect. "And we don't start really climbing until we reach the Glen Boulder Trail."

"Gotcha."

Will chuckled, thinking of two other searchers who had drawn the task of circling the opposite way. "You should feel lucky you're not with Levesque and Hatcher," he said. "That Huntington Ravine Trail is a real ballbuster."

"I know. I've been on it."

At a shade over 6,200 feet, Mount Washington is the highest peak in the northeastern United States and boasts some of the worst weather in the world. Elevation and weather aside, Will understood that it was also the unique topography leading to the peaks of Washington and the rest of the Presidentials—the numerous ravines, technically called glacial cirques, at Huntington, Tuckerman, the Great Gulf—that also posed danger. And now that kid was most likely off trail somewhere, moon-eyed tired, scared shitless.

Will established a quick pace. His legs felt stiff, and as he set his rhythm he reviewed what Lieutenant Randall Cody, Fish and Game incident commander, had told them about the lost boy. Part of a church group. Last seen at Hermit Lake Shelter. Reported missing around nine o'clock. Maybe wearing Air Jordans. This last piece of information was most valuable, and before setting out Will had consulted "the book," a compendium of pictures of nothing but the soles of shoes.

As Will walked, his eyes shifted to the ground. The trail was littered with numerous fresh prints, but so far he hadn't picked up anything that looked like the tread he had committed to memory: wedges of small nubs spoked out in a pattern of circles.

They hiked for fifteen minutes when Will suddenly stopped. He placed his hands on his hips and looked up and around, like a bear scenting the air.

"What is it?" Toby asked.

"Nothing. This is where we found that murdered woman about a month ago."

"Oh."

"I won't get her out of my mind for a while."

"Someone stabbed her, right?"

"Several times." Will let out some air and let his head drop. "It must have been a terrible death. She had obviously been running from the guy who did it and put up a good fight. There were defensive wounds on her arms."

"You know it's a guy?"

"Or a very strong woman."

Will lifted his ball cap, took it off, and wiped his forehead with the back of his hand. He scanned the area again. "I just don't understand why the killer would pick a spot so out in the open, so near a trailhead. With the traffic this trail gets, it just doesn't make sense."

"So, they never found who did it?"

Will shook his head no. "And probably won't. There's just

not that much to go on." He slapped his cap against his leg and put it back on his head. "Let's get out of here. This place gives me the creeps."

They passed several day hikers on the trail, most of them probably making their way back to Pinkham after cavorting around Glen Ellis Falls. Will and Toby exchanged hellos as they passed without giving away any hint of their mission.

When they reached the junction of trails, Will called in their location to headquarters. According to Cody, the kid was still missing. Seven others of search and rescue had showed up, the team now totaling eighteen, and a pair were working in behind Will and Toby. Will signed off.

"What channel are you on?" Toby asked.

Will told him the number. "AMC has its own UHF frequency with 216 channels," he added. "They're all filled up."

Toby shook his head. "You know, that's something I'm still not sure about. You've got your AMC, your Fish and Game, your USFS. I mean, who's in charge?"

Will winked at him. "Ah, you're obviously not aware of the MOU."

Toby rolled his eyes. "All right. What's an MOU?"

"Memorandum Of Understanding. You're in acronym heaven around here. People like to think in shorthand."

"Obviously. So what is it?"

"An agreement that says Fish and Game is in charge of anything that happens in the woods except for the Cutler River Drainage—Tuckerman, Huntington, and Gulf of Slides—from December first to May first, when Snow Rangers from the USFS take over."

"I see."

"I know this because I memorized what I just told you,"

Will said. "It can be confusing, but the organizations generally get along."

"They need to."

"Good point."

Backcountry Search and Rescue represented the volunteer wing in the Whites. Dr. Thomas Singleton, head of a local school for wilderness medicine, had succeeded in organizing under one banner what had been several "vigilante" groups of rescuers that had sometimes squabbled over jurisdiction. Singleton had tapped Will for his tracking skills. "We need you and your savvy out there," Singleton had told him.

As they hiked up the Glen Boulder Trail, Will concentrated on the terrain. He kept his eye to the ground but stopped every now and again to check for logical places the kid might have gone off trail and entered the woods. They headed past a birch stand and into a grove of mixed hardwoods, mostly beech and rock maple.

The sky was an angry gray. Turbid clouds puffed and skirted over their heads. Will could taste the rain coming in.

For a long time neither said anything. Will glanced at his watch. Almost three o'clock. He figured they had at most three hours of light left.

About halfway between Glen Boulder and the Avalanche Brook ski trail Will and Toby took a break. They sat on rocks on the side of the trail and shared apples and a bag of gorp.

"Have you done your three nights on Washington yet?" Will asked.

"Nope. As soon as the snow flies. I've completed everything else, though."

To join Backcountry Search and Rescue, you had to not only spend three nights alone on Mount Washington in winter, but also run a mile and a half under twelve minutes and lift a percentage of your body weight according to age, as well as do so many push-ups per minute. Will had puffed through the mile and a half in eleven minutes and change.

"You should get your pin sometime next spring, then."

Toby suddenly turned serious. "I don't know what they're going to do, though."

"What do you mean?"

"Well, are they going to keep the Old Man's face on the pin now that he's gone?"

Will smiled. Toby was referring to the recent loss of the New Hampshire icon. The Old Man had literally lost face, the granite chin and nose tumbling to the talus floor. Folks around here talked about the event as if they had lost a relative. "That's what mountains do. They fall down."

"Yeah, but . . ."

"I don't think you have to worry. The pin is just a symbol, anyway."

"So was the Old Man."

Their conversation was suddenly interrupted by the footsteps of another hiker coming down trail. Will immediately recognized him as Elwood Reese. Cody had told Will he'd be heading down from the weather station.

Elwood was a spry sixty-something with bandy chicken legs that stuck out of his shorts. He wore a sweat-stained cowboy hat, the brim pulled down over his forehead, and he was poking the ground with a single ski pole. "Well, I thought I'd run into you fellas soon." He wrung Will's hand.

"How's the weather above tree line?" Will asked.

He winked. "Blowing like Monica." He pulled at his wind shirt. "A little moist, too."

Elwood was not an official member of search and rescue, but he had been involved with the AMC since Will could remember. He was one of those odd ducks who couldn't get enough of the mountain and knew the trails in his sleep. He spent most of his time now working as a sign cutter.

Will introduced Toby.

"Good to meet you, young fella."

Will motioned with his head toward the trail. "Probably doesn't make sense to go up farther."

"I don't know," Elwood said. "My eyesight's not so good. I might have missed the little bugger."

"I doubt it." Will called back headquarters and told Cody that he had met up with Elwood. He was informed that other searchers were sweeping where Elwood had been, making it unnecessary for Will and Toby to continue up ridge.

"You know," Will said, map in hand, to Cody on the radio, "I'm wondering if we should head back to Pinkham along the Avalanche Brook ski trail. If the boy came down this way, it's possible he might have thought it was the Glen Boulder Trail."

Cody agreed.

Will signed off. He had never been on the ski trail, but the map showed it running parallel to the Direttissima. The kid could very easily have gotten off course. Or maybe he saw them coming and took off down the ski trail to hide from them. It wasn't the first time Will had heard of such a thing, and, as Cody had mentioned earlier, the boy had been teased by a bully in the group before his disappearance. He might be hiding out for spite.

Will, Toby, and Elwood worked their way down the path and in another ten minutes reached where the ski trail crossed the Glen Boulder.

The ski trail was less defined, grown over with grass and stumps cut close to the ground. While Will wouldn't be able to easily pick up sole prints in this terrain, he could at least tell by the bent-over grass if someone had been down this way.

His spirits rose as he tracked, for the grass told him that there had been recent traffic. They trudged across a small ridge, then eventually came to an open area. Here it looked as if there had been some trail work, and not too long ago. The air smelled of fresh-cut spruce and the ground was muddied up.

"Wait a minute," Elwood said. "I need a break." He sat down on a log, his hands resting on his knees.

Will knelt and examined a boot print. Lug sole.

"I'm getting too old for this shit," Elwood said, wiping his forehead with a paisley blue handkerchief.

Will turned his head, still kneeling. "You okay?" he asked. "You're not going to crap out on me, are you?"

Elwood exhaled loudly. He shook his head no. "I'm too ornery."

"What happens when it gets dark?" Toby asked.

"What do you mean, what happens?" Will said.

"Well, do we keep looking?"

Will stood. "Wouldn't do much good. Cody'll probably work with the dogs. I can guarantee you he's already planning day two."

Toby looked down at his shoes, then back at Will. "What happens if they don't have anything—you know, any clothing—with the kid's scent?"

Elwood jumped in. "Oh, these dogs don't discriminate. You just run them up trail and station them at the head of ravines. Ravines are like chimneys, you see. The air blows right up them. These dogs just pick up human scent."

"And if they don't smell anything," Will added, "then tomorrow we'll probably be in those ravines poking around. That's usually the course of things, a quick search of the trails, then the ravines, then a line search—you know, you've seen it on TV. Whole bunch of searchers moving in a line, GPS at both ends."

"Doesn't sound like fun," Toby said.

Just then the two-way squelched. Will keyed the mike and copied. Cody's voice announced that the kid had been found.

State police had picked up the boy hitching on Route 16 heading south. He had come down from the shelter right behind the group, hid in the bathroom of the main lodge all morning, got scared when he realized the commotion was about him, and tried to make it all disappear by running away.

"Thanks, Cody. We're coming in."

"Son of a bitch," Elwood said. "That kid's in deep shit."

"Well, at least he isn't deep-shit dead," Toby said.

Will didn't say anything. He just stared at the radio. He was pleased that the kid had been found, but the sense of anticlimax left him deflated. Toby was right, though: At least the kid wasn't dead.

The wind gusted hard and the trees whooshed above their heads. In the distance, the rumble of thunder.

"Looks like it's time to move," Will said. He checked the dotted line on the map where the ski trail angled down and almost touched the Direttissima before emptying out at the base lodge. He did a quick guesstimate using the first joint of his little finger as a measuring device against the scale, then walked it along the dotted line. "We'll be out of here in about an hour," he said.

Will let Elwood set the pace along the ski trail, and he and Toby followed behind. As Will walked, he reviewed what had just happened. The day actually hadn't turned out too bad. He'd be home before supper, and afterward perhaps he'd stop in and see what Laurie was up to.

They weren't living together now. A consensual hiatus. The time-out didn't mean they were to avoid each other, though. In fact, the sex was terrific since they had decided to live separately, something Will scratched his head about.

Then he thought about school and the labs he had planned to set up before the rescue call had interrupted his schedule. It was the third Saturday in September, three weeks into the fall term. The labs would just have to wait until tomorrow.

They had been hiking for less than a half hour. The wind was blowing steadily now. Lightning flashed behind them. With luck, they just might make it back before the storm really let loose.

A strong gust pushed at Will's back, and his eye picked up something red fluttering off trail. He stopped. Elwood and Toby kept walking. Will scanned the edge of the woods beyond a small meadow. The wind howled and the red flashed again. It stood out in sharp relief against the green and brown foliage.

Up ahead Toby stopped, turned, and yelled, "What's wrong?"

"Just wait up a minute!" Will stepped off trail and into dense ground cover. As he approached, he could see a piece of red fabric that had caught on a tree. A few more strides and he was standing eye-level with what he reasoned might be a piece of shirt. As he reached for it, his foot knocked against something that he first thought was a stick.

He looked down casually, then drew back. Had he seen right? He stooped and carefully pulled aside some brush.

It was a human hand, the flesh partially decomposed, attached to a severed arm, still wrapped in the shredded sleeve of a red shirt.

Chapter 2

Will backed away. This was a crime scene now, and Will knew enough not to disturb the area.

Suddenly there was sharp crack of lightning. It struck something nearby. On its heels, a concussive wave of thunder.

Then the heavens opened and the rain pelted Will as he made it back to the trail again. He sought momentary shelter under a large maple near the trail edge, dropped his pack, pulled out his rain gear, and threw it on.

Toby and Elwood waited up ahead. He shouted at them and waved them back, and they huddled under the maple. Will told them what he had found.

Elwood scratched the stubble on his chin. "Well, you don't say so."

Toby was silent.

One thing Will had gathered so far about Toby was that he seemed slow to process information. The discovery of the severed arm had obviously stunned him into silence.

Will radioed in.

"All three of you stay where you are and don't disturb anything," Cody responded. "I'll get in touch with the Major Crime Unit right away."

Will copied and signed off.

Toby suddenly came to life. "Shit. I guess we won't get out of here for a while."

Elwood shouted back at him through the roaring wind. "You got a big date or something?"

"Yes!"

Elwood smiled. "What's her name?"

"Sarah Ann."

"Two names, eh?" Elwood yelled. "She must be from down South."

"What?"

"She a Southern girl?"

"New Jersey."

Elwood snorted. "That's south of here. What's she look like?"

Will suspected their loud banter was due to frayed nerves and served to take their minds off what Will had found. While Toby raved on about his girlfriend's beauty, Will paid little attention. He watched the water drip off the bill of his cap and thought about the severed arm.

The wind suddenly ripped through the branches above their heads, and a limb snapped. It crashed down and just missed Toby.

"Shit. What the . . ."

Will grabbed Toby's arm and led him into the meadow. He took out an Ensolite pad from his pack and told the others to do the same. Elwood didn't have one, so Will used his knife to cut his pad in half. He handed the piece to Elwood.

Lightning flashed again. The storm closed in. They were exposed in this open meadow, but they couldn't chance another limb falling.

"Spread out," Will yelled. "Do what I do."

Using the pad as an insulator, he squatted, with only his toes touching the Ensolite. The theory was that if lightning struck the ground, only a small part of his body would act as a potential conductor.

Toby and Elwood followed suit.

Will had heard of people sitting upright, hugging their knees when lightning hit close by and getting killed when a bolt sent current up the feet, through the legs, arms, and chest, and out the butt. A perfect circuit.

The storm rose in intensity and the winds hit gale force. Will leaned into the wind on his toes and struggled to keep his balance. He worried about Elwood. There wasn't much to him, and he might just sail off like Dorothy.

It took at least fifteen minutes for the storm to pass over. Will figured the worst was finished, so they all moved back to the trail again and inspected the damaged maple. "That was close," he said. "You guys okay?"

"I've been better," Elwood said.

Toby gave a weak nod of the head.

Finally the wind dropped enough so they could speak without shouting. Will pulled out energy bars from his pack and offered one each to Toby and Elwood.

"My teeth can't handle those things," Elwood said. "I got a Hershey's somewhere. I can usually manage to gum it to death."

"I don't know how you guys can think of eating at a time like this," Toby said.

Will studied him for a moment. "You should get something in your stomach, too. Keep your blood sugar up."

"What did it look like?"

"You mean what I found?"

"Yeah. The hand."

Will described it. "Once the cops get here, you can have a look for yourself."

Toby stood in the middle of the ski trail, staring blankly at the ground. "I'm not sure I want to."

Will chewed, then took another bite of his energy bar. "I can understand that. But if you want to do rescue work, you've got to get used to seeing some pretty bad shit. You might want to watch and learn when the Staties get here."

Toby didn't respond at first. He squatted on his haunches, pulled out pieces of wet grass, and flung them into the wind. Then he looked up. "I'll take that energy bar now, if you have one."

An hour passed. Then two. Elwood had curled up against a tree, arms folded, and was snoring like a bull moose. Toby paced back and forth on the ski trail, now and then picking up rocks and chucking them in order to pass the time. Will reached into his pack and found his headlamp. He reversed the bill of his cap and strapped on the light but didn't turn it on.

The rain was intermittent now, but the storm was still all around them, the air electrically charged with a trace smell of ozone.

Will called Cody on the radio again for status and was told through the crackle that the Major Crime Unit van had just pulled in to the parking lot. In a few minutes, they'd be leaving the base station to head on their way up the ski trail. Will woke Elwood. "Cops! Better look sharp."

Elwood snapped awake.

It took another half hour, though, before they heard the whine of a small engine.

"Sounds like an ATV," Toby said.

Elwood stuck his cowboy hat back on his head. "Well, it sure as hell isn't a snowmobile."

The engine noise got louder and the headlight of a fat-tire all-terrain vehicle danced up over a small rise. Will switched on his lamp to indicate their location. The driver stopped and momentarily idled the machine, then gunned it and raced up trail.

The ATV, pulling an equipment trailer, came to a stop a few yards in front of them. A man wearing a ball cap with a state police insignia cut the engine and got off his machine. "Which one of you is Will Buchanan?" he asked.

Will stepped forward.

"I'm Sergeant Art Macomber." They shook hands. "I'll be in charge of this investigation. My team's right behind on foot."

Macomber wore slick black rain gear. His face was sharply defined with a striking aquiline nose.

Will introduced the others, turned, and caught Macomber staring at him.

"So, apparently you found more than you were looking for," Macomber said.

"You're right there," Will said.

Macomber placed his hands on his hips and faced Elwood and Toby. "You two stay here for now." He handed Will latex gloves. "Let's see what you've got."

After they both gloved up, Macomber grabbed a roll of yellow crime scene tape and a large D-cell Maglite from a pack on his trailer. Then they headed back to the severed arm. On the way, Will related the story of how the dancing red cloth had caught his eye.

As they got closer, Macomber slowed the pace, taking his time to check with his flashlight for anything that might be in

front of the find. Will knew that he would eventually be looking to establish a perimeter.

It was almost completely dark now, but Will's sense memory
was so strong he had little trouble locating the hand sticking up
out of the brush. A bony finger pointed to the sky as if there
were some sort of answer up there. Macomber carefully parted
the heavy, wet saw grass.

Will waited as Macomber considered.

Macomber finally stood and glanced around the area but still
said nothing.

"What do you think?" Will asked, finally.

"I think if we take a look around, we might find the rest of
the body. My guess is that there's a shallow grave somewhere
some animal got into."

Will stared blankly. He had thought the same, but hearing it
from Macomber made something hard drop in his stomach.

Macomber took a few steps to his left. "I'll start over here."
He motioned in the direction of the piece of red shirt caught
on the branch. "You take it from the right. And be careful
where you step."

Will moved in, mindful of his foot placement, his headlamp
aimed at the ground. The terrain dropped slowly downhill, and
he utilized a sharp zigzag approach. He kept Macomber's flashlight in sight.

Will didn't smell anything, which meant that if there was a
body nearby, decomposition had pretty much run its course. He
wasn't sure if it made him feel better knowing this or not, but
by the looks of the condition of the hand and the arm, the flesh
deteriorated but partially visible, the body had been out for a
month or so.

Will could feel his heart tick faster as he realized the timing coincided with the girl found stabbed on the Direttissima Trail. The areas were certainly contiguous, and from what he could surmise about the hand, it was eerily delicate, definitely female.

Walking slowly, eyes to the ground, Will soon ran in to a place that looked disturbed. Dead leaves had been mashed flat and branches on the forest floor had snapped, as if someone or something weighty had stepped on them.

He could feel sweat on his palms and tasted acidic honey in the back of his throat from the energy bar.

Then he saw it. The one-armed body lay partially exposed in mud, a hank of hair about a skull with a partial fleshy nose, the toothy mouth open as if about to speak.

Will had trouble finding his voice. Macomber had been right about the shallow grave. The body had been dug up and violently scattered about. He didn't know how much time had passed before he was able to finally shout Macomber's name.

Will held his position as he listened to Macomber's approaching footfalls. Then he heard them stop. "Over here," he yelled, moving his head up and down.

Macomber got a read on his lamp and was soon standing next to him. He aimed his flashlight at the ground. "Holy shit," he said under his breath.

Will and Macomber shared another moment of silence. For Will, it wasn't out of respect for the dead, but out of shock. It was as if death's grin were taunting them, saying, you are all nothing but sinew and bone.

Macomber broke the silence. "Did you touch anything?"

Will kept staring. "No."

"Think it was a bear?"

"Something big got at it. I don't think it was human."

Macomber sighed. "Well, whatever it was, it must not have liked it too much."

"What's that?"

"Well, it spit it out."

Will was momentarily taken aback by Macomber's gallows humor, but he immediately figured it was his way of facing the unthinkable. Will gestured at the yellow tape in his hand. "Want to start stringing?"

Macomber shook his head. "You don't have to do that. I'm sure my team is here by now. Let them do the work."

Will swallowed hard. He still tasted honey in the back of his throat. "I don't mind keeping busy."

"You've done enough already." Macomber placed a hand on his shoulder. "What say you and I go back to the trail and chat some more about this."

Macomber tied yellow tape to a tree close to the body, then strung it along behind him as they headed back out of the wooded area. He attached the other end to some deadfall close to the ground near the severed arm, effectively creating a direct yellow line between the two artifacts. He flagged a tree so that the location could be seen from the trail.

When they arrived back at the ski trail, Macomber interviewed Elwood and Toby for a few minutes, then told them they could go. They both left quickly, Toby apparently more interested in his date than dead bodies.

Will stood on the side of the trail leaning against a tree and watched as the Major Crime Unit went into action. He took off his ball cap. With the passing of the storm, the temperature had dropped considerably, but the cap had sweated through.

It was near dusk now, and Will reached for his pack and put

on another layer underneath his rain gear. He could hear a generator fire up, then the growl of the small engine as work lights snapped on. Shadows played against the dense foliage like a *danse macabre.*

Macomber came over to where he was sitting. "You doing okay?"

Will nodded. "What do you want to know?"

"I just need a narrative of what happened. Everything you can think of, the more detail the better." Macomber tested the mini tape recorder, then let it roll.

Will spun his story, running over what he could recall of the day.

Macomber interrupted. "So, you were actually the one who suggested going down the ski trail."

"That's right. It made sense to me, especially since other searchers were coming up from where we had just been."

"And you were the only one to see the red piece fluttering?"

"Yes. They were ahead of me."

"And they didn't go in with you to check it out."

"That's right."

"So, they never saw the severed arm."

Will didn't answer at first. He wasn't sure he cared for this line of questioning. "That's right, too. Why?"

"Why what?"

"You're thinking I had something to do with this?"

Macomber waved his hand as if he were brushing away a pesky insect. "Of course not. I'm just trying to double-check to make sure I understand the story right."

"Well, that's the way it happened."

"Will, look." Macomber pushed his cap back on his head. "I think you're taking this the wrong way. I merely asked if Toby and Elwood saw the arm to rule out any other disturbance in the area."

Will stared at Macomber a moment, then dropped his head. "Sorry. I guess I'm a little edgy."

"Understandably. And if you had anything to do with it, then why would you have pointed it out to us?"

"Yeah, why would I? I get it. I said I was sorry."

Macomber clicked off the tape recorder.

Will lifted his head. "That mean we're finished?"

"We are, but I think you should stick around until the ME gets here. She might have a few questions for you."

"Amy Liu?"

"You know her?"

"Unfortunately, yes. I met her at that Zealand Falls incident two years ago."

"Sure. I wasn't here then, but I've heard about it." Macomber pulled the brim of his cap down tighter on his head and pocketed the mini tape recorder. "I'm going to be joining my team now," he said. He reached out his hand.

Will stood and shook it.

"I want you to know," Macomber said, "it's been an honor to work with you. Everything I heard about you is true."

Will cocked his head. "What have you heard about me?"

"Oh, I think you know. You fill in the blanks."

It was completely dark by the time ME Amy Liu showed up on another ATV, driven by Lieutenant Cody. The rain had slowed to a trickle.

In the lights of the ATV, Will could see that Liu wore patterned slacks underneath a trench coat.

Will watched as both approached. Cody stood at least a foot taller than the diminutive Amy Liu.

"Well, Mr. Buchanan," she said, shaking his hand, "you seem to have a knack for this sort of thing." She squeezed hard, a grip that belied her stature.

Will supposed she meant finding bodies. "Yes, I guess so."

"You must be tired, my friend," Cody said.

"Not any more than you. That kid okay?"

Cody nodded agreement. "His backside might be a little sore."

Liu glanced at the lighted-up activity happening off trail at the crime scene. "Who's in charge?"

"Macomber," Will said.

"And he's already interviewed you?"

"Yes."

"Well, he certainly knows what he's doing. I don't see any reason why you have to stick around."

"Really?"

"If I have any questions, I know where to find you."

She left them to put on a pair of dark blue coveralls she had stowed in the ATV. She took out her kit, gloved up, put on a pair of safety glasses, and headed toward the crime scene.

Will watched her. "You think she could have radioed in that I could leave with the others."

"Maybe she just didn't think of it. She didn't even know who was in charge."

"Guess you're right."

"Come on," Cody said. "I'll give you a lift back."

Will didn't say anything for a few moments. "I don't know, Lieutenant. What the hell is going on in our woods?"

Chapter 3

I t was nearly ten o'clock by the time Will got back to his
truck. He was surprised to see his girlfriend, Saxton Mills police chief Laurie Eberly, waiting for him, her arms folded,
leaning against the driver's-side door.

"Hello, you," she said, and embraced him.

He held her a long time, running his hand up and down her
back, feeling her smooth fleece jacket warm on his fingers. He
whispered in her ear, "I guess you heard."

"It was all over the scanner. Cody told me everything. You
must be tired."

"Hungry."

"Follow me home. I'll feed you."

Inside her two-bedroom apartment, she handed Will a beer.
The bottle hissed at him as he unscrewed the cap. He was about
to sit on the sofa when he remembered how dirty he was.

"Maybe I should take a shower first."

She waved her hand dismissively. "The couch has a throw on
it. I can always wash it."

He shrugged, brushed the back of his muddy pants, and sat down. He ran the cool bottle over his forehead. That was another difference Will couldn't understand. When they shared a house she was always at him to wipe his feet and pick up after himself. Now it didn't seem to matter a hoot.

She yelled from the kitchen. "A sandwich okay? Ham and Swiss?"

"Sounds wonderful."

"I could grill it if you want."

"No. Don't bother."

"It's no bother, really."

"No. Please."

She delivered his sandwich and positioned a hassock in front of him, kicking it into position. She sat on it holding a beer, her arms resting on her knees.

"You're not having anything?"

She looked at the bottle in her hand and lifted it. "This."

"You just going to sit there and watch me eat?"

"I like to watch you eat."

"No, you don't. You want to ask me questions. You want to interrogate me."

"Oh, stop it. I just want to know what happened, that's all."

"Not until I finish my sandwich."

She smiled at him. "Fair enough." She took a sip of her beer. "I do like to watch you eat, though."

Will bit into his sandwich and chewed vigorously. "Like this?"

"Well, not quite like that."

He watched her watch him. He liked the way her new jeans fit, the way her hips flared from where he sat across from her.

Every once in a while, she hooked her dark hair over her ears. He liked the way she did that, too. He finished his sandwich and wiped his mouth with a napkin. "What do I get if I tell you what happened?" He wagged his eyebrows, Groucho Marx style.

"A cookie? I just baked some Toll House."

"Hmm. I'll need something else."

"Vanilla ice cream."

"Deal."

She put on some coffee as well. Having filled his stomach and downed his beer, he settled back on the couch. This apartment certainly was an improvement over her previous one at Marchesi Meadows. At least here she had a separate entrance, and he liked the idea that the front window looked out into the woods. He sipped coffee and told his story.

When he had finished, Laurie suddenly let her head drop to her hands. Her body shook as she cried silently for a few seconds, then began to sob.

Will could tell by the look on her face as he was describing events that she was getting increasingly troubled, but he hadn't expected this reaction. He rose from his chair and went to her side. "It's okay." He put his arm across her back. "Shh."

She began rocking, then suddenly got up. "I'm sorry. I didn't mean to do this." With her fingertips she wiped at tears that streaked her face. She folded her arms and turned away from him. "I'm not like this," she said to the window. "You know I'm not like this, at all."

"It's all right, Laurie." He moved toward her and touched her shoulder.

She turned slowly around back into his arms. "Stay with me tonight."

"Of course." He held her, gently rocking.

She pushed him away. "You *do* need a shower first, though."

By the time Will got out of the shower, Laurie was already in bed. He slid under the covers. Not sure of her mood, he still wore his boxers.

Will reached over and touched her. She had nothing on.

"I want you to take your time," she whispered.

"I'll try. But it's been over a week. I might get too excited."

"Always thinking of yourself."

He parted the covers and ran his finger down her stomach.

"You smell like me," she said.

"What?"

"The lavender soap. You smell like me."

"That's all there was in the shower."

"Sorry."

"I'm your alter ego." He kissed her belly. "Just getting in touch with my feminine side."

She shivered, then suddenly grabbed him by the hair. "Come on."

"I thought I was taking my time."

"I was just kidding." She pushed him back on the bed. She was breathing heavily. "What's with the shorts?"

"Just take them off."

She shimmied them down to his ankles and mounted him.

Will kicked off his shorts in a frenzied motion, grabbed on to her hips, and, with her guidance, easily entered.

"My, you are ready, aren't you," she said.

He was surprised at the eager force and rapidity of her thrusts. It was almost as if she was angry with him and using her body as a weapon. It was over for both of them in less than a minute.

Laurie rolled off him and lay on her back. "I'm sorry. I don't know what got into me."

"Are you kidding? That was great."

"Will, hold me. Don't go this time."

"Okay." The recently set rules of engagement usually called for one to leave after sex, depending on whose house. Staying the night was not allowed.

She lay in the crook of his arm. Will dropped off into a sound sleep and woke about three o'clock to Laurie playing with the hairs on his chest.

"You awake?" she asked.

"I am now."

"Don't you think it's funny that we use separate soaps? I mean, even that we can't agree on."

"I don't think it's odd. Lavender isn't your typical manly soap."

"I know that, but I should be able to compromise. You know, choose something more neutral."

"Like what?"

"I don't know. Oatmeal?"

"Oatmeal?"

"Yes. Wouldn't that be better?"

"Oh, sure. I love smelling like a breakfast cereal."

"You're impossible."

"Apparently." Will rolled over, crooked his elbow, and rested his head on his hand. "Why are you awake?"

"I couldn't stop thinking about the body, who she is."

"Was. You're not going to get upset again, are you?"

"No, I'm over that. Now I'm just pissed off."

"Uh oh."

"What?"

"It's just that when you get mad, you usually do something that gets you in trouble."

Laurie had no response.

Will thought he understood Laurie's emotional reaction to the news of the body, the way she broke down earlier sitting on the hassock. She was an evangelist when it came to her work, and the thought of someone out there killing young women in *her* woods was a sharp slap in the face.

Laurie said, "And you think there might be a connection between this murder and the one last month?"

"Well, don't you? Almost the same location. Probably about the same time."

"What does Macomber think?"

"I don't know. We never talked about it."

"Why not?"

Will let out some air. "Laurie, for God's sake. We found the body less than twelve hours ago. We were a little too preoccupied for theories."

"There's probably no way to tell if they're connected or not."

"It's the woods, Laurie. It's been over a month."

"Take me there."

"What?"

"Tomorrow. It's Sunday and I'm off duty all weekend. You're not doing anything, are you?"

Will groaned. He thought of the lab planning that still needed to be done. "Oh, no. I have no life."

"Come on. You know you want to go with me." She poked him in the shoulder.

He hated when she did that. He didn't respond.

"I'll give you another cookie."

Will suddenly recalled the map and how close the Direttissima was to the ski trail. He had to admit he was curious about what he might find in the wilderness between the two trails. He knew the exact spot the first body was found, and he could easily look at notes of yesterday's coordinates when he reported in the location of the severed arm. Connect the dots. See what he could come up with.

"Two cookies," she said.

"Deal. Now go to sleep." Will closed his eyes. The room was silent for a while. He almost drifted off.

"Will?"

"What is it now!"

"I think I'm finally ready for you to take your time."

Will hesitated.

"I promise not to rush."

Will took his time.

Will and Laurie were back at Pinkham Notch by nine o'clock the next morning. The sky was overcast with the threat of more rain. They had packed away a big breakfast at a local diner and were ready to search.

Before they got going, Laurie very much wanted to contact Macomber out of professional courtesy. It was his baby, after all. She thought she might have to make a few calls to track him down, but they found him upstairs in the Trading Post, the center for AMC recreational and educational activities.

"You want to do what?" Macomber said.

Will explained his belief that the two murders were connected.

"Yes, we've considered that." Macomber drummed his pencil on the desk. "And if they are," he mused, "our perimeter should certainly be wider than it is now."

"Exactly," Laurie said. "I don't know if we'll find anything, but I'm thinking the area between the trails at least needs a quick going over."

Macomber thought a moment.

"Have they moved the body yet?" Will asked.

"Yes. One officer is still on scene, though. I'll let him know you'll be in the area."

"So, we have your permission."

Macomber rubbed his face with both hands. The effort left him blinking at Will and Laurie. "I was just sitting here thinking of what to do next, so your timing is impeccable."

"You want to come along?" Will asked.

"No. If it were anyone but you two, it would be different. I need to catch some z's. Let me know immediately if you find something."

In the parking lot, Will pulled a pair of gaiters out of the utility chest on the truck bed. If he was going to bushwhack, especially through wet, cloying berry bushes, he wanted protection.

Laurie put on her own gaiters and checked her pack for latex gloves and evidence bags.

It took them less than a half hour to reach the spot on the Direttissima Trail where the first body had been found the previous month.

"Okay," Will said. "Here's my thinking on this. I'm going to let it fly, so just listen and try not to interrupt."

"You might be asking too much."

He pointed to the ground. "From the defensive wounds on

this woman's arms, it's obvious she put up a fight, which means she was most likely in flight from the guy. He caught up to her and killed her here. The question is how long had she been running, and where was she coming from? The perp wouldn't have killed her on this spot unless he was desperate. It's just too open and heavily traveled." Will paused.

"Can I say something now?"

"No. I need to spew this out."

"Go."

"You see, I don't think this guy planned to kill this woman. I think he had to do it. And now I'm more convinced than ever because of the second body. I'm guessing that if we ever find out the identity, then we'll discover a connection between the two." Will stopped talking.

"That it?"

"Yeah. I think so."

"First, I think we should stop referring to her as 'this woman.' Her name was Jeanne Conroy."

"Sorry. I didn't know."

"When you say the 'second body,' you're referring to the second one found, right?"

"That's right."

"So assuming these murders both happened at about the same time, was Jeanne Conroy"—Laurie glanced at the ground—"killed second or first?"

"Second."

"Why?"

"Because she was running away from the guy. She might have seen something she wasn't supposed to."

Laurie turned and looked into the woods. "Just playing devil's advocate here, but why couldn't it be the other way around? How do we know the other woman wasn't the one running away?"

"We don't." Will paused. "But it's silly to be thinking like this, anyway. What difference does it make who was killed first? The important point is that there's probably a story somewhere that connects the two, and we have to find it."

Laurie smiled. "We, Mr. Policeman?"

"That's what you asked for, isn't it? My help?"

"So, what's your plan?"

Will pulled out a compass. "I've already set this up." He handed it to her. "You remember how to use it?"

She sent Will an exasperated look as if she couldn't believe the question, but she played along. "Magnetic arrow inside the housing arrow. Follow the direction-of-travel arrow."

"That's right. Just put the dog in the doghouse, and it should take you directly to where the body was found yesterday."

"I get it already." She adjusted her pack. "You're going with me, right?"

"Obliquely. If Jeanne Conroy was on the ski trail and witnessed the killing, and the perp chased her through the woods, then I think it's worth scouting the Dirittissima to see if I can spot anything that might indicate where she came out. I'll enter the woods from there, and I'll meet up with you at the crime scene tape."

Laurie didn't particularly like the idea of splitting up, but she went into the woods, following the compass course.

Will walked slowly down the Direttissima Trail. He kept his eyes peeled for any anomalies that might strike him. He had no idea what they might be, but he had learned long ago to rely on his hunches. There was a highly developed atavistic part of his brain, he was convinced, that went beyond reason, some place a tiny bell dinged when seemingly random events in the universe collided. There were no coincidences. These bodies had to be linked. Jeanne Conroy was killed second, despite Laurie's challenge. He just knew it.

Will stopped about thirty yards down the trail. He looked into the deep woods and could see nothing abnormal. He walked ten more yards and stopped again. He closed his eyes and tried to imagine the woman running, terrified.

Convinced there would be nothing to signal where Jeanne Conroy had come out onto the Direttissima Trail, Will got his bearings with the GPS, set his compass, and took off into the woods, heading up an incline in the direction of the crime tape. He fought his way past thick raspberry bushes growing close to the trail.

He decided on a wide sweeping pattern. Moving in this manner would take him longer to meet up with Laurie, but he didn't want to have to come back in here if he could help it.

He felt a raindrop and soon heard the pudding of light rain on the leaves above his head.

As he walked, his eyes locked in to the terrain, scanning methodically across the ground cover. Even if he found nothing on the bushwhack, he could at least establish a good sense of the distance between the two trails.

He began to muse on the possibility that both women had been on the Direttissima to begin with. In that case, the guy would have had to haul Ski Trail Woman up through the woods after having killed both women—a hard thing to do, but not impossible, especially if the perp was in shape. Will's dinging bell told him the guy was not only well conditioned, but also familiar with these woods.

Will's head spun with ideas. He admonished himself to keep his mind free of speculation. It was just too distracting. He focused on the job in front of him.

By his watch, Will had been searching for over an hour. He had made his way up through a spruce grove, and the terrain started to flatten a bit. He reasoned he was getting close to the ski trail.

Then he saw what at first he thought was the hind end of a whitetail deer. He froze. There was no movement.

Will studied the area before taking another step. He approached closer, moving slowly, and discovered a white hat. It was a floppy one, an Annie Hall hat, and it was blotched with brown stains. Blood?

The hat was on the ground in front of a large poplar. Will quickly scanned the woods and set a perimeter in his head. If the person who owned the hat was walking or, especially, running, there might be broken branches about the height of the person's head. Will's gaze drifted upward in the direction of the ski trail. And if the person had been running, it was most likely downhill. You could pretty much bet the farm on it. Was there more blood somewhere else?

Will pulled out his GPS and recorded the location. He and Laurie had come into the woods without radios, so he would have to find her and come back to the site. She had the evidence bags.

Armed with the coordinates, he set out on a compass course toward the crime scene tape to meet up with Laurie.

. . .

It was Laurie's decision to go back to Pinkham and report what Will had found rather than returning to pick up the hat herself. Will wondered why she had even bothered to bring the evidence bags into the field, but she no doubt had reconsidered, once out there, in deference to Macomber's being lead in the investigation. The last thing she wanted was to appear to be grandstanding. She needed Macomber. Will sensed that her involvement in this case—and by association, his—was just beginning.

It was after one o'clock in the afternoon, and back at the base camp Laurie phoned Macomber and woke him up with the news. He thanked her and passed his regards on to Will for his efforts.

When she hung up the phone, Will said, "Lunch?"

Laurie hesitated. "I'm not hungry. I think I'll stay here and go back in with the guys Macomber's sending."

"Don't start obsessing, Laurie."

"I'm not. I have a responsibility."

Will was about to say something but thought better of it. He had learned long ago not to try to reason with Laurie. The state police had this well under control, and as a small-town chief of police her "responsibility" wasn't all that great, but that didn't mean too much when Laurie got personally involved with a case.

"You go on, Will. I know you have things to do. I'll catch a ride back home."

It was the dismissive tone in her voice that always set him on edge, and he had heard it so often lately that he had come to recognize it as the signal that he was to go away. Now. She was finished with him.

He hated when it happened, and it always made him grumpy.

Her emotional swings came on without warning and were the root cause of their not being able to share the same roof. At least that was his side of the story. "Fine. I'll see you later."

"You're not mad, are you?"

"Of course not." He turned to leave, but Laurie grabbed his arm.

"I'm doing it again, aren't I."

"Yes," Will said. "But at least you're beginning to realize when you do it."

In the parking lot, he threw his pack on the front seat of his truck and slammed the driver's-side door. He took off out of the lot. The rain had stopped, but it was still muggy and in the mid-seventies; he rode with his arm out the window as he headed back to Saxton Mills.

He tried to get Laurie out of his mind as he drove, but he couldn't stop thinking how good it was last night and how abandoned he was feeling now. Maybe it really was time to leave her. Maybe it was like when he gave up smoking. Cold turkey. None of this in-between stuff.

He wondered vaguely what would happen if he announced to her it was over and took up with another woman. That would send the sparks flying. But who would that be? He ran through a list of local prospects, but none stood out as appealing. Maybe he could ask out the new math teacher, a recent divorcée who had been giving him the eye. He just hated feeling like a wimp and an idiot for letting Laurie manipulate their relationship. Perhaps counseling would help. But then they'd probably argue over the counselor's being male or female. Ah, fuck it!

Will returned to the house he had built back in rosier times, when he had imagined himself and Laurie settling down to a bucolic life in the country. It was a simple Cape. There was no white picket fence, but Will had once thought they would get married and have kids. Now that he was fifty-two, it all seemed rather silly to him. He began to look at the house simply as a wise investment and often congratulated himself that finally he was building equity.

That afternoon, he had plenty of time to head over to school and set up his lab, but he was so enervated he couldn't seem to get out of his overstuffed chair. He started doing shots of Laphroaig at about four o'clock. By eleven o'clock he was pissed. All he had for supper was half a bag of stale Cheetos.

He slept in his chair that evening, vaguely aware that the local TV news had something about the body being discovered.

Will decided for his classes the next day he would honor the time-tested tradition of all teachers. He would wing it.

Chapter 4

Usually Will hit his stride a few weeks into the fall term, but he stumbled through the next week, always a little behind and never seeming to catch up. When he took on the commitment of search and rescue, he knew the time involved would be a challenge to his normal schedule, but he hadn't counted on the emotional toll. The classes he gave were lackluster, and he hadn't enjoyed them because he knew he wasn't giving enough.

By Wednesday he had heard no word from Laurie, and he refused to call her. The way he had left her at Pinkham, he figured it was her place to get in touch with him. As the weekend approached, he finally began to settle into his routine and thought only occasionally about the body in the woods. Thankfully, there were no other search and rescue calls.

He looked forward to Saturday to catch up on work he had let slide on the school's woodlot. It was part of his job to make sure the wood-fired furnaces in five dorms on campus were kept supplied, and he still had another seven cords to cut before the snow flew. He would start early Saturday morning, turn off his pager, and forget the world. On search and rescue you were always on call, so it was always your choice whether to respond—no pressure there.

After Will's first class on Friday, he checked the messages on his office phone and found one from Laurie: "Call me right away."

He immediately punched in the speed dial for the police station. Her deputy, Ray, answered and put her on.

"I think we may have caught a break."

"What's that?"

"Well, that hat you found? It had a label in it. It came from a small shop in Springvale, Connecticut."

"And?"

"Macomber had me call Springvale police, and there's been a missing person out on a young woman who fits the description of the body you found. Same age, height, and hair color."

"What about the stains on the hat?"

"Probably blood. They're backed up at the lab and haven't completed the testing."

"So, you don't know yet if the hat belongs to that woman or not."

There was a pause on the other end of the line. "No, but we're pretty confident it does. We'll know for sure when the DNA results come in."

Will pressed. "The hat could belong to anybody then. What makes you so sure it's hers?"

"Because she has a connection with the Whites. It was a few years back, but she used to come up here a lot to rock climb when she was younger. Apparently she lived up here for a while."

Will considered that. If she had been up in the Whites rock climbing for any length of time, there would be people around who no doubt would remember her. But then he caught himself thinking too much about the case. It had taken him too long this week to right his keel and here he was beginning to founder again. "Well, thanks for keeping me informed."

"That's not the main reason I called, though. I want you to go to Springvale with me."

Will paused. "I don't know, Laurie. I've got a lot of work to catch up on."

"I've made an appointment with the chief. I want to see what he knows about Samantha."

"That's the missing person's name?"

"Samantha Rayley. Thirty-two-year-old single mother."

"How many kids?"

"One boy. Her mother has him now. It's tragic, really. The child has leukemia."

Will didn't say anything. He wasn't sure he needed this. "Why don't you just take Ray?"

"Because you're closer to the case."

"But I'm not a cop. And I don't want to sit in the car while you chat up the chief."

"You won't have to. You'll be my consultant. I'll deputize you."

Will laughed. "Deputy Will." But then he thought again of the seven cords of wood, to say nothing of his classes. "I don't know, Laurie. This case has taken too much out of me already."

"I would really appreciate it."

The solemn tone in her voice suggested he had better go with her or else. "And you have Macomber's blessing?"

"Of course. He wants me to go."

"What's in it for me? And don't say a cookie."

"I just thought you might enjoy a road trip, get away from

this place. It would also give us a chance to talk. I think we need to talk."

Laurie picked up Will the next morning at ten o'clock. She was driving Ray's Chrysler minivan.

"Where's the Cherokee?"

"In the shop."

"So, you finally bit the bullet, huh?"

"Had to. I lost full compression in one cylinder Thursday. There was just no power."

Will settled into the front seat and placed his travel mug full of black coffee into the cup holder. "Well, I certainly feel domestic."

"I hate this thing."

"You should have told me. We could have taken my truck."

She rolled her eyes.

"Hey, what's wrong with my truck? It's gotten you a lot of places." It was hard to believe his truck wasn't preferable to this vehicle.

Ray had two small kids and three dogs. The minivan smelled like a cross between used Pampers and flea powder. The Pampers won out. The passenger seat was tacky with some large, unidentifiable stain with matted dog hair stuck to it. Will couldn't avoid sitting on it.

"Which reminds me," Laurie said. "I don't know how long I'm going to be without wheels, but I would appreciate your help ferrying me around for a week or two."

"Sure thing."

As they headed down I-93, Will was ready for the promised talk about *them,* but Laurie instead was full of theories about the two bodies. She was hoping that what she found out on this trip would help establish a clear connection between the two women.

"If there is a link," she said, "it should lead us to the killer."

"We've been over this before."

"I'm just thinking out loud. Bear with me."

Will hadn't thought about the case for quite a while. "And we do know that the woman near the ski trail was murdered, right? She didn't die from exposure or anything like that."

"She was stabbed several times, Will. Liu has established it as the cause of death."

"Okay. I just didn't hear the final results of the autopsy, that's all." He paused. "Tell me more about the other one, Jeanne Conroy."

"MBA. Worked in the fashion industry. Liked to hike. She was staying at Joe Dodge Lodge doing day trips."

"What was her PLS?"

"People last saw her at the summit of Boot Spur having a bag lunch, heading in the direction of the Glen Boulder Trail."

"Oh. Pretty close to where I was the day we were searching for that kid."

"I'm looking for more of a connection than that."

"Doesn't sound too likely."

"What do you mean?"

"Well, you've got an MBA working in the fashion industry and what looks like a country girl who likes rock climbing. They probably don't know each other at all."

"Maybe they were roommates in college."

Will shrugged. "And maybe they both knew the perp. Rival lovers, perhaps?"

"I considered that, but it turns out Jeanne Conroy preferred women to men."

"She was a lesbian?"

Laurie looked over at him. "That's usually what that means, yes."

Neither said anything for a few moments.

"Suppose we're wrong and there is no connection between these two women at all," Will said finally.

Laurie glanced over at him. "Then we've got a bigger problem on our hands."

"That these killings were random."

"Exactly. That's the media's take on it, anyway. According to them, there's a psycho out there indiscriminately stalking young female hikers. I'm sure you've read the papers and seen the news on TV."

"I haven't. I've pulled my head into my shell this week."

"Well, it's terrible. We've got hikers cancelling at Joe Dodge. The hut traffic is way down."

Will thought about the skittish public. He felt funny not knowing what had been going on in the news, but he could understand the paranoia given the circumstances.

"We've got to find this guy, Will. And soon."

Springvale, Connecticut, lies just over the border from Massachusetts, about a half hour northeast of Hartford as the crow flies. Route 19 goes directly through town and winds around the village green. The police station is at the far end of the green situated in the town hall offices, and the date 1875 is carved into an arch of granite over the doorway.

As they made their way past a local bank, Laurie said, "Look. There's Katydids. That's the store the hat came from." Her eyes fixed on the store as she slowed the car.

"Worth paying a visit?"

"Definitely. It seems like a trendy kind of place Samantha might have frequented a lot."

"You don't know that. You don't know anything about her."

Laurie pursed her lips. "I feel her. Maybe it's a chick thing, but the hat tells me a lot."

"Like what?"

"Like I don't know. You're obviously not a chick if I have to explain it."

Will almost told her that he was grateful for small favors but wisely let it go.

For a Saturday afternoon, the town looked pretty sleepy, and Laurie had little trouble finding a parking spot in front of the town offices, housed in a brick edifice with a clock tower that rose dramatically above their heads.

Inside, a fortyish woman with a terrible red dye job told them to wait on the slatted bench and Chief Anthony Spagnolli would be right with them. The officer's name made Will think of cannoli and how hungry he was. It was just before two o'clock and they hadn't had time to stop for lunch.

It took only about five minutes for Spagnolli to make his appearance. He emerged from an inner office that had his name printed in gold lettering on the smoky glass. It looked as if the police station had been remodeled recently and every effort had been made to maintain the feel of the old building.

Spagnolli came to the waist-high mahogany fence, newly varnished, that separated the waiting area from the office space and swung open the gate. "You must be Chief Eberly," he said. Laurie shook his hand and introduced Will as her "partner," an elusive and purposely deceiving term.

Spagnolli smiled crookedly and, Will felt, a bit self-consciously, as he briefly grasped Will's hand.

Spagnolli wore a crisp white uniform shirt, the creases sharp, and the left sleeve featured a patch with a rendering of the clock tower of the very building they were in. He stood several inches below Will's six feet, which had the effect of drawing attention to his sparse comb-over, the part beginning somewhere close to his right ear.

"I appreciate you seeing us on short notice," Laurie said.

"Not at all." Spagnolli walked them back to his office and showed them to two steel folding chairs in front of his desk. He sat down in a high-backed brown leather throne that looked comfortable for nap taking.

Will figured the hard folding chairs were designed to ensure that Spagnolli's visitors wouldn't stay long. He settled in as well as he could and told himself to let Laurie handle all the questions. He stared over Spagnolli's head at an oval-framed picture of a gray-haired man in a police uniform with fierce mutton-chop whiskers who appeared to be scowling at them.

"As I told you on the phone," Spagnolli said, "we had pretty much run out of leads until you called."

"And no one really knew where Samantha was going? She told no one she was heading for New Hampshire?" Laurie asked.

"No. But I think you should talk to the mother before you leave town. I told her you were coming. She was the one who last spoke to Samantha."

"And the one who reported her missing?"

"Yes."

"Did Samantha live with her mother?"

"No. She had her own apartment. She lived with her boy."

Laurie pulled out a legal pad from her briefcase. "How's the boy doing?"

"Not so well," Spagnolli said. "Mother's taking care of him." He looked down at his desk, ran his hand over the desk calendar, then glanced back up to Laurie. "Look, if you don't mind, I think it would be beneficial for us to talk to the mother together. You might ask her a few questions that I haven't thought of."

"So, she's expecting us?"

"Yes. She very much wants to talk with you."

Laurie looked over at Will. "Sure. Whatever works."

Will nodded, but he wasn't sure he wanted to talk to the mother. He just hoped that she wouldn't ask about the condition of her daughter's body.

"Before we go, I want to show you two something." He walked to a file cabinet, produced a small manila envelope, and tossed it on his desk.

Laurie picked it up. She squeezed together the tin pins, opened the flap, and pulled out six photographs.

"We found this envelope in her studio downtown," Spagnolli said.

Laurie studied the photographs.

Will looked over her shoulder. The photos depicted a series of outdoor shots of a wooded area that looked as if they had been taken from various angles, a large oak taking center stage.

"You say studio?" Laurie said. "Was she an artist?"

"Photographer. She did family pictures, weddings, that sort of thing."

Laurie studied the pictures again. "So, what's so special about these? I'm sure you found other photographs in her studio."

"They were taped to the bottom of a drawer in her desk."

Will stared hard at Spagnolli, who wore a deadpan expression. Spagnolli ran his hand over his head and repositioned a rogue strand of hair.

Laurie stated the obvious. "So, they were important enough to hide?"

Spagnolli simply nodded. "And I can't for the life of me think what could be so special about pictures of the woods."

"Do you think they were taken around here?"

"I have no idea. I've looked at those pictures for hours, and there's just nothing there that would identify location."

Laurie handed Will the photographs. He flipped through them, but Spagnolli was right, at least at quick glance. The only thing that caught Will's eye was that the rotted-out oak had a hole in the center of the trunk like a mouth and one branch raised like it wanted to ask a question.

"Did you find any photographs like these anywhere else in her studio?" Will asked, violating his self-imposed silence.

"No. Nothing."

"Even in her apartment?" Laurie asked.

"That's right."

Laurie placed the photos back in the envelope and handed them across the desk to Spagnolli.

He waved his hand dismissively. "Those are for you. I made copies."

"I appreciate it."

"I'm not sure what they mean, but I know they mean something. If this body you found turns out definitely to be Samantha, I figure it's the only thing so far we've got to play with."

. . .

Mrs. Anna Rayley's house was a modest raised ranch that stood lonely in what had most likely once been a farmer's field. The lawn in front needed tending, with splotches of grass that had gone to seed. The cruiser kicked up dust from the dirt driveway as they pulled in.

Spagnolli opened his door and batted at the dust. "We sure need rain," he said.

Will struggled out of the rear seat. Cruisers were notoriously uncomfortable in the back, something he remembered from his arrest on a trumped-up felonious sexual assault charge. To this day, he couldn't look at a cruiser without recalling the nauseating, humiliating feeling of being cuffed and transported to the Carroll County House of Correction because he couldn't make bail.

He placed his hands on his hips and stretched his back. He caught a quick glimpse of a woman's face watching from the picture window in front. He followed Laurie and Chief Spagnolli to the side door that opened into a breezeway.

Spagnolli took off his hat and knocked softly. In a few seconds, the door opened.

"Please come in," she said.

Spagnolli made the introductions.

Anna Rayley was a stout woman built low to the ground. She wore a short-sleeve blue-striped blouse that revealed fleshy, almost puffy arms. Her salt-and-pepper hair was pulled back and pinned unevenly, so that strands fell about her ears. Her eyes were red rimmed, no doubt from worry and lack of sleep.

She led them through the living area to the kitchen. At the far end of the living room was a brick fireplace painted white.

The kitchen had a large breakfast nook with an oval oak table that looked like an antique.

As soon as Will walked into the kitchen, he smelled the brownies. His stomach clenched and his spirits rose. He could put up with almost anything as long as he was fed.

Anna went to the counter and sliced into the brownies. "These just came out of the oven," she said. "I hope you'll have some."

Will smiled. "They look delicious, Mrs. Rayley."

"I've got coffee on, too. Would everyone like some?"

All three nodded compliance. At the table, Will dug in to the plate of brownies. After his second, Anna said, "Well, Mr. Buchanan. It's sure nice to meet someone with a good appetite."

Will sent her a closemouthed, squirrel-cheeked grin. He felt embarrassed at having been nabbed for wolfing brownies.

"Will loves to eat," Laurie said, as if that weren't already evident. The statement landed flat and created an awkward silence.

Anna's face suddenly turned sad. "Ben used to, too, before he got sick."

"Ben is your grandson?" Laurie asked.

"Yes. I wish he was here so you could meet him, but he's back in the hospital for another round of chemo." She looked down at her coffee cup. "I'll be visiting him tonight."

Spagnolli said, "Anna, as I told you, Officer Eberly would like to ask you a few questions." He reached over and put his hand on her arm. "I know this must be hard for you."

Anna's eyes welled up. She nodded, then stiffened her back. "Chief Spagnolli tells me you think you found my daughter's body."

"Yes," Laurie said. "Do you know why she might have been in New Hampshire?"

Anna shook her head. "She didn't say she was going there. She wouldn't tell me where she was going. Are you sure it's her?"

"Not absolutely—not yet, anyway—but I guess, well, did she used to live in New Hampshire?"

"Yes, but that was about twelve years ago. I know because she came back to live with me when she had Ben."

"Ben is twelve?"

"Going on thirteen. His birthday is in two months." She daubed at her eyes with her cloth napkin. "He said just yesterday that he hoped to live long enough to be a teenager."

Will felt the brownies become a rock in his stomach. This poor woman's daughter was most likely murdered, and now she was heartbroken with a very sick grandson. Suddenly Will's problems seemed small.

"I'm sorry, Mrs. Rayley," Laurie said. "If this is a bad time, we can always come back."

"No, please. I need to talk about my daughter."

"If she didn't tell you she was going to New Hampshire, what exactly did she say?"

"That she had thought of a way." Anna wiped her nose.

"A way for what?"

"A way to get more money. You see, Ben's hospital bills are astronomical and she has no health insurance. We have piles of bills I have no idea how we're going to pay."

"What about Ben's father?" Laurie said. "Can he help?"

Anna didn't answer for a few seconds. She held the napkin in a ball on her lap. "I don't know who the father is."

"Did Samantha?"

"She always said she didn't, but I know that's not true. She knows, but for some reason she's protecting his identity. Every time I'd bring it up, she'd get mad at me. But I know she knows. I'm her mother, after all."

Laurie thought a minute. "So, it's possible Samantha went to New Hampshire to ask Ben's biological father to help out with the hospital bills."

"It could be, yes. But I don't even know if Ben's father lives in New Hampshire."

And the father killed Samantha. That's what Will concluded, and he was sure everyone else at the table was thinking the same thing. But still, there were too many *ifs*, and it was much too early to draw conclusions.

Laurie must have also sensed this indeterminacy because she tried another tack. "Do you know if your daughter knew a woman named Jeanne Conroy?"

Anna paused. "No. At least I never heard Samantha mention her."

"How about someone she might have known in college?"

"Samantha dropped out of college."

Laurie wrote this down. "She never went back?"

"No. She thought it was a waste of time and money since she already knew what she wanted to do. She wanted to take pictures for a living."

Laurie sat forward. "Do you know if she ever did any freelance work in New York? Perhaps the fashion industry?"

Anna frowned. "No. She worked around here, mostly. Why do you keep asking me questions about this woman? Who is she?"

Laurie finessed her answer. "Just someone we think might have known your daughter."

Anna nodded. The vague response seemed enough to satisfy her.

"Do you have a recent picture of Samantha?" Laurie asked.

Anna pushed herself away from the table. "Yes, I have several. I thought you might want one." She left the kitchen.

In her absence, Laurie said to Spagnolli, "I had no idea Ben was that old. You told me she had a sick boy, and I expected six, maybe seven."

"Sorry. I didn't mean to mislead you. I guess Ben will always be a boy to me. I watched him grow up."

"I was just surprised, that's all. Does Anna have a husband?"

"Dead," Spagnolli said. "My sixth-grade teacher. He was a good man."

Anna returned with a wooden box full of pictures. She pulled out one that showed Ben and Samantha leaning close, their heads almost touching. "I love this one," she said. "Taken last year. Ben had such beautiful hair before the chemo made it fall out. They look so happy together."

"Do you mind if I borrow this?" Laurie asked.

"Oh, no. I have several copies."

Laurie looked at the box. "And I wonder if you have another showing Samantha about twelve years ago. That might be helpful."

Anna fumbled through the box and pulled out a shot of Samantha rock climbing. It was obviously taken from the perspective of someone on the rock close to her. She was smiling at the camera, her long hair falling out the back of her climbing helmet. Her lifted leg was muscular. She had a trim, athletic body.

"Was this taken in New Hampshire?" Laurie asked.

"I think so. She used to love to go up there and climb. The only other place she went was somewhere in New York State. I can never remember it. It's some strange Indian name."

"The Schwangunks," Will said.

"Yes, that's it."

"Thank you, Mrs. Rayley. You've been a big help," Laurie said.

"Oh, I hope so." She thought a moment. "Then again, I hope you're all wrong about that body being Samantha's. I keep expecting her to walk through that door at any minute."

By the time they returned to the police station, it was after four o'clock. Katydids was closed and wouldn't be open the next day, Sunday.

Chief Spagnolli offered to show them Samantha's studio, but Laurie declined. "I'm sure you've gone over it pretty well. If the body we found is really Samantha, and we should know that soon, I'll probably be back here anyway. I'm sure there will be some sort of a service for her."

Spagnolli smiled, clearly impressed by this sentiment.

The original plan called for staying two days in Springvale, but after they had thanked Chief Spagnolli and Laurie promised to keep him informed, she said to Will in the parked minivan outside of the town offices, "Why don't we drive a little bit, find a place to stay about halfway, and have a nice time by ourselves."

Will interpreted that to mean they were finally going to have their talk.

They stopped for a burger at a Denny's before hitting the

highway. As they waited for their order to come, Will said, "So, after talking to Mrs. Rayley, do you still think there's a connection between Samantha and Jeanne?"

"The roommate angle is most likely out the window. Apparently, Samantha didn't think much of college."

"So maybe these women aren't connected at all," Will said.

"Maybe they aren't."

Will considered. "You know, I'm beginning to feel it probably doesn't matter. What's more important is finding out who Samantha went to see in New Hampshire about money."

A motorcyclist roared out of the restaurant parking lot, and Laurie glanced out the window at the retreating figure on the bike. "Money and murder go together, that's for sure," she said to the window. She turned and looked back at Will. "I'm still going to keep looking into their backgrounds, though. Photography and modeling go together, too, even though the mother professes to know nothing about it."

"But if that doesn't pan out, it doesn't necessarily mean these killings were random either and a psycho's on the loose. Ben's father is probably key here."

"If Ben's father's from New Hampshire," Laurie said. "Mrs. Rayley wasn't too sure about that, remember?"

"You think Mrs. Rayley's being up-front?"

Laurie took a moment to answer. "I don't think she's hiding anything."

It was nearly six o'clock by the time they headed north in earnest. It was Will's turn to drive, and Laurie tried to adjust the passenger seat before leaving the Denny's parking lot.

"Do you know if this thing tilts?" She worked the mechanism and with a thunk almost ended up on her back.

Will laughed. "I think you found the lever."

Laurie positioned the seat about halfway. "There. That's better."

They drove in silence for a few miles.

"I'm glad you came with me," Laurie said. "I know I ask a lot of you sometimes."

"That's okay." Will sensed this was a good time to begin. "I guess I'd like to know, first, how you think our little arrangement is working?"

"Is that the way you think of it? A 'little arrangement'?"

"Well, that's what it is, isn't it?"

Laurie sighed. "I guess so."

Will shook his head. "We're not going to start quibbling over what to call it, are we?"

"I don't know. I just don't think it's very romantic, that's all."

"Well, what would you call it?"

"I don't know. How about 'love agreement'?"

"Well, of course it is. But it's love according to certain rules that I'm not sure I like."

"Look, Will. We're in this unique situation, but I happen to think it's working. I need my space and you need yours. We find each other when we need to."

"Sometimes I get confused when that is."

"That's what makes it exciting."

"Laurie. I just want to say a few things I think are wrong. Do you think you could just let me talk for a while without coming back at me?"

"Is that what I'm doing? Coming back at you?"

"See what I mean?"

"All right. I guess I am doing that." She folded her arms. "Talk to me, Will."

Will stared at the highway and composed his thoughts before

beginning. Wasn't it ironic, he began, that he was the one who wanted the more traditional arrangement? Not that he was pushing marriage or anything, but he missed having her around. If she would recall, he built that house for them, and the problem with what they had now was that there were no rules to keep them together. And here Will paused for dramatic effect.

"So, I was thinking the other day, since there are no rules, what's to keep me, or you for that matter, from seeing someone else? I mean, because we're living apart does that then mean we can sleep with someone else if we want to?"

The upward rise in his voice suggested that the question was not rhetorical, that he wanted an answer.

He looked over at Laurie. All he got in response was her heavy breathing. She was asleep.

At first he thought he'd wake her, but then decided against it. He didn't want an argument, and he knew that if he said something his anger would win out. He just drove, seething.

After an hour, Laurie was making bull moose noises like Elwood on the trail. To hell with a romantic evening. Will was wide-awake now. He would push on back to New Hampshire.

By the time he made it to his driveway it was close to ten-thirty and Laurie was still asleep. He stopped the car in front of the house. When he opened the door, the overhead courtesy light didn't even wake her. Her mouth was wide open. He had seen this deep sleep before. It usually came on when she was overworked.

He went inside for a blanket, came back, and covered her with it. She snuggled underneath it.

Will closed the car door quietly and went upstairs to his own bed.

Chapter 5

At dawn, Will felt Laurie crawl into bed. He turned away from her, opened one eye, and glanced at the digital clock: 5:32. She reached her arm around him and held him close. They both slept nestled together and didn't wake until almost noon.

Will rolled over.

Laurie lay on her back, staring at the ceiling. "I guess I was bad last night."

"Yes, you were."

"Thanks for covering me with the blanket. That was sweet."

"Sweet?"

"I know you don't like that word, but that's exactly what you were."

"Okay. I was sweet."

"My muscles are a little stiff, though. Why didn't you wake me?"

"Because you needed your sleep."

"You could have just helped me into the house. I probably wouldn't have even woken up."

Will sighed. "So, I guess I'm not sweet, after all. Now you're mad I left you in the car."

"Not mad. Just stiff."

Will shook his head and rolled away from her. He didn't say anything, but he was thinking he would never understand the right way to act around Laurie.

"Hey." She pulled on his arm. "You're still sweet. Now get over here and continue . . ."

"With what?"

"What you were talking about last night. I think I dropped off when you were saying something was ironic. A 'conventional arrangement' or something like that."

Will thought about his long speech. No wonder she couldn't stay awake. "I must have bored you to tears."

"Not really. I was just tired."

Will thought about mentioning his big idea that there was nothing to stop him from seeing other women, but now it didn't feel right. He didn't want to see anyone else. It was just too much work. "It doesn't matter."

"Come on, Will. What's on your mind?"

Will scratched his ear. "I just wish we could be together like this all the time."

She reached over and touched his hand. "Well, you *are* going to see a lot more of me."

"I am?"

"Sure. With the Cherokee in the shop, I can't expect you to drive me to work *and* back to my apartment."

Will thought a moment. "You're staying here then?"

Laurie smiled. "What part of this don't you understand?"

"But that's great. When did you decide this?"

"Just now. I was lying here thinking about our schedules."

She played with the hairs on his arm. "It's just too much to ask you to do." An inflection in her voice suggested that she was holding something back. He knew her too well.

"You don't have to live here if you don't want to," Will said. "I'd be happy to cart you anywhere."

"Cart me? Now *that* doesn't sound so sweet."

"What are you up to, Laurie?"

"I don't think I'm up to anything." She removed her hand from his arm. "I'm just offering to stay here to make things simple for you, okay?"

Will hesitated. "Okay." He rolled over and held her. For a moment, neither said anything.

"So, what else did you talk about in the car last night?" she asked.

"I told you it doesn't matter."

"Well, it mattered last night."

He leaned closer and kissed her ear. "I was just babbling."

"I don't believe you."

"Laurie, for God's sake, what's wrong?"

"Do you really want to sleep with other women?"

He sat up. "Aha! I knew it had to be something."

"Well, do you?"

Will hesitated. "I've thought about it."

Laurie propped herself up on her elbow. "Well, go ahead then."

"I don't want to."

"Then why did you bring it up?"

"Because I've been frustrated with the way things are. I don't like our 'arrangement.' I think we have to work at living together. If not, I might just as well sleep around."

"Is that a threat?"

"Look. Stop." He gestured with his hands for emphasis. "Just stop." He ran his fingers through his hair. He slowed his voice down. "I don't want to sleep with anyone else. And I don't want to argue." He lay back and waited for a reaction, but none came. "Especially with a little liar like you," he finally added.

"Little liar?"

"Yeah. You heard everything I said in the car last night and you pretended to be asleep."

"Not true."

"Oh, I'm sure you fell asleep for real eventually, but you heard everything. Otherwise, how did you know I was thinking about seeing other women?"

She didn't answer.

"Little liar. Little Liar Laurie."

"Stop saying that."

Will rolled closer to her again. "Okay. Look me straight in the eye and tell me you didn't hear everything I said last night."

She met his eyes and said, "What's for brunch?"

That afternoon, Will and Laurie sat together and spread out on the kitchen table the six photographs Spagnolli had given them.

Will scratched his chin, then reordered the sequence of pictures.

"You think they're interconnected?"

Will frowned. "It doesn't look that way, does it? I was kind of hoping that if we pieced them together they would make one big one."

Laurie picked up one of the pictures. "Mind if I reshuffle them?"

"Knock yourself out."

Laurie tried various combinations. "Nothing adds up."

Will tilted his chair back and placed his hands behind his head. "So, the question before us is why did Samantha tape seemingly random shots of the woods underneath a desk drawer?"

Laurie finished his musing for him. "She obviously figured they were important and valuable enough to hide."

"And we're not seeing what it is."

"Let's keep saying the first thing that comes to mind. No ruminating."

"Okay."

"Do you think she knew what she was getting into was dangerous?"

"Yes. It feels like some kind of insurance policy. They were hidden, but in probably the most conspicuous of places. If something went wrong, she knew the cops would search there as a matter of course. She wanted them to be found."

"Good. Now what do the pictures tell you about the terrain?"

"Mixed hardwoods. Maple, oak, poplar, hop hornbeam. Relative height of trees suggests lower elevations."

"What else?"

"Rocks. Berry bushes."

"New Hampshire or Connecticut."

Will hesitated.

"No thinking!"

"New Hampshire."

"Why?"

He shrugged his shoulders. "Gut sense."

"Come on, Mr. Big Shot Woodsman. What else do you see?"

"Nothing."

Laurie looked at the picture in her hand, then back at Will.

"What's wrong?"

"What?"

"What are you staring at?"

"Nothing."

"You were looking at my hair, weren't you?"

"No. I was just spacing out."

She hooked her hair behind her ears. "Do you like my hair this way? It's a little shorter, you know."

"What?"

"Come on. No ruminating."

"Sure."

"Liar."

"I think it's fetching."

" 'Fetching'! What am I, your dog?"

He reached his hand out and stroked her hair. "I think it's divine."

She poked his shoulder. "Liar."

"Exquisite."

She singsonged, "Little Liar Willy."

The next Thursday, test results were made public that showed the blotchy brown stains on the hat were blood that belonged to Samantha Rayley, and dental records confirmed Samantha's body as the one Will discovered near the ski trail.

But Will had little time to consider these findings because he was preparing for Fall Family Weekend at Saxton Mills School.

In the old days, it was called "Parents Weekend," but with a nod toward political correctness and with the withering away of the nuclear family, the more generic title was preferred.

Friday night was reserved for a marathon of ten-minute conferences with real parents, significant others, grandparents, guardians, divorcées, sponsors—in short, anyone who had anything to do with kids in classes who cared enough to find out about their academic performances.

Will enjoyed this time but found it impossible to keep to his schedule. He certainly wasn't voluble, but the "parents" were. And he refused to cut off conversation just because the ten minutes were up.

As a consequence, he was there most of the evening without a break. Partway into the conferences, he glanced at his list to see how many he had left and was surprised to find Brian Hatcher's name penciled in in the last time slot.

Hatcher was a fellow member of Backcountry Search and Rescue, the person Will mentioned to Toby who, along with René Levesque, had taken the reverse route up the Huntington Ravine Trail when they had been searching for the lost nine-year-old boy.

Hatcher was a good friend and colleague. He headed up the rock climbing program at Saxton Mills School. He was only a part-timer, though. He owned Climb High, an outdoor equipment store, which also served as the base for his rock climbing school.

His daughter, Celia, a junior now, was Will's advisee, and usually Hatcher just chatted about her with Will occasionally when he met up with him at school. For Hatcher to make a formal appointment suggested there was something urgent.

When Will finally got to see him, Hatcher looked troubled. His eyes were drawn and tired. "What's going on, Brian?"

Hatcher was fidgety. "I'm sorry to keep you. I hesitated about signing up, but I figured that I wouldn't get a chance to talk to you until after the weekend."

Will motioned to the chair by his side. "Sit down, Brian. I'm guessing this is about Celia."

Hatcher flopped down in the chair and spread out his legs. "I'm exhausted," he said. "I've been worried sick about her." He leaned forward, elbows on knees, and looked directly at Will. "I think she's starting to hang with the wrong crowd, smoking dope."

"You know that for sure?"

"Naw. Hell, you know how it is with these kids. They got their own little network. Can't find out shit." He made a poking motion at his eyes. "I can see it here, though. You know the eyes don't lie. And she's been out at odd hours. I think she snuck out the other night."

"It doesn't sound like her."

"I know. But I guess all kids have to test the limits, you know what I mean?"

"Some of them, yes."

"Have you noticed anything different about her lately?"

Will hesitated. In truth, he hadn't even spoken to her in over a week. With all that had been going on in finding Samantha Rayley's body, he had thought little about Celia or any of his other students. "I haven't seen anything suspicious."

Hatcher clapped him on the shoulder. "Well, I wanted to let you know. You're a good man, Will. I appreciate all you've done for her. Her grades are pretty good now."

But Will didn't feel like such a good man. He felt negligent.

"I'll make a point to have a talk with her over the weekend," he said.

"I wouldn't do that."

"Why not?"

"She gets on the defensive pretty easily these days. I think it would be better if you just watched and waited. If you suspect something, then talk to her."

Will wasn't so sure it was the best approach, but he acceded to Hatcher's wishes for the time being. He wondered vaguely why, if Hatcher didn't want him to see her right away, there was the immediate need for the conference. He chalked it up to his just being an antsy father. "I'll try to see what I can find out on the sly."

"Thanks, my man. I sure appreciate it."

"Otherwise she's doing okay?"

"Her math grades have slipped a little, but they're still respectable, I guess." Hatcher sat back, interlaced his fingers, and placed them over his stomach. "So, how are you holding up?"

"Me?"

"No, the guy sitting next to you."

"Okay. It's been a little hectic."

"I guess Levesque and I missed all the action on that lost-kid call."

"You were the lucky ones."

"And they found out who it was—the body, I mean?"

"Samantha Rayley. It was confirmed yesterday."

"Yeah, and I was talking about it with Laurie this morning."

"You were?"

He nodded. "She was making the rounds of climbing stores and stopped in to show me Samantha's picture. See if I remembered her."

"And?"

"I'd seen her before. She used to work at Glen's Pizza, I think. She came in the shop a few times."

Will thought about that. So, there was a connection. He would have to find out from Laurie if Hatcher told her anything else.

"And I guess you and Laurie also went down to see the police in Samantha's hometown."

Will was taken aback. "Laurie tell you that?"

"No. Her deputy, Ray. You missed an emergency call last Saturday. I just wondered where you were, so I asked him."

"What exactly did Ray say?"

"That you were checking out a hat, or something."

Will didn't respond. He made a mental note to talk to Laurie about Ray's loose lips.

Hatcher sat forward. "Did you find out anything?"

Will hesitated. "You know I can't discuss the case, Brian."

"Right. Sorry. I was just curious, that's all." Hatcher got up to leave. "Well, I won't take up any more of your time. Like I said, I appreciate everything you do for Celia. She's lucky to have you as an adviser."

As Will drove back home that evening, he mulled over what Hatcher had said about Celia and made a commitment to be more attentive to her. He admired Hatcher for bringing up a teenage daughter on his own. Hatcher tended to be coarse at times, but he had a good heart.

Will recalled the terrible moment years ago when Hatcher returned home from a fishing trip over the weekend to find that his wife and year-old child had been kidnapped out of their house. Police eventually found his wife's abandoned car on the side of Route 16 with baby Celia still in it, but there was no sign of his wife. She was never found.

If there was anything Will could do to help out Hatcher, he knew that as his friend—hell, just as a human being—it was his responsibility to do so.

The meetings that evening reconnected him, after a wayward start to the term, to his true calling of working with young people. From now on, he would try to focus more on his teaching—maybe even take a break from search and rescue—and while he would still try to help Laurie with the Samantha Rayley case, he would do all he could to place it on the back burner.

Chapter 6

A t home that evening, Will told Laurie about his meeting with Hatcher. "I guess you scored with him," Will said. "What do you mean?"

"Well, he told me he remembered quite a bit about Samantha Rayley."

Laurie looked puzzled. She sat on the edge of the bed in her bathrobe with a towel wrapped, turbanlike, on her head. She smelled fresh from her shower. "He told you that?"

Will leaned one hand against the doorjamb. "Well, yeah. He said he thought she worked in that pizza shop next door to Climb High."

"And . . . ?"

"And . . ." Will considered. "And I guess, now that I think of it, that's all he told me."

Laurie grabbed the bottle of nail polish from the nightstand. She twisted off the cap, raised her right leg onto the bed, and started painting her big toenail. "Hatcher didn't remember anything other than that. He really wasn't much help at all."

"So, you checked out the pizza shop?"

"That place has changed hands so many times. The guy who runs it now just moved into Conway last year."

"A dead end."

"You could call it that."

"What about the photography angle? Have you found out anything that would connect Samantha with Jeanne Conroy?"

"Nothing so far. It's looking like the two women didn't know each other." She glanced across the room at him. "You going to stand there all night, or are you going to come sit and give me your opinion." She patted the edge of the bed.

"About what?"

"Which color do you like best? Mango or passion fruit?" She swung her leg back to the floor and put both feet together. Her big toes were painted different colors.

"Which one is passion fruit?"

"I'm not going to tell you."

Will scratched his chin and made show of selecting the color. "Well, I pick passion fruit."

"Point to it."

Will hesitated. "They're pretty close."

"I know what you're doing. You're choosing passion fruit just because of the name. You don't care about the color."

"You're right. I don't. Why don't you use both? You know, one foot mango, the other passion fruit."

Laurie sent him her long, suffering look.

"What? What's wrong with that? I mean, it's not like it's summer and you're wearing sandals. It's like caring about the color of your underwear. Who's going to see it?"

"You don't like my underwear?"

"I love your underwear."

"So, the color of my nail polish is important. *You* see my toenails. I want you to like them."

Will let out a long exhale. "Okay." He pointed. "That one."

"Good choice."

"What color is it?"

"Mango."

"Damn."

"Sorry, no passion fruit tonight." Laurie turned away from him and began painting her toenails in earnest.

Will studied her back. "For someone who just hit a dead end in an investigation, you sound pretty chipper."

"Oh, Hatcher wasn't my only lead."

Will waited to hear more, but she wasn't forthcoming. "You know something, don't you. You *have* had a breakthrough."

"Oh, I guess you could say I've learned a few things I didn't know before."

"Come on, Laurie. Stop painting your damn toes and tell me."

She kept her back to him. "I think that's privileged information."

He got up from the bed and faced her. "Okay, little Ms. Coy, sneaky-type person. Tell me what you found."

"Such language." Laurie kept painting her toes. "I think I know who Samantha was having an affair with twelve years ago."

"Who?"

"I can't tell you that, not until I follow through with a few things, just to be sure."

"Oh, for God's sake, Laurie. Of course you can tell me."

Laurie sighed. "I'm serious, Will. You have to respect my concerns here." She finished painting her toes, twisted the cap, and placed the bottle back on the nightstand.

"You know, I just don't get it sometimes."

Laurie stood and unwrapped the towel from her head. "What is it you don't get, Will?" She shook her hair and began patting it with the towel.

"Why sometimes I'm your toady rent-a-cop and sometimes not."

"I think I usually refer to you as an associate."

"Only when it's convenient."

"Of course." Her tone grew serious. "I guess this is not one of those times when you need to know something. I'll tell you sometime."

"When?"

She didn't answer.

Will took a step toward her. He grabbed her around the waist.

"What are you doing?"

He lightly shoved her back on the bed.

"Will, stop it."

"Let's see the color of that underwear." He parted her bathrobe and stepped back.

She smiled. "I don't wear underwear in the shower, dummy."

"Oops. My mistake." He didn't move.

"Will, what on earth are you staring at?"

"Beautiful mango toes."

"Try looking a little lower."

Saturday morning dawned brightly, but there was a brisk chill in the air. Will dropped Laurie off at the police station on his way to another round of teacher conferences. "So, I'll pick you up around five?" he said.

"If that's okay. If you're too busy, Ray can always give me a ride home."

"No. I want to pick you up. I like taking you home." He paused. "I like the way that sounds."

She smiled at him and got out of his truck. "Teach your parents well."

Will watched her walk into the station. He liked the way all that stuff on her belt—the leather holster, the cuff case—jostled as she moved.

The remaining conferences went smoothly, but at lunch Will couldn't stop thinking about Celia. He was hoping to catch her in the dining room, but she never showed.

Although Hatcher lived close by, he and Celia had decided it would be best for her to live on campus her junior and senior years as preparation for college life, but she went home most weekends that had no Saturday classes.

Despite what Hatcher had said about not confronting his daughter, it was against Will's nature to be secretive, and if the kid was into drugs, then she might be in danger right now. It was an issue that couldn't wait.

Will always figured that being up-front with kids was the best way to deal with them. He checked the athletic schedule for the starting time of the girls' varsity soccer match. He knew she would have to be back on campus at least by then and thought he might try to catch up with her before the game started.

He had time before Celia's game to find a computer in the faculty room and double-check her grades on the database. As was the case with most kids who might be in trouble, Will knew it was good to have an opening gambit, and grades might be a good place to start.

What the computer told him, though, confirmed that she was actually doing well, just slipping a little in math as Hatcher had mentioned, but hardly a concern about her performance. He searched through her file for teacher comments but found nothing about her behavior that would tip off drug usage.

A little before two o'clock, Will left the faculty room for the day-student parking lot. He soon spied a truck with the Climb High logo on the door coming up the road. Celia was driving. He waited until she parked to approach her. She bustled out of the cab and, with her back turned, began rummaging through the truck bed.

"Hi, Celia."

She wheeled. "Oh, Mr. Buchanan. You startled me."

Celia Hatcher was a tall girl, a shade under Will's even six feet, and had her father's gray eyes. Her dark hair was pulled back and held by a scrunchie, the ponytail falling in a storm of mismanaged curls.

"Sorry. Got a minute?"

"Just about that. I'm supposed to be meeting in the locker room at two-fifteen."

Will looked at his watch. "You'll make it. This won't take long."

"Am I in trouble?"

"I don't think so. I just wanted to let you know I talked with your dad last night." The news didn't provoke much of a response, no doubt because he and Hatcher were always talking. "In a parent conference," Will added.

"My dad made an appointment with you? Why?"

"He's concerned that you might be hanging around with the wrong crowd."

She didn't say anything at first. "That's the way he put it? The 'wrong crowd'?"

"Yes."

Celia looked down at the asphalt and spoke to it. "It's because of what happened last summer, isn't it?"

"What exactly happened last summer?"

"Not much, really. My dad just doesn't like the people I hang with." She looked directly at Will. "And it's not a 'crowd,' either."

"And probably not 'wrong.' Who are they, Celia? Do they go to Saxton Mills?"

"No. They're older." She stuffed shorts, cleats, and a towel into her gym bag and slung it over her shoulder. "I really have to get going, Mr. Buchanan."

"Mind if I walk with you?"

"If you want to."

Will shoved his hands in his pockets as they made their way to the locker room. "Look, Celia. I know this isn't the right time or place but I think we need to talk."

"I don't get it. What's the problem?"

"That's what I want to find out."

"I mean, just because my dad doesn't like guys who are pierced and happen to have tattoos doesn't mean I'm doing things I shouldn't."

Will thought it sounded like the wrong crowd. "Your father's concerned, that's all."

"Yes, you said that. I can't believe he made an appointment to see you. What else did he say?"

They stopped outside the door of the locker room. "That he thinks you're using."

Celia looked at him, startled. "Using?" She lowered her voice. "You mean drugs?"

"Pot." Will read her expression, more thoughtful than scared. "Well, I'm not."

"Suppose we meet sometime soon. It might be a good idea to talk about this so I know what to tell your father. You know where my office is."

"Do you believe me?"

"If you tell me you're not using, then I believe you."

Celia looked away from Will. "That's nice to know."

He put a hand on her shoulder. "I'm leaving this up to you, Celia. I'm expecting you to seek me out."

She shrugged. "Okay. You coming to my game?"

"I'll catch the first part. I've got some work to do. Sharpening axes, that sort of thing."

Celia smiled. "You need to take some time off, Mr. Buchanan. You work too hard."

As Will drove to pick up Laurie at the police station, he reflected with satisfaction on his day, feeling more connected to his work as teacher and adviser than ever. He was pleased that he had spoken with Celia, and his tack of being direct with her suggested he was back in the rhythms of his work. If he knew Celia at all, he was sure that she would eventually show up at his office to chat. In the meantime, he at least had got her thinking.

At a little after five o'clock, Will waited in his truck outside the police station with the engine running and heater ticking. The temperature had dropped twenty degrees since noon.

Will had stayed through Celia's game, watching her score a

goal in the fading early October light, the sun an orange flare on the horizon. If this kid was doing drugs, it wasn't affecting her play much. She was a born athlete, and watching her skills with the ball, Will could see in her the agile movements of her father on rock.

At first Will chose not to go into the station in deference to Laurie's sometimes chaotic schedule, where the unexpected was commonplace, but after a half hour, he figured he would at least find out how long she would be.

As he opened the front door, he was almost run over by a man rushing out. They both ended up bunched together, a stalemate in the open doorway. Will excused himself, then recognized the man. "Nelson Carpenter?"

"Oh, it's you, Will."

Will held out his hand. "How the hell have you been? I didn't even know you were in town."

Carpenter looked at Will's hand like he didn't know what he was supposed to do with it, then shook it limply. "Just here for the ski season."

"God, I haven't seen you since—"

"I'd love to talk, Will. I'm late for work."

"Sure. Where you working?"

"Burger and Brew."

"I'll stop in."

Carpenter scurried away, leaving Will in the empty doorway. Will studied his retreating figure. Carpenter was lean and hard and wore his hair shoulder-length despite a growing bald spot, like a target on the back of his head. Will proceeded into the station. He found Laurie in her office, putting on her coat. "You ready?"

She glanced at the clock on the wall. "Oh, I'm sorry. Have you been waiting long?"

"Nope."

"Something came up at the last minute."

Will smiled. "You mean Nelson Carpenter?"

"How did you know?"

"I'm psychic."

"No you're not."

"I have superpowers." Will raised his arms triumphantly. "So, what did ol' Nelson want?"

"If you're psychic, you should tell *me*." She punched him playfully on the shoulder. "Come on, Wonder Boy. Beam me home."

In the truck, Laurie said, "Do we have time to stop at the mini-mart for a paper?"

"Sure. I was planning to anyway."

"Oh, good. Do you need gas?"

Will looked over at her and grinned. "You're really funny, you know that?"

"What do you mean?"

"You act like it's a big surprise that you want to stop at the mini for a paper when you do it every day. You're such a creature of habit."

Laurie looked out the passenger-side window. "I guess I am pretty predictable."

They drove in silence for a while.

"Something wrong?" Will asked.

"No. I was just thinking, that's all."

"About us?"

"About Nelson Carpenter."

"Yeah, I guess he just sort of blew back into town."

"He owns a house here, Will."

"I thought he rented. He's kind of transient, isn't he?"

"Comes and goes." She leaned her head back and closed her eyes. "But he usually shows up every ski season." Laurie paused. "How well do you know him?"

Will downshifted and turned onto a dirt road, a shortcut that would bring him in a few miles just north of the mini-mart in Saxton Mills. "I actually got to know him a few years back when he was part of the climbing scene. You know, when he first worked as an instructor for Cloutier at North Country Sports."

Laurie folded her arms. "What's he like?"

"Carpenter's a good climber."

"I mean as a person."

"Loner. Drinks a lot, or used to anyway. Never said much about himself, but he liked the ladies."

"Do you remember if he had a steady girlfriend?"

"I don't think so. Always played the field, is what I remember." Will came to a full stop at an intersection and waited for traffic to pass. "Why? What's all this about, anyway?"

Laurie sat up in her seat. "Will, I wonder if I could run something by you. It's really got me thinking."

"Shoot."

"Carpenter came to see me this afternoon to report his pistol stolen. Someone broke in to his house."

Will thought a moment. "And?"

"And, it puts an interesting spin on things."

Will pulled in to the driveway of the mini-mart and cut the engine. "I think I'm missing something here."

"It was Guy Cloutier at North Country Sports who told me he had to fire Nelson Carpenter fourteen years ago for having an affair with a customer." She looked directly at Will.

"You mean, Cloutier's the stronger lead you were talking about last night?"

"Yes. And you know who the customer was."

Will finally got it. "Not Samantha Rayley."

She nodded. "I guess she and Carpenter were quite a number."

Chapter 7

Nelson Carpenter's alleged affair with Samantha Rayley temporarily sparked Will's interest in the case, but with a busy week ahead of him, he kept his resolve to focus on teaching.

He usually counted on Wednesdays, with its half-day schedule meant to accommodate sports events, to get work done in the woodlot situated on the school's two thousand acres. He still needed to buck up three cords and had help from a group of kids on his "woods team" who chose to cut and stack wood rather than play a sport.

It was an Indian summer day, the sky Wedgwood blue, lightly puffed with fair-weather clouds. He gassed up his chain saw at the school barn and felt that the chances were good that they'd get at least a cord split by the end of the afternoon.

Will was about to load up the stake side with kids and equipment when Brian Hatcher's truck skidded into the driveway.

Will approached him. "What's up, Brian?"

"We got toned out. You didn't hear it?"

"My pager's off."

"Well, get your gear. We've got trouble on Cathedral."

Will hesitated. If there was trouble on Cathedral Ledge, the "gear" Brian was referring to was technical rock climbing equipment.

"You've got your pack with you, don't you?"

"In my truck, but I don't have a climbing rope."

"I've got two with me. Come on, Will. We need to move fast."

Will quickly gave his kids instruction to take the afternoon off, grabbed his climbing pack out of the truck bed tool chest, and jumped into the cab of Hatcher's new Tundra.

Hatcher sped away, gravel flying from the rear tires.

"What have we got?" Will clicked his seat belt and hung on to the door handle.

"Climber down." Hatcher looked over at Will. "No brain bucket." Hatcher didn't say anything else, but he didn't have to.

Depending on the height and severity of the fall, Will knew that with no helmet they would be looking at anything from a mild concussion to summer squash.

Hatcher radioed in that they were both responding, and Will sat disoriented from having been suddenly ripped away from a planned schedule. Emergency calls often began for Will with a boost of adrenaline but were quickly followed by a thoughtful period when he imagined the worst.

Hatcher's voice yanked him out of his reverie. "Good thing I was about to head off with my kids."

"What?"

"My climbing kids. I've got lots of gear with me." Hatcher's afternoon climbing activity was limited for safety reasons to ten students.

Will nodded, but the thought of climbing brought him up short. He hadn't been on rock in a while. Hatcher was always trying to get Will to partner with him on weekends, and right now Will was wishing he had done just that. Sure, he had been a pretty good climber in his day—a 5.9 was something he could accomplish with relative ease—but he knew enough about the sport to realize that it was dangerous and skills had to be practiced. "Which route? Do we know?"

"Standard."

Will felt better. The Standard Route on Cathedral Ledge was the oldest. He had climbed it about ten years ago and remembered it being a 5.6. Climbs are rated by a numbering system developed by German alpinist Willo Welzenbach that differentiates between hiking (classes 1, 2, and 3, which are non-technical or non-roped activities) and technical rock climbing (classes 4, 5, and 6, which require a climbing rope and a variety of gear for safety). For Will, a 5.6 would be a moderate challenge, usually with pretty good handholds.

Hatcher entered the town of Conway, drove by the high school, and waited in traffic to turn left on the back road that paralleled the main tourist route. The stretch between Conway and North Conway had developed into a shopping mecca with trendy outlet stores, and the road was always busy.

It took another fifteen minutes to get to the climbing area. To the right of Cathedral loomed Whitehorse Ledge, precipitous and inviting for climbers. Both ledges, part of Echo Lake State Park, were popular destinations, offering challenging routes for novice and expert alike, but because they were so accessible—just three miles from North Conway—they attracted all sorts of inexperienced climbers who sometimes got themselves into trouble. Climbing without a helmet might make you look cool, but it could also make you look dead.

When Hatcher's truck came to a stop, both men exited the

cab without saying anything. Will grabbed his pack and a climbing rope.

Following a path that led around the rock face, it took another ten minutes before they reached the base of the Standard Route. Hatcher radioed in again that they had arrived on scene.

Upward at an acute angle, an immense expanse of granite, like a massive tabletop on edge, spread out before them dramatically.

Hatcher stepped back farther to get a better look at the situation on top. Will could hear him as he reported on the radio seeing a figure dangling from a rope, describing him as having a medium build and wearing a red bandanna. He could make out another figure to the victim's right waving frantically and shouting at them.

Will dropped his pack, found his climbing shoes, and, with socks removed, began putting them on.

Hatcher rejoined him. "We're first on the scene."

"Great." Will was less than enthusiastic about Hatcher's observation because as "first on scene" they would be in charge of operations.

"How do you want to do this?"

Will appreciated the gesture of deference but it wasn't necessary. Because of Hatcher's experience, there was no question he would do the lead climbing. Will couldn't think of anyone he would rather have belaying him. "It's your call."

"You've been on the Standard Route, right?"

"Just once."

"How are you with crack climbing?"

"Okay, I guess."

Hatcher squinted up at the cliff. "Then I think the best way up would be to traverse over on the Standard Route but switch to the Toe Crack to make the ascent. The guy looks like after he slipped he swung closer to that route." He winked at Will. "Some fun, huh?"

Will put on his climbing harness over his canvas work pants. He much preferred climbing in shorts, but at least the pants crotch was gusseted. As he ran one end of the rope through loops in the harness, he said to Hatcher, "Are we the only ones here?"

"Levesque is rappelling from up top. He'll meet us at the Cave. I imagine we'll eventually have more support from below, too."

While the Standard Route was pretty easy going at first, the climb led directly to an anomaly in the rock, a small, dank cave that climbers used as a way station before attempting the next pitch.

In his mind's eye, Will recalled the route above the Cave. Lead climbers had to scale the famous Cave Wall to the right without protection until they could clip with a carabiner into an existing sling on the right. They then had to ascend up through a chimney—a crack large enough for a climber to fit into—maneuver around a nasty overhang, and eventually tie into another tree on a ledge in the upper chimney to belay from. The climb was tricky and the accident could have happened at any one of those points.

"Who called this in, anyway?" Will asked.

Hatcher pointed to his left. "A climber on Thin Air—you know, the route next to Standard—heard the partner yelling and saw the dangling guy. He finished the climb and called from a cell phone up above."

The access road that switchbacked up to the tops of the cliffs sometimes drew gawkers who looked on with great interest at those struggling up the cliff. Will imagined that if news had gotten out that there was an injured climber, there might already be a crowd swelling at the top.

Will finished tying into his harness with a figure-of-eight, and they both checked each other's knots before Hatcher slung a large rack of hardware over his shoulder—the carabiners, slings, cams, and chocks that served as protection as he climbed. They both strapped on their helmets.

Hatcher looked up at the rock, toed in, and with several quick, deft moves, climbed ten feet up and away from Will.

Will, as his belayer, was tied into an anchor with the rope around his waist, and his job was to feed out slack to Hatcher as he moved up the rock.

Hatcher removed a small nut from his sling and wedged it into a fissure in the rock. He clipped in a carabiner and snapped the climbing rope through it.

He glanced down at Will. "This traverse is pretty easy. I don't think we have to worry about it."

Will nodded. But he had second thoughts as he fed rope out to Hatcher, who moved rapidly up and across the rock face. The idea with lead climbing is to set protection along the way so that if there is a fall, the drop is only the distance of the length of rope from the last anchor. Hatcher was, except for the three anchors placed that Will could count, effectively free climbing the traverse.

Soon Hatcher was out of sight. Will waited, feeling the sun beating on his helmet. Sweat trickled into his eyes, and he wiped them with the back of his hand. The rope uncoiled in front of him like a huge umbilicus and soon there was little left.

Then, faintly, he heard Hatcher's voice from above and felt a tug on the rope. Even though he couldn't see Hatcher, Will knew he had reached the first pitch and was tied into an anchor. Now it was Will's turn to follow.

Will acknowledged Hatcher and shouted the traditional command. "That's me!"

It was Hatcher's turn to shout back. "Climb when ready!"

Will made his first move. "Climbing!" he yelled, completing the command sequence.

The pressure of the rock through Will's shoes felt foreign, yet familiar. He tried to recall the last time he had been on rock and settled that it was almost two years, too long ago to be at the top of his game now. But Will told himself to concentrate on his moves, to climb with his legs, which have much bigger muscles, and not blow out his arms.

Will reached the first nut that Hatcher had inserted. He unclipped the rope and jiggled the nut until it came out of the crack. He clipped the carabiner, nut attached, to a sling he wore over his shoulder. Now that he was on belay, Will's responsibility was to strip the protection as he climbed and collect what Hatcher had inserted.

Will glanced up ahead where the rope stretched at a sharp angle. From his perspective, he couldn't see where the next anchor was placed. He took a deep breath, thrust his right leg out, and found a solid nub. He put pressure on his right toe, found a handhold, and smoothly brought his left leg to the same nub before thrusting out his right leg for another move.

He felt the reassuring tug on the rope as Hatcher picked up the slack. He told himself not to hurry. If the dangling victim above was still alive, he would just have to wait a little longer. Will's own safety, according to his EMT training, was paramount. But it was also important to establish a rhythm, and Will made his moves more efficiently as he ascended.

Finally he reached the next point of protection. Hatcher had used a cam, a device with offset serrated half circles that is triggered by pressing a button with the thumb. The solid anchor, wedged into the space between a small rock overhang, was "bombproof," and it took some time to work it out. He clipped it on to his sling.

The next part of the climb rose even more steeply and the rope trailed ahead over an outcropping. Again Will had trouble spotting the next protection placement. He took a moment and looked down, something he usually avoided, and he was stunned at how much elevation he had gained.

When he turned back to the rock to begin climbing again, he suddenly lost his finger grip, and in grasping for a handhold, his foot slipped. Before his brain could register what had happened, he was swinging on the rope, tearing across the side of the cliff.

He could feel the rope catch on something, then release with a rip as his body pendulumed in a wide arc, banging against the granite as he went, his helmet knocking now and again against the rock with a hollow thud that momentarily stunned him. When he had gathered his wits, he found himself dangling from the rope.

Then he heard Hatcher's voice booming. "Will! Are you okay? Will!"

Will glanced up. He could see Hatcher looking down at him. "I'm okay." Then he noticed the frayed rope above his head and immediately knew he wasn't okay. With a rush of clarity, he understood that on his swing across the rock face, his protection had zippered, and when the rope got caught up, the rock razored it as it released. He could see feathers of nylon sticking out where the rope had been cut.

Given the urgency in his voice, Hatcher must have seen it, too. "Can you stand anywhere?"

Will checked his position. The rock face was smooth. There was a reason there were no routes in this area. "It's pretty slick." Then he felt the rope snap, and he dropped an inch.

"You've got to hook in somewhere," Hatcher yelled. "Use a nut!"

Will ran his hand over the rock, searching desperately for a place to wedge in protection. He fought a wave of panic and told himself to calm down. Despite his fear, he couldn't resist looking down again. He was a good sixty feet above the ground. There was little doubt that if he plunged, he was a dead man.

Instead of adding to his panic, the glance at the talus floor forced him to concentrate on the rock face. Off to the left, his fumbling hands discovered what might be a place to hook into. The rock looked flaky, though, and he wasn't sure that if he wedged in the nut, the whole crack wouldn't crumble. But he had to get off the rope.

He crabbed to the left, unclipped the nut from his sling, and, with hands shaking, attempted to wedge it into the small crack. It was just a small wire stopper, but it was too wide for the crack. He tried to force it and almost lost his balance again. As he had suspected, the granite flaked, but in doing so it created a larger opening for the nut. Will jammed in the nut and almost screamed with relief when it held. He hooked the carabiner directly into his harness and splayed out his legs on the rock face, praying the nut would stay wedged.

"I'm in!" he yelled.

"Can you hold it there?"

"Not forever."

"I'll send you down rope until you get above the frayed part. Then you can tie in again and I'll lower you!"

Hatcher's instructions had the effect of emboldening Will, but he could feel his legs getting weaker as he tried to hold his position and feared developing "sewing machine legs"—spasms caused by muscle fatigue. He helped guide the rope as Hatcher lowered it and it looped down past him, the frayed part slowly dropping toward him. Finally it was close enough to touch.

The cut part of the rope revealed broken strands, and those that remained were threadlike. He doubted that he would have lasted another minute on the damn thing.

As Will looped the good part of the rope through his harness and tied in again, his legs began to shake, but he soon felt the comforting tension on the rope and released.

Hatcher lowered him slowly to the ground while Will used his feet to guide his descent.

Will stood for a moment experiencing the joy of terra firma and fumbled with the knot until he eventually untied himself from the harness. Then his legs gave out and he slowly collapsed.

He sensed someone nearby and twisted around to see Toby Winston approaching. "Mr. Buchanan, are you all right?"

Will tried to speak, but the words were tough coming. It was then he realized his heart was racing and he was breathing heavily.

"Can you move?"

"I don't know. I just kind of fell over."

"Man, I thought you were dead. That was quite a swing."

"You saw it?"

"The whole thing. I was just coming in with Mr. Smith and we were going to follow you guys up."

Will struggled to identify who "Mr. Smith" was, then realized Toby was referring to Skanky, a veteran rescuer so nicknamed because of his propensity to pick up cheap women. Apparently Toby called everyone "Mr."

Toby held Will's head steady as he looked into his eyes. Then he cleared his C-spine. "Can you wiggle your fingers and toes?"

Will complied. He was okay. He was still here.

With the help of Toby's arm to steady him, Will got to his feet, but his pins were still shaky.

"Come on, Mr. Buchanan. I'm going to walk you out of here."

"You don't need to do that, Toby. I'm all right. Really I am."

"There's an ambulance waiting in the parking area to take in that other climber. You need to get checked out."

Will was too tired to argue.

Toby hooked his arm through Will's and they stumbled their way along the path that led back to the waiting ambulance.

Chapter 8

I t was warm inside the ambulance, and Will sat on a stretcher waiting for his blood pressure to be taken by Sharon Olds, a paramedic he had known when she was just an EMT. She was in her early twenties, but her tiny stature and cherubic face made her look as if she were still a freshman in high school.

Sharon placed the stethoscope on his arm, pumped the cuff, and listened as she slowly released the valve. Will didn't have to be told that his blood pressure was high.

She smiled. "I think you're still on the rock."

He tried to return her smile but felt silly and stupid having to be attended to. "I'm all right," he said dismissively.

She grabbed his wrist and took his pulse. "Eighty-five," she said.

"See, it is better."

Sharon frowned. "Are you sure your head feels okay?" She palpated his scalp with both hands one more time.

"Look, I'm fine. Really I am."

"You've got some nasty bruises."

"And what about you?" he said. "You're really something. When did you become a paramedic?"

"Last year. And stop changing the subject."

"I had no idea you were going on with your training."

She let her hands drop to her side. "Lie down, please."

"I need to get back out there, Sharon."

"You're not going anywhere." She gave him a gentle shove on his shoulder. "Be a good boy or I'll get Ralph to sit on you."

Will could see EMT Ralph Collen-Binder out of the corner of his eye smirking at the thought. Ralph stood a few inches over six feet and weighed in at two seventy-five and change. Will couldn't understand why such an overweight man would get involved with the health profession, especially since he was a heavy smoker.

On his back, Will stared up at the roof of the ambulance as Sharon checked his eyes again and behind his ears for signs of ecchymosis, then for any discharge from his ears that would indicate brain injury.

Sharon finished her examination and popped off her latex gloves.

"Can I get up now?" Will asked.

"What's your hurry?"

"I told you. I need to get back and help out."

"Why don't you just take it easy until they get the guy down." She paused and smiled at him "Do it for me. I know I'd feel better about it."

Will resigned himself to playing a waiting game as Sharon and Ralph prepared an IV drip, just in case, for the guy still on the rock.

He knew Sharon was just being careful with him, but he felt like a caged animal. As he lay there, he ran over what had happened and tried to quell the guilt that rose steadily. He had screwed up. Because he hadn't kept his skills sharp, he had slipped on the rock and fallen, putting others in danger.

Will swung his legs to the floor and stood.

The movement was so abrupt, Sharon turned to him, startled. "Are you okay?"

"Couldn't be better."

Before Sharon could say anything more, Will hopped out the back of the ambulance.

The parking lot was just a turnaround, a slot big enough for the ambulance to wedge itself into and not much more. Most of the cars belonging to climbers were parked along the edge of the access road. Will stood by himself in the turnaround.

Will headed back up trail. His legs felt stiff, but his respite in the ambulance had helped. He felt stronger as he moved, but his progress was soon halted by the sight of his fellow rescuers coming toward him, struggling with a Stokes litter, a basket-weave metal-alloy stretcher, along the narrow trail. The men were quiet, and a few, including Hatcher, acknowledged Will with a head nod. From their silence, Will figured the climber was dead.

Will quickly moved to the side and fell in at the back to help with the carry-out. From his position at the rear of the litter, Will could glimpse the head of the fallen climber.

Hatcher had been wrong. The climber wasn't wearing a red bandanna, but a light beige one soaked with blood.

In Hatcher's truck on the way back to school, Will said, "You saved my life."

Hatcher glanced over and winked at him. "All in a day's work, my friend."

"I mean, I wouldn't be sitting here if it hadn't been for your quick thinking."

"Forget it, Will. You'd do the same for me."

Will wondered about that. A couple of hours ago his life had literally dangled from a thread, and now, for the first time in a while, he had doubts about his abilities. Maybe it was time to hang up his climbing shoes and turn in his pin.

"What do you say we stop for a drink?" Hatcher said. "A few brewskis would go down pretty good."

Will looked at his watch. Four-thirty. The Burger and Brew was open. "As long as you let me buy."

"Suit yourself."

Will figured he could call Laurie from the bar and let her know he'd be late. More than likely, from radio chatter she would have already guessed he had been out on a call.

At a booth inside the Burger and Brew, Hatcher talked about bringing down the climber's body and how the accident had happened.

The victim, a twenty-three-year-old college student from Massachusetts, had just begun his ascent out of the Cave and had clipped into an old piton. His partner said it was the first time he had climbed the route, and he was unfamiliar with the best place to put in protection. The climber ended up far away from the piton, slipped, and fell backward. The rope caught him but only after he fell twenty feet and slammed headfirst against the side of the cliff.

Hatcher quaffed his beer. "It turned out we didn't have to hurry at all. The guy probably was toast as soon as he smacked his head."

Will raised his glass. "Let's hear it for helmets."

Both men drank.

Will tried to relax, but he couldn't shake the feeling that somehow the accident had changed him, that he was a different person from when he rolled out of bed. He attempted to replay the incident, but the slip had happened so fast he couldn't pinpoint the moment when he had misjudged.

Hatcher ordered another beer.

Will declined and nursed what he had. He probably shouldn't be drinking at all with the Tylenol he had taken.

"You know," Hatcher said. "I'm really sorry for getting you into that pickle. It was stupid."

The comment brought Will up short. "What are you talking about? The whole thing was my fault."

"I was going too fast. I should have put in more protection."

Will appreciated what Hatcher was attempting to do, but he couldn't let it slide. "Look, Brian. It was a 5.6. Both of us should have been able to free climb it. It was my fault. I could have brought us both down."

Hatcher paused and smiled at him again. "Lighten up, Will. Don't be so hard on yourself."

"I can't help it. I'm not used to feeling this way."

Hatcher sat back. "What happened was an accident. Accidents are the reason there's a rescue team. It's nobody's fault."

"Somehow that doesn't help."

"Shit happens, Will."

Will stared at the dregs. He downed what was left and checked his watch again. A little after five-thirty. "We should get going. I need to pick up Laurie."

"You guys are back together, eh?"

Will eyed him. "I didn't realize we were ever apart."

Somehow he thought the "arrangement" with Laurie was a private affair, but he should have realized the whole town knew something was up when she moved into her own apartment.

"Her car's in the garage getting fixed. I need to call her."

Hatcher looked puzzled. Will knew he hadn't given him enough information to make sense, but he excused himself and stepped outside to call the police station from his cell.

Deputy Ray picked up. Laurie was on another line but Ray said he'd deliver the message that Will would be late.

When Will returned to the booth, Hatcher had ordered another beer and was half finished. Will's glass had also been refilled, the bubbles rising energetically to the top.

Hatcher said when Will sat down, "Everything okay?"

"Everything's ducky."

Hatcher grinned. "If you say so."

Will took a sip. "I take it you don't believe me."

Before Hatcher could respond, both men felt a draft as the outside door opened and Nelson Carpenter walked in. He headed toward the bar, removed his coat on the way, and disappeared through the rear swinging door that led into the kitchen.

"That son of a bitch," Hatcher said.

"Carpenter?"

Hatcher sat forward and wrapped his hands around his mug. He lowered his voice. "Every time he comes back into town there's trouble."

"Like what?"

"Like I'm sure he's dealing. I catch that bastard and I'll slice his balls off."

Will was temporarily stunned by Hatcher's vehemence. Then he realized the likely cause. "You're saying Carpenter's the source? Celia's buying drugs from him?"

"That's what I'm saying."

Will toyed with telling Hatcher he had spoken with his daughter, but given Hatcher's mood, he wasn't sure how he would take it.

"Look, Will. You want to do something for me?"

"What?"

"Talk to that cop girlfriend of yours and tell her to keep an eye out for that bastard. I don't know why he's still walking the streets."

"You know for sure he's dealing?"

"No. But I've got a big fucking hunch."

"I'll talk to her."

"And tell her if she doesn't get him, I will."

Will woke with a start. The alarm clock read 3:13. He threw off the covers and sat on the edge of the bed.

"What's the matter?" Laurie placed a hand on his back.

"Nothing."

"Bad dream?"

"I don't know. I don't remember." He ran his hand over his head and felt a lump above his right ear. "I'm just wired. I want to sit here for a bit."

"Talk to me?"

"There's nothing to say."

"I think there is. Come on. Lie back."

Will reluctantly responded to the gentle urging of her hands on his shoulders. He lay on his back and stared at the ceiling. He could barely make out the shadow of the exposed beams above his head. "How did I get old?"

"What? What are you talking about?"

"I think it might be time to turn in my pin . . . before I kill someone."

"Oh, for God's sake, Will. You're not old."

Neither said anything for a few moments.

Laurie finally broke the silence. "You just had a bad day. It was an accident."

"That's what Hatcher said."

"Well, he's right."

"But I don't have accidents. That's the point."

Laurie rolled onto her side and propped her head with a crooked elbow. "Are you going to tell me you've never slipped rock climbing before?"

"No."

"I didn't think so." She ran her hand lightly over the hairs on his chest.

"I felt like an elephant out there, though."

She patted his chest. "So go practice with Hatcher. And stop feeling sorry for yourself."

"Is that what I'm doing?"

"That's what it sounds like." She paused. "You know, I like doing this."

"What?"

"Talking."

Will considered. "What's going to happen to us, Laurie?"

"What do you mean?"

"Are we ever going to have a normal relationship?"

Laurie rolled over on her back. "This feels pretty normal to me."

"It's not. And I'll tell you why."

"I imagine you will."

"The only reason you're in bed with me now is because your

car is in the shop. As long as there's a reason for you to stay, then we get along fine. When we have to face each other on our own terms, we fail."

"I don't think that's fair."

"Then you tell me what's going to happen after your car is fixed."

Laurie didn't respond.

"Ever think of just chucking it all?" Will asked. "Just saying the hell with everything?"

"Sometimes."

"I mean, look at us. We're both doing things that could get us killed any day. And for what?"

"Because we like what we do."

"Well, maybe it's time to find something else to like." He paused. "If we care at all about our relationship."

"So, our jobs are the problem?"

"You have to admit, they tend to get in the way. Would it be so bad to just take off and go south?"

"And do what? You hate the heat."

Will couldn't mount a defense. It was true. He couldn't stand being anywhere he had to wear shorts. "I don't know. Maybe I could dust off my bass. Start another singing group."

"You haven't played your bass in three years."

"I know. That's what I mean. There are things I want to do."

"You really want to get back into music? That was a while ago, Will."

"So, I am getting old?"

"Oh, for God's sake. Let's go back to sleep. Things will look better in the morning."

"You really think so?"

"It's just the witching hour talking."

Will tried to close his eyes, but they kept snapping open.

Laurie suddenly started chuckling.

"What's so funny?"

"I don't know. I was just thinking about that story. You know, the one about the woman who kept a bunch of boy-friends away because she was knitting on something and kept pulling out the yarn and . . ."

"Penelope? The *Odyssey*?"

"Yeah. I think that's it."

"What about it?"

"Well, maybe you could break into the garage every night and keep doing things to my car. That way we could keep talking."

Chapter 9

In his truck on the way to work the next morning Will said to Laurie, "Hatcher seemed pretty sure about it in the bar. I was just wondering if Carpenter was in your crosshairs for drug dealing."

Laurie took a moment before answering. "His name hasn't come up, but I'll see what I can find out."

"I guess this drug stuff comes in waves."

"It's not my sense that it's gotten worse around here." She glanced across the seat at him. "What's the buzz at school?"

"Weekends are always tough, but this year the drug of choice is supposed to be alcohol. Vodka, especially. Hatcher seemed really sure about this pot, though."

"Yes, you said that. You think he knows more than he's letting on?"

Will shook his head. "What do you mean?"

"Just from the way you described his reaction when he saw Carpenter. Like he really knew."

"I'm only telling you what Hatcher said."

For a mile or so, neither spoke.

Will mulled over his years hearing the same old stories about drugs and alcohol. Schools that thought they didn't have these problems were deluding themselves. Campuses just mirrored society, and Will was certain kids would always use drugs as the preferred means to challenge authority. It also meant schools had a responsibility to recognize the problem for what it was and work overtime to combat it. But to feed off this culture by dealing was unconscionable, and he thought he understood Hatcher's wrath. "What kind of pistol did Carpenter report missing?" Will asked.

"A 9mm Beretta."

"Why was he carrying that? I mean, isn't that a pretty serious firearm?"

"Self-protection. At least that's what he claimed."

"You buy it?"

Laurie took a moment before responding. "Let's just say I'm rethinking. Hatcher's claims about Carpenter add yet another thing to the mix." She paused. "You say you confronted Celia about her using pot?"

" 'Confront' isn't the word I would use. I suggested that she come and talk with me, but it would be up to her to initiate it."

"I see."

"You think I should force the issue?"

"It's up to you, Will. I know you have your ways of doing things."

"Thanks for that."

"But do you think she's telling the truth?"

"It's hard to know." Will pulled into the police station and came to a stop near the entrance.

Laurie put her hand on the door handle and hesitated. "How are you doing this morning?"

"Better. I think."

"Your work is important, Will. All of it."

"No going south, then? No Florida?"

"Maybe when Miami freezes over."

After Will's first-period wildlife ecology class, he checked his e-mail and found a message from Celia Hatcher reminding him that her college recommendation was due soon. She was applying early decision at one of the Ivies. Will saw it as an opportunity to talk, so he checked her schedule on the school's database and wrote back that he would like to see her at his office during her free period before lunch.

When she arrived, she said, "I hope you don't think I was harassing you about this, Mr. Buchanan. It was just a friendly reminder."

Will motioned for her to sit down. He scooted his army surplus rolling chair from behind his desk and positioned himself beside her. "I don't think anything of the kind," he said. "I was just wondering if you wanted me to emphasize anything special in my letter."

She smiled. "Just tell them that I'm the best student you ever had."

"The academics are the easy part."

Her brow furrowed. "What are you saying?"

Will leaned forward, elbows on knees. "I want to ask you more about your father's concerns."

She looked away from him. "I thought so. You don't really want to know what to put in the letter, do you? I mean, that's not the reason you called me in here."

"Well, what you have to tell me now will help me figure out what to say in the letter."

"But we talked about this. I told you I wasn't using."

"I know what you told me. I just want to hear more about why you think your father suspects you."

"He just builds things up in his head."

"I don't understand why you say that. I think I know your father pretty well."

Celia chewed the corner of her lip. "You're not going to write that I use drugs, are you?"

"You should know me well enough, Celia. If that's what you're doing, then I can't lie about it."

"You would actually put that in a letter?"

"Probably not. I just wouldn't write the letter."

"Oh."

"I think it's time you told me what happened."

She faced him. "All right. I tried pot once this summer. It was at a party."

Will sat back in his chair. It was his cue to listen. He watched her body language as she spoke. Her hands, cupped on her knees in front of her, looked relaxed, and even though she didn't make eye contact, he sensed what she was saying was true. When she finished her story, he said, "So, only once?"

"And I didn't like it." A hitch in her voice suggested that this claim was questionable.

"But your friends must still be after you to join in."

"All the time. It's hard, Mr. Buchanan. I mean, you don't want to be thought of as a loser." The statement sounded lame in spite of the realities of peer pressure.

"I appreciate your being honest with me."

She looked relieved. "So, are we okay?"

"Do you know Nelson Carpenter?"

"I know *of* him. My dad talks about him."

"Then you know he thinks Carpenter's dealing."

"I don't know where the stuff came from, Mr. Buchanan. I only know that it was at that party."

"And just that one time."

She nodded. "I really didn't like the way the pot made me feel. Like I wasn't in control. You believe me, don't you?"

"And your friends never mentioned any supplier at all?"

"I don't think they wanted me to know anything." She looked at Will directly. "Besides, they're no longer my friends."

"You don't see them anymore?"

"No. I want to get in to a good college, and I don't want to blow it."

Will studied her earnest glance. "Then I guess I'll have to see what I can do to help you get in."

She brightened. "You'll write me a good recommendation?"

"Everyone's entitled to a slipup, I guess. Especially if you're not seeing those so-called friends anymore. I could say even better things if you can get that math grade up."

"Funny you should say that." She beamed, then reached into her book bag and pulled out a math exam paper. The grade circled in red ink was a 97.

"Wow. Good for you." He handed it back.

She replaced the paper in the bag and rose to leave. "I'm glad you called me in," she said. "I feel much better about this now."

"Can I ask you something before you go? Were you planning to come in to talk to me, anyway? You know, when I said it was up to you?"

She slung her bag over her shoulder. "I wanted to, but I was afraid. That's why I e-mailed you."

"Then I'm glad we finally had a chance to talk about this."

"I really appreciate it." She studied him a moment. "How about you, Mr. Buchanan? Are you feeling better?"

"There was something wrong with me?"

"Well, my dad said you had a pretty rough day on that rescue at Cathedral Ledge."

"Oh, yeah. I am feeling better, thank you."

A distant look came to her eyes. "You know, sometimes I worry that my dad's the one hanging around with the wrong crowd."

"Why do you say that?"

She shrugged. "He'll leave the house and not say anything about where he's going. He just tells me he's a big boy and can take care of himself."

"Well, he is away a lot on rescue calls."

"Not that many," she said. "Last month he was gone two whole days without telling me anything. I just worry about him, that's all."

Her eyes fell to Will's desk. "Oh, I hate that thing." She pointed to the stuffed fisher cat that had been a fixture on his desk since he had been at the school.

It took a brief instant for Will to realize what she was talking about. "You mean Festus?"

"It gives me the creeps. It's like a giant weasel or something."

"Actually, Festus has recently been raised to venerable status. They just named the new Manchester minor-league baseball team 'The Fisher Cats.' "

"They couldn't think of anything better?"

Will laughed. "The name beat out five other entries, including 'The Primaries.' "

"Now *that's* hard to believe."

"I can't wait to see the mascot. Go Cats!"

After work, on the way to the mini-mart for the paper, Laurie sat with her arms folded, deep in thought.

"You want to talk about it?" Will asked.

"What? Oh, sorry. I guess I'm not being very social."

"Something's weighing on you. I can always tell."

"It's that obvious?"

"The folded arms. Always gives you away."

Laurie let her hands drop to her sides. "God, I *am* tense. It's like I've been in the dentist chair all afternoon."

"So . . . are you going to tell me about it?"

She stared straight ahead. "Spagnolli called today and said the memorial service for Samantha Rayley is this Saturday. I couldn't stop thinking about her today."

"And you're still planning to go?"

"Of course."

"Then I'm there, too."

She looked over at him. "That's nice. Thanks for volunteering without me asking." Then she did something Will couldn't remember her ever doing. She unbuckled her seat belt and slid across the seat. She hooked her arm through his and rested her head on his shoulder.

"What's this?"

"I guess I just need to hold on for a few minutes."

"Want me to pull over?"

"No. I'm mad at you, though."

"Me? Why?"

"You didn't tell me everything about Cathedral."

"Sure, I did."

"The frayed rope?"

Will paused. "A slight detail."

"You really almost bought it, didn't you?"

"But I didn't."

She squeezed his arm tighter. "You would have left me all alone, you bastard." She smacked his arm with her other hand.

Will slowed the truck down. "Who've you been talking to?"

"That's privileged information."

"Come on."

"Sharon Olds. In the diner on my break."

"Oh." Will tried to think of something else to say but ended up, instead, focusing on the divided line of the highway. Her reaction surprised but pleased him. Her hanging on his arm was so unlike her that he didn't want to break the mood by saying something stupid.

Behind Will's truck, a kid in a muscle car pulled up on his rear, hit his horn, then roared past him doing about eighty.

"Too bad we aren't in the cruiser," he said. "We could nail the bastard."

"I got his plate." She shifted in her seat, took her pen from her pocket, and wrote it down on a pad she drew from her hip pocket. She left the pad on the seat and reassumed her position next to Will.

"So, tell me about this guy who was harassing women at Lake of the Clouds Hut," Will said.

"How did you hear about him?"

"It was all over school. I guess one of the women is the mother of one of our students."

Laurie didn't respond.

"So, this is more *privileged* information?" Will pulled into the parking lot of the mini-mart and drove into a space in front of the store.

"There's not much to say, especially if you think he might have had something to do with Samantha Rayley. According to the state police, he was just a lonely guy trying to get a date."

"On top of a mountain?"

"He was looking for athletic women."

Will grinned in disbelief. "You're kidding. That's what he said?"

She nodded. "But when he found out he was being questioned in a murder case, he freaked. He was eventually cleared because he could prove he wasn't anywhere near the area when the murders happened."

"They let him go?"

"Well, he still faces harassment charges."

Will considered. "So, it's Nelson Carpenter or nothing. He's the best lead? Still no connection with Samantha and Jeanne Conroy?"

"Nothing. I suppose there's always the possibility the killings were random."

"Which you still don't believe."

"Do you?"

Will shook his head. "Here we go again."

She patted his arm. "I'll tell you what. You sit and mull it over while I go get the paper."

"I'd be glad to go in for you."

She smiled. "No. I have to talk to the owner anyway, if he's in."

"Wallace? What about?"

She slid across the seat, looked back, and smiled. "Now, that *is* privileged information."

As Will waited in the truck, he didn't think about the Samantha Rayley case as much as he did Laurie. He could still feel the faint trace of her arm through his.

Since his accident at Cathedral, Will thought almost losing his life might have been the best thing for their relationship. She was actually being openly affectionate with him. Laurie was never one to talk about her feelings, which made her holding on to his arm like a schoolgirl at the drive-in all the more compelling.

But these good thoughts were abruptly shattered by the sound of gunfire coming from inside the mini.

At first, Will sat stunned, not sure he had heard right. Then another shot, and he sprang out of the truck. He sprinted to the entrance and found Laurie lying in front of the door, her shoulder pushing against it.

He carefully opened the door, and her head lolled as her upper torso rolled across the doorsill. He knelt and saw blood pooling on her shoulder.

Laurie's eyes were open, and she was staring straight ahead at nothing.

"Laurie. It's me!"

Her lips quivered as she spoke. "I've been shot." She said it absently as if she was trying to confirm what had happened. Her eyelids fluttered and closed, and Will sensed her slipping away from him.

"Stay with me!" Will shifted into his EMT mode and quickly assessed her injuries. Laurie was talking, so she had an airway and was breathing. But her circulation? He ripped off his jacket and used it to stanch the blood on her shoulder.

Will kept pressure on the shoulder wound, looked up, and found the attendant behind the counter with his hands in the air. Will had been so focused on Laurie he hadn't even determined if the scene was safe for him to enter. *Who shot her?*

Will looked up and glanced at the rear of the store, but his vision was blocked by the aisle shelves. He snapped his head back to the attendant. "Where's the shooter?"

The attendant just blinked at him, his hands still raised.

Will tried another tack. "What's your name?"

The attendant finally came to life, a kid with a shaved head and a nose ring. "Willy," he said.

"Call 911."

Laurie groaned.

"It's okay," Will said.

She reached up and pulled him closer with her good hand. "Go after him, Will. He went out the back. I'm okay, really I am."

Will's spirits soared. The sound of her voice had a clarity that was missing a few short moments ago. "I'm not leaving you."

"Go after him!"

Will was suddenly aware of others milling around. They must have been hiding when the shots were fired and had just come out of the woodwork.

A bald man wearing a checked lumber jacket stepped forward. "I'll keep pressure on that." The man dropped to his knees. "Go on. I know first aid." He placed his hands next to Will's on Laurie's shoulder.

Will stood. His hands were covered with Laurie's blood, and he wiped them on his pants.

He took a second to double-check Laurie.

"Take my gun!" she said.

Will grabbed her Smith & Wesson, then tore off down the aisle, ducked down the rear corridor, and hit the crash bar on the rear door.

Outside, his breath made plumes of condensation as he quickly scanned the area. He tried not to think that he might be heading into a trap, but he knew he couldn't be overly cautious or he would lose even more time.

The rear of the store bordered the woods, but there was a path that Will quickly determined was the direction the perp had headed. He dropped to one knee and examined the stirred-up leaves and a heel print in the mud. He had never been on the path, but he reasoned the guy had to be running and would stay on it wherever it led.

Will felt him slipping away. He broke into a sprint and followed the path as it meandered deeper into the woods and across a slowly running stream, until it emptied out onto a turnabout on a dirt road. It felt as if he had been running forever, but his watch told him he had been gone for a little over ten minutes.

Will stopped, hands on hips, to catch his breath. He knelt again and discovered tire prints in the gravel. A few more yards revealed where a car had peeled out. Will calmed himself and listened intently to see if he could hear a vehicle in the distance, but the woods were quiet.

At least he had found where the perp's car had been parked, and something might turn up with a formal investigation of the site. The Major Crime Unit would be all over it.

His thoughts quickly turned to Laurie, lying in her own blood. He started jogging back in the direction of the store when his attention was diverted by something lying on the edge of the path. It was gray and hard edged, and it stood out against the fallen birch leaves that flecked the muddy trail. He moved closer and discovered, partially hidden in the leaves, the butt end of a pistol.

He reached into his pocket and pulled out a ballpoint pen. He hooked the pen through the trigger housing and lifted the pistol.

It took just a few seconds to identify it as a semiautomatic, a 9mm Beretta.

Chapter 10

When Will returned to the mini-mart, Laurie was just being loaded into the ambulance. Her deputy, Ray, was helping out with the wheeled stretcher as Will approached. "I'll take over, Ray."

Ray looked up at him. "You sure?"

Will lifted the pistol he had found and dangled it gingerly toward the deputy. "You need to take care of this."

Ray took the ballpoint from Will's grasp and handled the pistol as if it had just come out of the oven.

"I'll explain later."

Sharon Olds bumped shoulders with Will as they both maneuvered the stretcher and shoved it into the back of the ambulance. "Want to ride along?"

"You bet I do."

"I could use your help."

The stretcher locked in with a sharp, metallic *click,* and Will jumped in the back and closed the rear door.

The driver wasn't Ralph Collen-Binder, but a young woman Will had never seen before. Conway Memorial must be experiencing a turnover of personnel, he thought.

Will gloved up. "What can I do, Sharon?"

"Keep pressure on that wound while I get some fluids into her."

Will studied Sharon, trying to read her assessment of Laurie's condition.

Sharon must have intuited his concerns, for she smiled weakly and flashed him a thumbs-up sign. "Keep talking to her," she said. "She's lost a lot of blood."

Will knelt down and placed his hand on top of a trauma dressing, and it was then that he realized Laurie was staring at him. At least he thought she was. Her gaze was distant. "How you doing?"

She said something that Will couldn't understand at first. "Did you get him?" she repeated.

"No. He left a calling card, though."

"What?"

"His gun."

"Well, that was nice of him." A troubled look immediately came over her face, and Will imagined she was bothered, even in her vacuous state, by the same thing he was. Why would the perp leave his gun behind? Unless he just dropped it accidentally.

The ambulance lurched as it cornered hard, and Will clung to the edge of the stretcher. "Sorry about that," the woman said from the driver's seat.

"Just keep it on the road," Sharon said.

In another twenty minutes, they pulled into the emergency room of Conway Memorial. Doctor Wilson Ford took over and was briefed by Sharon; then he shooed them both out of the trauma unit.

In the waiting room, Will asked Sharon, "How bad *is* it?"

"I think she got lucky. From what I can tell, she took two shots, both hitting in close proximity. One nicked the collarbone; the other, the fleshy part of her shoulder."

"Exit wounds?"

"It looks like one round went through the shoulder. The scapula feels like mush. I don't think there's any bullet left inside her."

So, there was good news of sorts: no bullet to go scrounging for. But Will knew enough about gunshots from a 9mm to realize that there still could be more extensive damage.

"I've got to get going. You okay, Will?"

"I'm fine."

"You've had quite a week."

"Really, I'm fine."

"I've heard you say that before."

Sharon left him to get the ambulance ready for the next call, and Will settled for a long haul on the couch in the waiting room.

In a little over an hour, Ray showed up at the hospital. "How's she doing?" he asked.

"She's in surgery."

"But she's doing okay?"

"I don't know, Ray. I can't tell you anything for sure."

Ray Flemmer had been Laurie's deputy as long as Will could remember. He stood now looking down at Will, running his hat brim through his hands, his head, with slicked-back hair, lowered as if at a viewing.

"Have a seat, Ray. You make me nervous." Will patted

the chair next to him. "If I know Laurie, she's going to pull through." But as soon as Will said it, he thought about her on the table. Anything can happen in surgery. Just last week a woman had died in a Boston hospital from complications from a staple operation to shut off part of her stomach.

Both men shared a nervous silence.

"I turned that pistol over to Sergeant Macomber," Ray said finally.

At the mention of Macomber's name, Will flashed the moment he discovered the severed arm of Samantha Rayley. "So, the Major Crime Unit is on scene now?"

Ray nodded. "I think they got some footprints, too. I mean, besides yours."

Will recalled the heel print in the mud. "And I think the perp should try another line of work."

"Yeah. Seems kind of clumsy."

"I'm curious. Have you had a lot of this kind of thing going on?"

"You mean robberies?"

"Well, especially mini-marts."

"Not that I know of."

"You interview the clerk?"

Ray let out a sigh. "Man, that kid was scared shitless. He was stumbling all over his words."

"So, what did he say?"

Ray looked askance at Will. "I don't know if I should tell you."

"It's your call." Will knew Ray well enough to understand that challenging him only led to digging in his heels. He also understood Ray sometimes considered Will a meddler who had no business being involved in police affairs. Better to bring Ray around slowly.

"There's one thing I don't get, though." Ray shifted in his seat and faced Will. "Why the guy didn't move faster."

"The shooter?" Ray had a way of saying his mind without giving much direction as to his turn of thought.

"Well, the kid said he held a gun on him for a long time."

Will puzzled a moment. "Why don't you start from the beginning, Ray."

"The guy comes in the store. He's wearing some kind of ski mask, I guess. And he tells everybody to get down on the floor."

"Except the kid?"

"Yeah. Except him." Ray looked as if he was trying to replay the scenario in his head. "He tells the kid to empty the till. Then he just holds the gun on him."

"For how long?"

"I don't know. The kid thought it was at least ten minutes."

"And the perp didn't say anything all that time?"

"He just kept pointing the pistol at his head. Unnerving, man. The kid was about to pee his pants."

Will rolled his hands to urge him on. "So, then what happened?"

"So, then I guess Laurie walked in. And the guy didn't hesitate. He opened fire. The kid said he thinks Laurie saw him at the last minute, and when it registered what was happening, she reached for her pistol."

No doubt her reaction, her quick move for the Smith & Wesson, was just enough to keep the bullet away from her heart.

Will didn't have to be told much more to suspect that the perp knew Laurie's habits and had been waiting for her.

The robbery was a setup.

. . .

Will spent the night in the waiting room and woke, disoriented, with a stiff back from having been contorted on the half-size couch. He hadn't planned on falling asleep but had underestimated how tired he was.

He stepped outside into the biting air of a late September morning, the wind blowing steadily against his thin jacket. It was Friday. The sky was gray and dull as concrete. He called the school on his cell to say he would not be in and gave instructions for his students to follow the syllabus.

He checked with Emergency and found that Laurie had been transferred from ICU to a hospital bed—a good sign—but when he showed up at the nurse's station, he was informed that while she was stabilized and resting comfortably, she was sleeping. He was not allowed in to see her.

As a result, Will felt a momentary pang of conscience over having cancelled his classes but then realized he wasn't in any shape to face his students, anyway. Everything about the start of this school year seemed to be working against him, and he doubted whether he would ever get into a rhythm.

He settled on having a good breakfast at the hospital cafeteria. The over-easy eggs and hash browns went down well, and he sat watching the nurses and orderlies in scrubs as he relished his second cup of black coffee.

His brain was still fuzzy from yesterday's events, and the whole scenario bothered him the more he replayed it.

He was sure there were probably a lot of Berettas out there, but if it turned out the pistol belonged to Nelson Carpenter, then he was obviously a prime suspect as the shooter. But since Carpenter had reported the pistol stolen just recently, it was also

possible the perp who shot Laurie was the guy who stole his
pistol. Or did Carpenter report it stolen just to make it look
that way?

Will's musings were interrupted by his awareness of someone standing directly in front of his table.

"Hello, Will."

Will's eyes followed up the length of torso and found Sergeant Art Macomber staring down at him.

"I'm glad I caught up to you."

Will nodded. "Sergeant, you've been looking for me?" He
pulled out a chair. "Have a seat."

"How's Officer Eberly doing?"

Will informed him of all he knew.

"It's terrible. Just terrible what happened."

"Somehow I don't think that's the reason you're here."

"Well, I *did* want to check on her, but you're right. I also
want to talk to you about what happened yesterday. I figured
you'd be at the hospital."

"I'd be glad to help out if I can."

Macomber took off his black ball cap with the embroidered
state police shield and placed it on the table. Macomber was
dressed in his standard issue coveralls. He smiled at Will.
"How've you been doing? I understand you had a little accident
on Cathedral."

God, does the whole world know about that? Will recalled the respect Macomber had afforded him at the Samantha Rayley
crime scene and wondered if, with the slip on the rock, he had
also fallen from grace. "I'm fine."

"I just want to run a few things by you, Will."

"Fire away."

"Why don't we begin with you telling me your impressions.

What you did when you heard the shots. What you found. The sequence of events. That sort of thing." Macomber reached inside his coveralls and took out a small fold-over notebook from his shirt pocket.

Will gave his version of the story.

"So, you don't think this was just a robbery." It was a statement, not a question.

"The guy was waiting for Laurie, Sergeant. According to the kid, he opened fire as soon as he saw her."

"And your guess is that the shooting is related to the Samantha Rayley case?"

Will hesitated. "How much have you discussed Nelson Carpenter with Laurie?"

"Not at all. My last talk with her involved those photographs taped beneath the drawer of the desk in Samantha Rayley's studio."

"So, she made copies for you?"

"She did."

"And what do you think about them?"

Macomber shrugged. "Could be photos from almost anywhere."

"But you think they were taken around here?"

"That's my guess, but I've searched through them several times for anything that might indicate location and came up with zilch."

Will nodded, then related the story Laurie told him of Nelson Carpenter's connection with Samantha Rayley twelve years earlier and his recent arrival at the police station to report his allegedly stolen pistol. "I'm surprised she didn't let you know about him."

"I'm sure she was going to. She's usually good about keeping me up-to-date." Macomber was thoughtful a moment. "So, the bottom line is that you think Nelson Carpenter staged the robbery at the mini-mart."

"That's right. He had to get Laurie out of the way because she was getting too close to knowing he killed Samantha Rayley."

"Because she wanted money from him for medical bills."

"Yes."

"Well, we have motive then." He hesitated. "And the Beretta used to shoot Officer Eberly does belong to Carpenter. It's registered in his name."

Will blinked at Macomber. He had mentioned this bit of news in an offhand manner, but it landed with the force of a dropped cinder block. Anger and frustration surged through Will as he heard his suspicions confirmed about Carpenter being the shooter. "So, did you bring him in?"

"Can't locate him. We're checking through his place as we speak."

"Nelson Carpenter shot Laurie." Will said it slowly, as if hearing his own words could make the unthinkable real.

"He also left boot prints."

"I know. I saw them. You know for sure if they're his?"

"Not yet."

But Will had a strong hunch the boot prints belonged to Nelson. Will had a passing, cautionary thought not to leap to conclusions. Carpenter did, Will reminded himself, report his pistol stolen, but that was more than likely a ruse. The evidence may be circumstantial, but it certainly all pointed Carpenter's way. If Nelson Carpenter had somehow suddenly materialized, Will was sure his hands would be on his throat, and he wouldn't let go until the little weasel's eyes popped out of his head.

Macomber looked uneasy, like a bomb expert about to take the first steps to defuse. "We'll get him, Will."

"That son of a bitch."

"I know you're upset."

"You have no idea how upset I am."

Macomber reached across the table and placed a hand on Will's arm. The gesture was avuncular, meant to reassure. "I think I do. That's one reason I'm here."

Will looked down at Macomber's hand on his arm, then met his eyes. "What are you talking about?"

Macomber released his hold. "I wanted to be the one to tell you that the pistol was registered to Carpenter. I wanted to make sure it was *I* who told you he was on the lam."

"Okay. You told me."

"I'm not finished."

Will folded his arms and waited.

"I don't know you well as a person, Will. Only by reputation. And I know how much you care for Officer Eberly."

"Get to the point, Sergeant."

Macomber's voice was emphatic. "Stay out of this. Leave Carpenter to us. I don't want you to do anything you'd regret."

Will kept his arms folded. He could feel his muscles tensing. "Is that what you think I'd do? Go after Carpenter?"

Macomber didn't hesitate. "Given your history, that's exactly what I think you'd do."

After Macomber left the cafeteria, Will walked the hospital grounds. The wind gusted and pushed against him, reddening his nose, and he hunched his shoulders and shoved his hands inside his jacket pockets. He considered seeking momentary refuge behind a large willow but decided that the cold wind had the desired effect of helping clear his mind, and like Lear on the heath, he threw himself against the elements.

Macomber's news about the Beretta belonging to Carpenter and his caution to mind his own business had the effect of strengthening Will's resolve to do the opposite. Just a few short days ago, he was ready to wash his hands of the Samantha Rayley case, but now he knew that he had a responsibility to Laurie to do what he could to find Nelson Carpenter. This was personal now.

He was sure Laurie had been on to something about Carpenter and Samantha being together twelve years ago. Laurie would be out of commission for a while, and he would just have to pick up the slack.

Ray was a good by-the-book cop, but Will doubted his abilities to think on his feet. Macomber was smart, but he was also busy with other cases. Will wouldn't break the law, but if it meant that he had to bend it in the name of justice— well, then it was his prerogative, wasn't it? He was no lawman, and that probably was a good thing. Will would have to be careful, though, and make it look like he was being hands-off.

As he walked, Will was systematic in his review of the case. He was sure he was missing something. He went back to the beginning and tried to imagine Samantha Rayley checking in that day at Joe Dodge Lodge, the clerk at the desk recommending the day hike along the Direttissima Trail, she not showing up that evening. What else did he know for certain? Her visit to New Hampshire no doubt had a purpose. She wasn't here just on vacation. That purpose most likely was to see someone about money to help with the medical bills. That person was

Carpenter, the father of her child. Or was it someone else she knew? No. It had to be Carpenter.

The pictures? That seemed to be the best place to start. But he had already gone over them. There was something else eating at him.

Will stopped. A heavy gust hit him in the face, making his eyes tear. *Yes, that was it. That's what he'd been missing.*

He needed to talk to Laurie.

It was after two o'clock in the afternoon when Will finally got in to see Laurie, and he was surprised and pleased to see her sitting up.

He rushed to her side, bent down, and gently kissed her on the cheek.

She looked at him and smiled. "That's all I get?"

"You want to make out right here?"

"I guess not."

"How you doing?"

"I'm sore."

He took her hand. "You look super!"

"I do not. I feel like shit." She looked away from him, squeezed his hand, and fought back tears. "Thank you for coming to my rescue. You are my knight in shining—"

"But I didn't catch him."

"I know. I guess you *did* screw up." She gestured toward the wall. "Get that chair over there and sit down and talk to me."

Will snugged the chair to the edge of the bed. He took her hand again. "You *do* look great," he said. "I mean it."

"That's enough of that." There was a sudden steeliness in her voice. "You've got to get me out of here."

"Not a chance."

"I'm sure I can recover at home just fine."

"For God's sake, Laurie. You just got out of surgery. You're not going anywhere."

She looked away from Will and out the doorway into the hall. "They tell me I was shot with a Beretta 9mm." She turned back to him. "Nelson Carpenter's."

"It looks that way."

"It's just so hard to believe," she said absently. "I mean, I know him. I actually *like* him."

Will thought about Carpenter, back in the early days when he had climbed with him. Carpenter had a dry, infectious humor that made you want to be around him. "You must have been getting too close. He obviously wanted you out of the way."

A distant look came to her eyes again. "Obviously."

"Laurie, look. Let's not talk about this now."

"Why not?"

"I'm not supposed to get you upset." He lowered his voice. "They'll kick my ass out of here."

"But you always get me upset."

"I do?"

She smiled. "All the time."

He glanced at his watch. "I only have a few minutes left."

"You're on a timer?"

"They gave me ten minutes."

"Jeez. That's plenty of time to get me upset."

"I just have one question for you that's been bugging me. Then I'll go."

"But I don't want you to leave." She hesitated. "Wait a minute. What are you up to?"

"Look, Laurie. I did a lot of thinking this morning about what we know about this case. I went back to the very beginning, trying to piece together everything to see if we had missed something."

"Will, this case is something you need to stay out of. Is this about Carpenter? You're going to do something stupid, I just know it."

Will ignored her and pressed on. "So, there's one piece I don't think we ever talked about. I mean, I think it's important."

"Well, what is it, for God's sake?"

"What happened to Jeanne Conroy's car?"

"It was found in the parking lot at Pinkham."

"And Samantha's?"

She took a moment to consider. "It wasn't in the lot, and no one's looked for it, as far as I know. After you found Samantha's body, we just focused on finding out who she was."

"So, the car's still out there somewhere?"

Laurie met his eyes. "Don't go looking on your own, Will. Mention it to Macomber. Let him deal with it."

He bent down and kissed her forehead. "Good idea." He placed a hand softly on her arm. "You take care now."

"I mean it, Will. Talk to Macomber."

"I hear you."

She searched his eyes for a moment, then turned away. "It would be the first time."

Chapter 11

That evening, Will spread out his topographical map of the Mount Washington region on the kitchen table. It bothered him that Samantha's car had somehow slipped through the cracks. He imagined Carpenter taking Samantha's keys after having buried her, locating her car in the parking lot, and driving it somewhere nearby to ditch it. He wouldn't have bothered with Jeanne Conroy's car because her body was left so near the trail where she fell that it no doubt would be discovered quickly. Samantha's body, on the other hand, was buried out of the way, and it made sense that Carpenter would want to get rid of any evidence that could be traced back to her.

Finding the car, then, could be instrumental in establishing beyond a doubt that Nelson Carpenter killed Jeanne Conroy and Samantha Rayley. Will reasoned, given the horrific nature of both crimes, that Carpenter had to be covered with blood when he dumped Samantha's car, and it was likely that his fingerprints, and at least traces of blood from both women would be discovered inside.

According to Laurie's recollection of Spagnolli's police report, Samantha drove a light blue, nondescript Hyundai Elantra, and it had to be somewhere. Cars just didn't disappear.

Will's eye followed the dark line of Route 16 on the map as it moved north, bisecting the Presidentials and the Carter-Moriah Range, pausing as he went on his imaginary trip to check the contour lines on each side of the highway.

Where to hide a car?

Due north of Pinkham, the highway T'd at Gorham and met at Route 2. Will tried to think like Carpenter, imagining his state of mind. He must have been frantic to get the car out of the way as fast as possible.

As Will studied the map, it confirmed for him, even on the outside chance the perp wasn't Nelson Carpenter, that the killer had to be local and that he must have known where he was going and driven deliberately to a location. Otherwise, how had he been so successful in getting a major piece of evidence out of the way so efficiently?

As he focused on the road north of Pinkham, nothing stood out as being an obvious place to hide a vehicle, for the highway was well traveled, the terrain dense with trails on either side, which left the secondary roads as the only alternative. And there weren't many.

The road south of Pinkham, with its pronounced contours rising from the side of the highway, was an even less likely area to hide a car, and the only side road of note was more than fifteen miles from Pinkham: Route 16A, which led directly to Jackson.

Will lifted his head and rubbed his eyes, suddenly feeling this was a useless exercise. If Carpenter had had enough lead time, which was apparently the case, the car could be just about anywhere. He could have driven all night and even dumped it in another state, especially since Samantha's body was the second one found and not until a month after Jeanne Conroy's.

Will folded the map, got up from the table, and poured himself two fingers of Laphroaig, neat. He went into the living room and sat in his recliner. He swirled the single malt and sniffed it before taking a sip.

What the hell. He could at least look for the damn car.

Will spent most of Saturday morning driving his truck slowly north on Route 16A. He kept his eyes peeled for anything that might suggest a car had been driven off the road. A few miles up from Pinkham he found skid marks, but they led directly to a damaged guardrail, not a hiding place.

He tried his luck turning left off Route 16A onto the Pinkham "8" Road that led to the Dolly Copp Campground.

He drove the perimeter road of the campground but decided this was too populated an area to be an attractive choice for Carpenter. He then headed back to the Pinkham "8" and this time turned left onto an isolated road that was closed in the winter. It led up past the Barnes Field Campground and met with another road to the right that wasn't named on the map.

This one looked more promising. A road certainly less traveled. But the drive up seemed only to emphasize the futility of his quest. The problem now wasn't too few possibilities but too many. If he were Carpenter, he could think of a number of places to pull off and ditch the car.

Will headed back to the winter-limited access road, parked, and rethought his tactics. He checked his watch. He had already spent two hours on the road and was no closer to finding the car than he was when he started. He needed to think of something else that might limit the odds, and this aimless driving around was silly. But as he rechecked the map, he couldn't kick the feeling that the car was close by and the key to finding it was staring him in the face.

That afternoon Will returned to Conway Memorial to check on Laurie and was surprised to find her bed empty. Concerned that she might have taken a turn for the worse, he headed out to the nurse's station, but before he got there he spotted Laurie walking the hallway on her own, rolling an IV stand.

"Trying to make the great escape?"

She turned slowly and smiled. "I think I'd have to move faster than this."

He watched her walk. "Hey, you're doing great."

"Will you stop with the superlatives, Will. You're not very good at playing the upbeat, concerned loved one."

"Oh, come on."

"I'm doing okay." She stumbled. "Just not 'great.' "

Will grabbed her arm. "At least hold on to the railing."

She leaned into him and put her weight on his arm. "I think I'd better get back to bed."

Will helped her guide the IV stand as she turned and took mincing steps back to her room. She favored her injured shoulder, but Will was elated and amazed with her progress. She was one tough cop.

A heavyset nurse wearing a pink smock met them before they reached the door. "Ms. Eberly, what are you doing out of bed?"

Laurie smiled weakly. "Just taking a little walk."

"Well, you get yourself right back in there." She shot Will a glance that quickly implicated him in this subterfuge. "The doctor is not going to be pleased."

Before Will had a chance to defend himself, the nurse had bundled Laurie back under the covers and was taking her pulse. She studied her watch, frowned, then placed Laurie's hand back gently on the bed. "Now, are you going to stay there?" She said it softly, suggesting her sternness earlier was all bluster.

Laurie nodded.

"You don't want to open that wound." She did a quick check of Laurie's dressings, frowned again, and exited the room.

As soon as she left, Will caught Laurie's eye and wagged his finger.

"I guess I was a bad girl," she said.

"I should be surprised? Man, did you see the look she gave me?"

Laurie took a second to arrange her covers. "You just missed Ray."

"How is the intrepid deputy?"

"Picking up the slack. Jeez, I need to get out of here."

"And do what? You can barely walk."

"I think I've convinced the good doctor to release me in a few days. I want to set up shop at your place, if that's okay."

"Sure. At least that way I can watch you." Will pulled up a chair, reached out, and took her hand. "They find Carpenter, yet?"

"No." She paused. "Ray had some news from Macomber, though."

"Let me guess. They found something in Carpenter's place."

"How did you know that? And don't tell me you're psychic."

"I'm making an educated guess. Macomber and I talked when he came to visit you. He said he had a search warrant."

"They discovered muddy boots in the house that matched the footprints in back of the mini-mart."

Will nodded. "So, that does it, I guess."

"There's more. Underneath floorboards in his closet there was a stash of marijuana and twenty-six hundred in cash."

"Carpenter *has* been dealing."

"I'm not finished yet."

"It gets better?"

"You're going to find out about this anyway because we've decided to release the information."

"What is it?"

"Along with the weed, they found Samantha Rayley's wallet and driver's license."

Will stood, mouth agape. "You're kidding."

"Do I look like I'm kidding?"

"Then that's the proof we need."

"Especially if his fingerprints are on the wallet."

He bent to kiss Laurie. "Stay in bed. Otherwise Ms. Pink Smock will get you."

"Good advice."

Will visited Laurie again the next morning, Sunday. She looked even stronger than the previous afternoon, and if she continued to make progress, she was sure she'd be home in a few days. Of course, he didn't know if this was just Laurie's wishful thinking. The doctor might have other ideas.

Will spent the afternoon sitting in his living room trying to plan his classes for the week, but he had trouble focusing. He couldn't stop thinking about Samantha's wallet in Carpenter's house.

What it meant, of course, was that Will no longer had to be so concerned with finding her car, because now they had evidence to implicate Carpenter in her murder. But what about Jeanne Conroy? Would they also find her blood on the wallet?

If both women had been killed by Carpenter on the same day, as Will supposed, then it would make sense that there would be blood from each victim, along with his fingerprints. Or, if they got really lucky, they might find Carpenter's own blood on the wallet, too—also a possibility, considering the epic struggle that must have occurred on the trail.

But the more Will thought about it, the more he couldn't square why Carpenter would have held on to the wallet in the first place. He could understand why Carpenter would have taken it. Doing what he could to keep Samantha's identity a secret would have been a priority. But to hold on to it? Why didn't Carpenter just throw it in the landfill? Or leave it in her car after he dumped it? Perhaps it was a memento mori, a Carpenter fetish.

Will's musings were interrupted by the phone ringing. He picked up. It was headmaster Perry Knowlton.

"I hate to bother you on Sunday, Will."

"What's up, Perry?"

"I'm afraid your advisee's in trouble."

"Which one?"

"Celia Hatcher."

Will hesitated. "What'd she do?"

"She was caught smoking marijuana."

. . .

Will drove into school that evening and met Celia at his office. When he arrived, she was waiting outside his door, her arms folded across her body, handkerchief in hand.

When she saw him, she attempted a smile. "I'm sorry you had to come in, Mr. Buchanan." She started to say more, then broke down.

Will hugged her a moment. "Come on. Let's go in and talk about this." He guided her into his office, sat her down, and pulled his office chair next to her.

"I know this looks bad," she said, "but I didn't do anything wrong."

Will watched her as she dabbed her eyes with her handkerchief. He considered closing the door to his office, but there was no one else in the building to overhear. "Tell me what happened?"

"I went looking for Sandra, my roommate, because I just borrowed this new Eminem video and I wanted her to watch it with me. I asked around the dorm and somebody said she saw Sandra leave with another girl and head out the path that goes to Rusher Hall—you know, the one that runs out the back through the woods?"

"I know the path, yes."

"So, anyway, I figured that Sandra was heading to Rusher to see her boyfriend. So, I started walking along the path; then I heard someone call my name from the woods." She hesitated.

"Sandra?"

"Yes. She waved me over. That's when I found out what she and her friend were doing. They were smoking dope."

"I see."

Celia's eyes welled up again. "As soon as I saw what was going on, I turned to leave. You have to believe me, Mr. Buchanan. But just then Mr. Brodsky came jogging along the path and saw us." She shook her head. "Why couldn't he just sit inside and watch football on Sunday afternoon like everyone else?"

"Mr. Brodsky isn't the problem here."

"I know. I know."

Will waited a moment before responding. "Celia, will your friends back you up on this?"

"I think so."

"Then you should take your case to student court."

"You think I have a chance?"

"If your friends testify to your story, yes."

"But I was in the 'knowing presence.' " Celia was referring to a rule at school designed to keep students from entering a plea of not being culpable if they were present but not participating, an argument similar to Bill Clinton's story that he didn't inhale. Simply knowing what was going on by being there, in other words, was presumption of guilt.

"If you tell your story the way you told it to me, I think you've got a pretty good chance of convincing the court your intention wasn't to go in the woods and smoke."

"So, you believe me?"

"From what you've told me, yes."

"I just can't get into any trouble now, Mr. Buchanan. You know that. I just *have* to get into a good college."

"Does your father know about this yet?"

"No. I don't think I want to tell him."

Will sat back in his chair. "But you know he's going to find out anyway. The school has an obligation to inform parents of what's going on."

"Can't you make an exception? I mean, if I'm not guilty . . ."

"We can't short-circuit the process, Celia. You know that."

"Will you tell him, then? I don't think I can face him. You know he thinks I'm doing drugs and hanging with the wrong crowd, and I don't think he'll believe me."

Will took a moment to consider. "Tell you what I'll do. You call him tonight and let him know what happened. You're the one who needs to initiate this. But also tell your father to look me up tomorrow, and I'll do my best to support you."

For the first time since she entered his office, Celia smiled. "Thanks, Mr. Buchanan. You're a great adviser."

Chapter 12

A s soon as Will parked in the faculty lot the next morning, a car pulled in beside him. The driver leaned forward and motioned for Will to get in. It was history teacher Martin Brodsky.

Will killed the engine and hopped out of his truck. He opened the passenger door of Brodsky's car and slipped into the front seat.

"Little nippy this morning, don't you think?" Brodsky smiled at Will. He was a thin-featured man with an angular nose that tended to dominate his face. A former high school cross-country champion, now in his early fifties, he kept in shape by running the numerous trails that wove through the two-thousand-acre campus.

Will got the small talk out of the way. "Yes, winter's on our doorstep, Martin."

Brodsky took his hands off the wheel and twisted to face Will. "I probably shouldn't be talking to you before the student court, but I wanted to give you a heads-up about what I'm going to say." He paused. "You're still Celia Hatcher's adviser, aren't you?"

"That I am."

Brodsky shook his head. "I hate this stuff. This is the worst part of the job, don't you think? Why these kids can't stay away from—"

"What is it you have to tell me, Martin?" Will glanced at his watch. "I hate to rush you, but we've got five minutes before class."

"Oh, yeah. Sorry." He looked like he was searching for the best way to begin, then said, "I understand through the grapevine that Celia is claiming she wasn't smoking at all but came on the other two girls doing it."

"That's what she told me last night."

"So, you've already talked with her?"

"Yes. I'm guessing that her version of the story doesn't jibe with what you saw?"

"I have to be truthful about this, Will. These damn kids—"

"So, what did you see?"

"Granted, this was from a distance, but I swear I saw Celia passing a joint to another girl."

"Was the other girl her roommate, Sandra?"

"No. It was someone I hadn't seen before. Supposedly it was a friend of Sandra's who'd been visiting. The pot belongs to the friend, is what they're saying." He paused. "Now I find that convenient, don't you?"

Will didn't answer right away. He was too preoccupied with an image of Celia toking up on a trail behind her dorm, then telling Will a cock-and-bull story straight to his face. And who was this other girl? Was she part of the "wrong crowd"?

Brodsky kept talking. "I'll bet you that visiting girl will claim it's not her pot, either, that they just found it or something. So, it ends up that it's nobody's stash. These girls will lie about any-thing and—"

"I want to thank you for tipping me off about this."

Brodsky blinked. "Sure. I thought you should know. No sur-prises. Right?" He put both hands on the wheel again. "God, I hate this."

Will opened the car door. "Me, too."

The student court began at six-thirty that evening in a music classroom in the dark basement of one of the oldest buildings on campus. On the same floor was a large band room and ten cramped, windowless practice cubicles, known affectionately on campus as the "rabbit warrens," for their secondary appeal as trysting places.

Will and Celia sat in the hallway on a deacon's bench along-side Sandra and her adviser, ceramics teacher Ruth Stagpole, waiting until they were called into the court.

Celia had e-mailed Will earlier in the day that he didn't have to bother calling her father because he wasn't at home but that she had left a message on his answering machine about what had happened.

Will spoke softly to Celia. "Did you tell him about the court?"

"I told him everything."

"I was hoping you could talk to him personally."

"Believe me, I wanted to. But what could I do? It was a choice between telling him everything on his machine or noth-ing at all."

"Well, I guess you made the right choice."

She stared straight ahead and sighed. "A lot of good it's going to do me."

Will stirred in his seat. "Try to be upbeat about this, Celia. I know it's hard, but you need to be positive when you present yourself. If you're honest about what you have to say, you'll be fine." Will stressed the "honest" part. He had chosen not to tell Celia about his encounter early that morning with Brodsky and just let the proceedings of the court play out.

The door to the classroom suddenly opened and both parties were summoned. Will assumed that the other girl involved, the visiting friend, wouldn't be part of the court unless she decided to show up as a character witness.

Will followed Celia into the music room and sat next to her. Desks were arranged in a semicircle. The head of the court, dean of students Stephanie LeRoux, sat center stage at a lone desk next to a portable blackboard, which had musical notation written unevenly in yellow chalk along with a scrawled "Ozzy Osbourne lives!"

There was a lot of nervous looking away and clearing of throats when they entered. Will studied the makeup of the court: three student leaders and three faculty plus LeRoux as tiebreaker. The findings of the court would be recommendations to the headmaster in whose hands rested the final outcome.

Brodsky spoke first, and when he was finished, Celia and Will were asked to leave the room and wait in the hallway so that Sandra could tell her side of the story.

It took almost a half hour for Sandra to say her piece, and when she finally came out of the room, she turned her head away from Celia and leaned against the wall, her body language suggesting that her testimony wasn't going to help Celia's case much.

Celia and Will were summoned. Celia spoke quickly and concisely, and with little emotion. She was finished in less than ten minutes, entertained a few questions from the court, was asked if she had anything else to add, and, when she shook her head no, was summarily dismissed.

When they left the room, Will felt that her delivery would hurt her. Not showing any emotion had the effect of suggesting that she really didn't care what happened.

Celia turned and faced Will. "Now what?"

"Now we wait."

Will had gone through this process a few times before, and it was never pleasant. No kid ever meant to get into trouble and naturally tended to blame other forces at work for their own infractions. Such as, *The devil made me do it.*

Hearing Brodsky's story again in court suggested strongly to Will that Celia had been lying to him all along, and for that reason, Will felt if she received a major violation, it was probably the least she deserved. He hated being lied to.

Suddenly, at the end of the hallway, the door flew open and slammed against the side of the wall. It was Hatcher.

Celia gasped and rose to her feet.

Hatcher stormed toward them. "What's this about a trial?" he yelled before he even got to them.

Will got up quickly and went to meet him. "Brian, calm down." He grabbed Hatcher's coat sleeve to halt his progress.

Hatcher stared hard at Will, then down the hallway at his daughter, who stood paralyzed in front of the deacon's bench. "What the hell is going on, Celia?"

Across the hall was one of the small practice rooms, and Will tried the door. It was unlocked. "Let's go in here, Brian. I'll tell you everything you want to know."

Will guided him into the room, flicked the light switch, and closed the door. "Have a seat." Will motioned to a steel folding chair.

"I told you she was up to something."

Will pulled up another folding chair, flipped it around, and straddled it like a horse. "I know. And you might be right."

"What do you mean, 'might be'?"

"She says she wasn't smoking." Will related the story as Celia told it, then Brodsky's version.

When Will had finished, Hatcher asked, "And which one do you believe?"

"I think she was smoking."

Hatcher got up out of his chair and ran his hand across his mouth. "Yeah. I do, too."

Will studied his ruddy face. Tiny sweat beads began to form in the furrow of his brow. Hatcher was obviously distressed, but he gave the impression it was more than that, like he was starting to come unhinged. Will hadn't seen this anger from him before and it was scary. He wondered if Brian was like this at home, with Celia the target.

Will slowed his voice and spoke softly. "Brian, why don't you just sit down?"

"I don't want to sit down." His eyes darted around the room. "What the hell is this place?"

"It's a practice room."

"Feels like a fucking dungeon."

"It *is* kind of cramped."

"Shit."

Will got up from his chair and came closer to Hatcher, who

was sweating profusely now. Hatcher tugged at his collar, his respirations skyrocketing. He was panting like a Florida poodle in August. "For God's sake, Brian. Are you okay?"

Hatcher forced a smile. " 'Course I'm okay."

But Will was thinking heart attack. Maybe stroke. "Please, sit down."

"No. It's not what you think. It's just . . . just . . ." His hand swept around the isolated cubicle. "This place!"

It wasn't too hard to force Hatcher back down into his chair because he was limp and seemed to have lost all ability to resist. Will kneeled down and grabbed his wrist. Hatcher's pulse was tachycardic. Will put his hand on Hatcher's chest and spoke calmly. "Just try to slow your breathing. You're okay. It's going to be okay."

But there was panic in Hatcher's eyes as he hyperventilated. "I get terrible claustrophobia," he said between breaths. He tried to smile. "I bet . . . I bet . . . you didn't know . . . know . . . that about me."

"Let's get you out of here then."

"It's this damn . . . damn room. God, you teach kids . . . in here?"

Will helped him to his feet and put an arm around his waist, and they stumbled into the hallway. "Let's get you outside."

Hatcher ripped himself away from Will's grasp. "I got it now, buddy. Thanks." He lurched down the hall like some wounded creature, apparently forgetting all about the court, and disappeared out the door.

Will didn't get home that night until after ten-thirty. He had forgotten to leave the porch light on, and he fumbled with his house key as he tried to insert it into the lock. He entered the house through the side door.

In the kitchen, he threw his briefcase on the counter and, by force of habit, went directly to his liquor cabinet. He reached for the bottle of Laphroaig but immediately reconsidered. Given the lateness of the hour, a cup of tea before bed would go down better. He wanted his head clear. He put the kettle on and sat at the kitchen table to wait for the water to boil.

The upshot of the court proceedings was that Celia had, indeed, received a major violation, along with a mandate for drug counseling and random testing for her remaining days at Saxton Mills. What it came down to was that Martin Brodsky's testimony was more compelling than Celia's. But what Will thought about more was what had just happened with Hatcher.

As long as he had known the man, he had never witnessed any episode like the one that occurred just a couple of hours ago. Hatcher had always given the impression he was self-assured, not the kind of man you would think suffered from apparent phobias. Will considered him a highly intelligent man with many talents, so to see him suddenly reduced came as a shock. But the more Will thought about it, the more he recalled Hatcher spending most of his time outdoors, pretty much assigning others to handle the storebound retail end of his business.

The kettle sang and Will poured his mug. He let it steep a little before taking it with him into the living room. He reached for the light switch and froze when he heard a voice coming from the far end of the room. "Leave it off, Will. Just sit on the couch right where you are."

The voice was familiar and it took just a few seconds to place it. Will spoke his name. "Nelson Carpenter?" With the help of the light coming in from the kitchen, Will could barely discern the shadowed figure sitting in an overstuffed chair.

"That's right, Will."

"How did you get in?"

"You left your bedroom window open."

"How careless." Will took a step closer.

"I have a gun, Will. Just sit on that couch and drink your tea."

Will backed toward the couch and slowly sank into the cushions. He placed his cup on the coffee table in front of him. "What do you want?"

"I don't want to hurt you. That's the first thing."

"Well, that's a relief. I guess I can drink my tea then."

"But I am running out of options, and I need your help."

Will affected nonchalance, but he was churning inside. "You expect me to help you? After what you did to Laurie?"

"I didn't. I couldn't shoot *anyone.*"

"Then who shot her?"

"I don't know. That's why I need your help." There was a slight tremor in Carpenter's voice. "I just want to talk."

Will took a sip of his tea. His mind was racing overtime trying to figure out how he could gain the edge. Carpenter was smart enough to keep distance between them and use darkness to his advantage, but perhaps he didn't realize he was cornered. The only door on Carpenter's side of the room led to the bathroom and another bedroom. No egress. "Would you care for some tea?"

"That sounds so civilized, but I won't be staying long."

"So, talk."

"Someone set me up."

"Why should I believe you?"

"Because you're a smart man. You're logical. You know I wouldn't report my pistol missing to Laurie unless it was the truth."

"Or unless you were really clever."

"Believe me, I'm *never* that clever."

Will considered and realized he knew little about Nelson Carpenter's intelligence. "I have your word on that."

"And I had nothing to do with dealing drugs."

Will almost laughed out loud. "And I suppose the stash found in your house just mysteriously appeared along with Samantha Rayley's wallet."

Carpenter didn't respond at first. "As a matter of fact, that's just what happened."

"Then you'll have to forgive me if I don't believe you." Will took another sip of his tea. "If you're really innocent, you should turn yourself in."

"Oh, sure. That'll do me a lot of good. If I can't get you to believe me, how can I expect people like Macomber?"

"You'll get yourself killed."

"At least I'll die trying." Carpenter shifted in his chair. "They're saying on the news I killed Samantha Rayley . . . and that other woman."

"Did you?"

Carpenter paused. "We've known each other a long time, Will. Do you honestly think I'm capable of that?"

"We haven't known each other that long, Nelson. In fact, we've been out of touch for years."

"You really think I could have killed them?"

"I honestly don't know."

"But why? What's my motive for killing Samantha?"

For a moment, Will couldn't believe the question. Carpenter didn't know? "You just said you saw the news."

"I did. I'm supposed to be the main suspect in the killings. I just don't know why."

"You and Samantha used to be lovers, right?"

"We had a brief fling, yes."

"And you got her pregnant."

"What? No. That's not right."

"Then who's the father?"

"Wait a minute. Let's back up. Samantha said all this before she died? That I am the father?"

"No. Her mother claims Samantha didn't tell anyone who the father is."

"And you're thinking because we slept together once that I'm the father?"

"Once?"

"She was drunk. I was drunk. It seemed like a good idea at the time, but we both regretted it."

"It only takes once, Carpenter."

"Oh, really? Thanks for the news flash."

"So, someone else is Ben's father?"

"Who's Ben?"

Will could feel his neck getting red. "Come on, Carpenter. Your dumb act is just *that*. I can only swallow so much."

"He must be the child."

"Brilliant."

"Well, he's not mine. And now that I think of it, this is probably the best news I've heard all day. Give me a blood test."

"Turn yourself in and we'll do just that."

"Not until you tell me how I'm supposed to have killed those two women."

Will sipped his tea, but it had gone cold. He put the half-empty mug back on the table. "All right, I'll play along. Samantha came to see you because she needed money to pay Ben's hospital bills."

"The kid's sick?"

Will ignored Carpenter's feigned ignorance. "You refused to help her, probably claiming you weren't the father. But she knew something about you. She took pictures."

"Pictures? What do they show?"

"We're still working on that."

"You don't know?"

"We'd know a lot more if you told us what they meant."

"How can I tell you if I haven't seen them? It sounds like you've got nothing." He paused. "You're not going to tell me what's in the pictures? They show me doing something?"

"You're not in them."

"So, what do they . . . ?"

"They were taken in the woods. Someplace around here."

"That's it? That's what's supposed to be evidence against me?"

"I'm not telling you everything we know about them." But as soon as Will said it, he knew there wasn't that much more to tell.

"Look, Will. I know Samantha was seeing someone else after we decided to break it off."

"Who?"

"She wouldn't tell me. But she came to me one night and told me she was pregnant."

"Why would she tell you she was pregnant?"

"Because we got along. She trusted me."

"After one night?"

"All right. So we slept together more than once. I liked the kid. Hell, I lost my climbing job with Cloutier because of her."

Will suddenly thought about the photograph Anna Rayley had given Laurie. "Did you take a picture of Samantha on a climb?"

"I might have. She always had a camera with her." He hesitated. "But I didn't kill her. And I didn't kill that other woman. Who was she?"

Will ignored the question. "Okay, Carpenter. I'm tired of talking. Just for fun, let's say you didn't do it. What happens now?"

"I go away knowing I've told you the truth. And perhaps you'll help me find who's trying to bring me down."

"If you're so sure you're not the father, then you should have the guts to turn yourself in and take a blood test."

"I'll take my chances on the outside."

Will stood up suddenly. "Give me the gun, Nelson."

There was rustling from the other end, but Will could only make out the movement of shadows.

"Stay where you are, Will. I *will* shoot you if I have to."

Will called his bluff. "It looks like you're going to have to. If you're really not capable of shooting anyone, then I guess you'll have to prove it."

Will suddenly dropped to the floor and rolled. He came up near another chair and temporarily used it for cover. If he could get to Carpenter fast, he'd have him hemmed in.

Carpenter suddenly tried to sprint past Will to the door, and Will sprang from beside the chair and launched himself at

Carpenter's retreating figure. He tackled Carpenter around the waist and drove him to the floor.

Carpenter swung wildly with his pistol and clipped Will on the temple. Stunned, Will released his grasp and Carpenter scrambled to his feet. By the time Will recovered, Carpenter had reached the rear door. Will ran after him, but he got to the driveway just in time to see Carpenter's retreating figure, lit momentarily by a streetlamp, flit into the woods.

He's on foot.

Will stumbled back into the kitchen. His head throbbed. He touched his scalp, and when he looked at his fingers he found blood. He used a dish towel and pressured it to his scalp.

Chapter 13

The bleeding from his scalp wound had pretty much stopped, but as a precaution Will took the towel with him as he jumped into his truck. As he headed out, one hand on the wheel, he flipped open his cell phone and with his thumb punched in 911 to alert dispatch that Carpenter had just left his house.

The dim light cast from the sliver of moon meant the chances of catching up with Carpenter on foot were pretty slim, but Will suspected he might have a parked vehicle somewhere on a dirt road that bordered the woods by his house. If that was the case, Will would have to move fast to intercept him. He figured he'd still have time to double-back and meet Ray and the state police, who he supposed would soon be in the process of responding to his 911 call.

Will skirted quickly over the main road, and when he reached the turn he yanked the wheel hard left. The tires spun on the gravel and the rear hopped and stuttered. He over-steered, clipped some saplings along the side of the road, and floored it when he finally regained control.

If Carpenter was parked on the road, then Will had him

hemmed in. The thought suddenly sobered Will, and he had a glimpse of himself out of control, tearing off on his own after an armed and dangerous felon, with little more than a truck and a towel.

Will slowed the truck and kept his eyes focused on the road. His temple throbbed, and he patted it gently with the towel as he drove. The road dead-ended in a little over a mile and there was still no sign of Carpenter.

Will reversed direction and headed back along the dirt road at a slow, steady crawl. He sped up when he reached the junction of roads again and took off back to his house.

As he reached his driveway, staccato flashes of blue lights from Ray's cruiser greeted him.

Will parked beside the cruiser in the driveway and hopped out. The jarring when he landed sent a shot of pain through his skull, and he grabbed his head, stumbled back, and hit the side of the cab with his shoulder.

By the time he steadied himself, Ray was at his side. "Jesus, Will. You all right?"

"I guess I shouldn't have jumped."

He switched on his flashlight and aimed it at Will's face. "Let's get you inside. I'll call an ambulance."

Will gently pushed the flashlight away from his eyes. "I'm okay, Ray. I'm feeling better now."

"You sure you don't want to lie down?"

"That's the last thing I want to do." Will smiled at him weakly. "Where are the others?"

"I just got one state cruiser meeting me here so far."

"Is it Macomber?"

"No. I think it's Sharkey."

Will thought a moment. "Why don't you radio Sharkey to

come into Saxton Mills and fan out to the southwest when he gets support. We'll cover this end and stay in radio contact."

"We will?"

"I'm going with you, Ray. Either that or I'll follow you in my truck."

Ray shifted from foot to foot. "Maybe we should wait to hear what they want to do."

"For God's sake. We're losing time. If you've got a better idea then let's hear it."

Ray froze.

Will grabbed him by the arm, and shepherded him toward the cruiser. Inside, Ray turned on the dome light and radioed Sharkey, who concurred quickly with the strategy outlined by Will.

Ray signed off and glanced over at Will, who was looking at a map. "Where to first?"

"Kempton River Road."

Will and Ray traveled back roads into the early morning but came up with nothing. The search circle was a tight one, but Will realized that Carpenter knew these woods, and with the cover of darkness, he could be almost anywhere.

Around two o'clock, the search was called off until morning light.

"Like pissing into the wind," Ray said. "I'm ready to go home."

"You know where Carpenter lives?"

"Sure."

"Can you take me?"

"You mean now?"

"Ray, look. I know it's late, but Carpenter might be headed there."

Ray scratched his chin. "You know, if I were him, I would've parked on that dirt road below the hill in the back of your house."

"He wasn't headed in that direction when he first took off, Ray."

"Could've double-backed."

A possibility. But there was really no way of knowing. "Can you please take me to his house, Ray?"

"If he's there, he's pretty stupid."

"Just humor me, Ray."

It took another fifteen minutes for Ray to head up Route 16, turn right on 16A, and travel through Jackson on Wilson Road. Toward the junction of 16B, he pulled into the driveway of a darkened log house.

"What now?" Ray asked.

Will studied the house, a two-story gambrel with a farmer's porch. "Pretty nice place."

After a few moments, Ray said, "You in the market?"

"Let's check it out."

Ray looked out the car window at the house. "You really think he's in there?"

"Probably not. But it doesn't hurt to look."

Will studied the house for signs of movement.

Ray waited a few moments, then got hold of Sharkey on the radio. "Yeah, I'm sitting outside Carpenter's house, but I don't have a key with me. You planning to check the place out?"

"I'll swing by on my way out."

"Any sign of Carpenter."

"Negative."

Ray signed off.

Will smiled. "I bet you do have a key with you."

Ray's expression was deadpan. He didn't say anything.

"I guess you don't want me traipsing around the place."

"Something like that."

At his house, Will brewed coffee as he waited for light. His head throbbed when he lay down and he figured he might just as well stay up. He pulled out his topo map of the area around Carpenter's house and spread it out on the kitchen table. He kept coming back to one thing: Carpenter was still in the area, hiding out close by, where he had most likely been since he went on the lam.

Will would have to remind Ray to run a check for stolen vehicles in the area. The more Will thought about it, the more Ray's version of where Carpenter had left the car before breaking in to the house began to make sense. It would be an easy jaunt down the hill in back to the dirt road.

So, where was Carpenter?

As Will studied the map, the long Carter Notch Road near Jackson drew his attention, isolated in places yet accessible to civilization. He had been up there a few times hiking. He imagined Carpenter in a tent somewhere in that area, not far from his house. In the morning, he'd call in sick and have a look.

Will rolled out at dawn. The sun danced brilliantly through a stand of sugar maples as he drove up Route 16. This upcoming weekend, the second in October, would draw crowds of leaf peepers, especially now that the brilliant reds and yellows were almost at peak.

Will's head had stopped pulsing, but he had a nice lump as a souvenir from Nelson Carpenter. He recalled Macomber's admonition to keep his nose out of police business, but now that Carpenter had clocked him, Will was even more resolved to go after him.

As he drew closer to the town of Jackson, though, he was reminded that he was again driving roads with little information to go on, and like the other day when searching for Samantha Rayley's car, he was just chasing a shadow. But somehow, this time it felt different, especially when he realized he was now covering the area south of Pinkham, the direction Carpenter might have headed in Samantha Rayley's car. All he had to go on was his gut sense, but he had a strong feeling that he was on the right track.

Will banged a right onto 16A, then in a few miles, a hard left up Carter Notch Road, past the Eagle Mountain House, and through a low-lying area with Wildcat Brook to his right until he reached a sign that read: ROAD CLOSED FOR THE WINTER. The road ascended gradually from there, and he started up the rise when he suddenly stopped.

Something familiar had registered in his brain when he passed a section of road, and for a moment he couldn't place the sensation. He backed up the truck to the sign and again proceeded slowly up the road.

What was it?

He traveled a few more yards and slammed on the brakes. Off to his left, a marshy area with a distinctive rotten oak with a hole in its trunk, one branch raised like an arm.

In a surge of recognition, he recalled the scene in one of Samantha Rayley's photos. It was the same oak. To take the picture, she had to have been standing right on the road where his truck was parked.

Will sat, his mind racing. Whatever Samantha was attempting to communicate through her photographs no doubt began right here. He wished he had the photos with him but then realized that right now the most important thing was that he had, in all probability, found the surroundings that Samantha Rayley had most carefully documented.

Will pondered his next move. He could always go back and report his discovery, but he had already left a message on the school's answering machine that he wouldn't be in. He had the whole day ahead to explore.

He stared up the road, then glanced down at the map again and saw a parking lot at the terminus servicing three trails that emptied out onto the road. He decided to drive up and park there and work his way down on foot to see if he could find any other places that would remind him of the scenes in the photographs.

As he drove, he couldn't posit any connection between Samantha's pictures and Nelson Carpenter, though, and it troubled him. The question remained, why would she bother taking pictures of trees and bushes? He could hear Carpenter. *Sounds to me like you've got nothing.*

There had to be an arrangement of photos that made sense, and Will was emboldened by the idea that he had found photo number one. But he really didn't even know that for sure. He would have to get all the pictures together again and see if there might be one that depicted a scene closer to the main road.

As the scenery whizzed past the window, Will's thoughts were distracted by something else that caught his eye, a dilapidated structure set far back into the woods off to his right. He drove past it without stopping, then double-backed and parked along the side of the road just above the shack.

He shut off the engine. The place looked deserted. Part of the porch roof was missing, and the whole building was listing slightly to the left, but it no doubt at one time served well as a hunting camp. If Carpenter was looking for a place to hide out, this would be ideal.

Will decided to approach the camp from the side, bushwacking through a tight stand of spruce until he reached a clear-cut area. He could see the camp off to his right. He glanced up ahead. It looked as if the terrain stayed level, but he couldn't tell because his vision was blocked by a copse of bushes that bordered the property. The open area surrounding the camp itself was dotted with dense underbrush.

Will had now made it far enough in to approach the camp from the rear. He watched and waited.

The camp was still quiet. Above his head, the wind sang through a maple tree and leaves suddenly cycloned around his feet.

He took a few tentative steps, then ran in a crouch toward the rear of the camp. He approached the back steps, stood on the landing, and listened with his ear to the door. Nothing. The door opened to the inside. He twisted the knob and pushed. It was stuck, but it didn't seem to be locked. He threw his shoulder against the door, which scraped along the floor, out of kilter no doubt because of the tilt of the house. He stumbled into a kitchen, flailing at cobwebs that tentacled around his head.

A stale smell of kerosene and old linoleum immediately hit his nostrils. He scanned the kitchen for indications of recent activity, but the sink was streaked with mineral stains, the refrigerator unplugged. It was a Kelvinator, probably as old as the camp itself. He tentatively opened the refrigerator door, imagining mold or worse, but the inside had been scrubbed.

Will walked into the living room. The wind whistled through the eaves and drew his attention momentarily up to the exposed ceiling. He could see sky through a hole in the roof. He brought his eyes back to the room and studied the furniture, a rustic couch, the deal frame adorned with ripped and frayed denim cushions, veneered with dust. Of more interest was the matching chair next to it. The seat cushion clearly showed an imprint in the dust where someone had sat on it, perhaps not too long ago.

The recognition made Will whirl around, his eyes wide, senses sharp. The place started to close in on him, and he sped up his search. He quickly pushed open the door and found a bedroom. On top of a sagging bed, a sleeping bag. He had seen enough.

He escaped out the back door, his heart hammering. He placed his hands on his knees and caught his breath, relishing the infusion of fresh air into his lungs.

The camp could belong to anyone, but it would come as no surprise to Will if it turned out that Nelson Carpenter was using it as a hideout. The sleeping bag would most likely have hair fibers that would confirm the identity of the user.

He reflexively pulled out his cell phone to check for a signal, but he was in a dead spot. He'd have to drive back toward town to call Macomber, who probably wouldn't be all too pleased that Will had been trespassing on private property. Macomber would have to get a warrant and worry about probable cause, but that was his problem. He was a lawman and Will wasn't.

He suddenly recalled his recent encounter with Carpenter. Was Carpenter telling the truth about Samantha coming to him to talk about her pregnancy? Was there really another lover? Will doubted it. After all, Carpenter had lied in the beginning about sleeping with Samantha only once. He would make up anything to save his ass.

The wind was blowing more strongly now, and Will glanced at the sky. Clouds were building from the south. A front was scheduled to come through, and he could already feel the temperature dropping.

He made a quick scan of the area around the camp and found a privy, leaning a little, as if in sympathy for the camp itself. As he got closer, he didn't even have to open the door, for the ripe smell told him it had been used recently.

Not willing to risk exposure by skirting across the long, open expanse in front of the house, he decided to retrace his steps back to his truck. He headed toward the tree line that edged the rear of the camp and, once there, decided he might as well walk its perimeter. Was there rear access to the camp?

Will kept his eyes locked on the ground in tracking mode, a state where his senses were on high alert, the chatter of consciousness suspended. He soon came upon an open area off to his right and stopped when he noticed some bent-over grass.

He knelt, arm resting on knee, and found that there were two faint parallel lines of impressions in the underbrush that led into the open area. Ahead of him, as he followed the lines with his eye, were broken saplings. He walked farther in, and in a low-lying muddy area discovered the hardened tread of an automobile tire.

Will followed the signs where they led up an acute incline and soon came upon a point of land that dropped sharply a good twenty feet into a gully.

Just below his feet, he saw a large brush pile but not much else. He stood looking down into the depression. He let his eyes wander over the rest of the terrain and could see no signs of recent cutting, as if the brush pile had appeared out of nowhere.

He searched around the lip of the height of land and found a good place to descend. It took just a few minutes of digging his heels in as he carefully made his way down.

He approached the brush pile, pulled away a few limbs and branches, and discovered a light blue Hyundai Elantra hidden underneath.

The discovery instilled in him an odd mix of elation and sorrow. He had found Samantha Rayley's car, but actually seeing it made her seem too real, like she was no longer simply a statistic but a real person who once had driven this car and worried about oil changes and monthly payments.

A chill ran through him as he sensed her presence close by, imagined her smiling broadly, pleased that her car had finally been found.

He thought he felt breath on his neck and wheeled around, but it was only the wind.

Will drove back down Carter Notch Road until he found a spot with a strong enough signal to use his cell phone. He decided to call the hospital before getting hold of the state police and was informed that Laurie was doing well but couldn't talk to him because the doctor was seeing her. He was told to call back later.

That afternoon Will stood beside Sergeant Art Macomber and watched as two officers from the Major Crime Unit slowly removed the brush from Samantha Rayley's car.

"Tell me again how you found this," Macomber said. "I mean, how did you know where to look?"

"I didn't. I was trying to find Nelson Carpenter."

Macomber didn't respond at first, but Will could tell by the icy tone in his voice he wasn't too pleased. "And how did you know where to look for Nelson Carpenter?"

"I didn't. He found me."

"I'm not talking about that part of the story. What made you look for him around here?"

"I was guessing. I figured Carpenter had to be close by. I was studying maps last night and just got a hunch, I guess."

Macomber appeared satisfied for the moment; then a frown creased his forehead. "But why here? Why not 'close by' somewhere else?"

"I had already looked for Samantha's car in the area above Pinkham."

"And you did this after I told you directly to keep your nose out of this case?"

"You told me not to go after Carpenter. I wasn't going after *him*. I was just looking for Samantha's car because I thought it was a loose end. I figured you were busy and I'd help you out."

Macomber's steely expression didn't change.

"And I did find something else you might be interested in."

"And what's that?"

Will told him about the one-armed oak in Samantha's photograph.

"You're kidding. It's the same one?"

"I'll have to recheck the picture for sure, but I'd bet the farm on it."

Macomber puzzled for some time. "But wait a minute. Samantha had to have taken those photos before her car disappeared. Right?"

Will nodded.

"So, the pictures really couldn't have had anything to do with showing us where Carpenter hid her car. What's the connection?"

"I had trouble with that myself until I realized that we're still missing something. I'm thinking now that she somehow had the goods on Carpenter and was using the photographs to convince him she knew where he had hidden something."

"Or someone."

Macomber's knee-jerk comment brought Will up short. He hadn't considered another body somewhere.

"Why? What were you thinking?" Macomber asked.

"I was guessing money. Carpenter must have been taking in a tidy sum over the years from his drug operation."

"So, it was extortion?" Macomber shook his head.

Will thought he detected a smirk and felt the need to explain himself. "Like I said, I'm just guessing. I'm no investigator, but I do know Samantha's kid is sick, Sergeant. Maybe Carpenter had been secretly sending her money over the years, and when she needed more, he refused. She came up here that weekend to show him she had pictures of where his stash was hidden."

"And threatened to take them to the police if he didn't pony up? Blow the lid off his business?" The rise in Macomber's voice emphasized his disbelief.

Will could feel the back of his neck getting hot. Was the theory really that far-fetched?

Macomber placed his hands on his hips and glanced around the area. "So, somewhere out here there's buried treasure." It was a flat statement, spoken in mock wonder.

Will was getting tired of this. "Not buried. Maybe closer than you think, though."

"What do you mean?"

Will jerked a thumb toward the hunting camp.

Macomber took a step toward him and leaned in close enough that Will could tell he'd had a tuna fish sandwich for lunch. "Don't tell me you went in there."

Will didn't flinch. "I went in there."

Macomber blinked. His steady voice was laced with anger. "I could arrest you for trespassing. Breaking and entering."

"You could. But you won't because you need me to help find whatever's buried."

"I'm sure we can handle that on our own. That is, after all, *our* job."

Will gestured toward the Hyundai. "Just like you found Samantha's car?"

Macomber colored, but before he could respond one of the men called to him. "Sergeant, I think we have a positive."

Will looked over at the car. The heavy brush had been re-moved and one of the technicians was dusting the lock on the trunk lid.

Will and Macomber approached the car together, their con-tretemps temporarily defused by the discovery.

Once the prints had been lifted, Macomber gloved up and said, "Let's have a look inside the trunk."

Will watched as the technician—fireplug build with hair that grew on his head like a burr—slipped a picking tool into the lock and deftly maneuvered it while he stared ahead blankly into space, obviously feeling for the tiny lock gates in his mind's eye. Another twist, and the trunk hood broke open. Will wondered if he had once been a repo man. Or an ex-con.

Macomber fished around inside the trunk and pushed aside a neatly folded blanket and found a set of emergency triangular markers and a flashlight that no longer worked, the terminals corroded. Under the spare, though, he pulled out a manila envelope. Inside were pictures, a dozen or so.

Macomber took his time handling each one by the edge and holding them in such a way that his body blocked Will from seeing them.

"Anything interesting?" Will asked.

"Looks like more of the same. They're just more outdoor shots."

"Can I have a look?"

"I don't want you to handle them until we get them to the lab." Macomber was being a prick.

"Look, Sergeant. Can't you just show them to me?"

Macomber hesitated. He didn't say anything, but he hooked his arm through Will's and led him away from the other two men. When they were alone again, Macomber said, "We really have to come to an understanding."

"I know what you're going to tell me."

"You think so?"

"Yeah. You're going to give me the sermon you preached in the hospital, and you can forget it. Carpenter shot Laurie, the one person I care the most about, and he pistol-whipped me, to say nothing of killing two women in our woods. I'm going to do what I can to get this guy before he does any more damage. I know you've got a job to do, and I promise not to get in the way. But if you expect me to sit back and do nothing, then you're dreaming." Will took a breath.

"Are you through?"

"Yeah."

"Okay, then I'll tell you what I was going to say before you went off on me. I was going to tell you I think you're right that I probably need your help on this one."

Will hesitated, making sure he heard right. "You do?"

"Sure. I'm not stupid. What you know about these woods could come in handy, and I think your hunch about these pictures revealing something buried is a good one."

"You're not bullshitting me, are you?"

Macomber ignored him. "But you have to promise me you won't go off on your own like you did this morning. If you want to be a cop, then go to school and get hired. I'll take you on as an adviser, but we have to work together. You have to let me know everything you're doing on this investigation. Is that understood?"

Will nodded. "Okay. Can I see the photos now?"

"It's windy out here, Will. The conditions aren't right and I'm worried about mishandling them."

"So, when can I see them?"

"I'll give you a call."

Chapter 14

Will got home that evening and found Ray's cruiser parked in the driveway. He immediately suspected trouble.

He jumped out of the cab and walked briskly to the house. Through the glass in the kitchen door he was relieved to see Laurie standing near the sink, talking to Ray.

When he walked in, Laurie said, "Well, there you are."

"More important, there *you* are." Laurie smiled, and Will's spirits soared when he saw the high color in her cheeks. "Shouldn't you be lying down?"

She waved the idea away. "I've had enough of that." Her smile slowly faded. "Seriously, where have you been? I called the house to have you pick me up at the hospital." She glanced over at Ray. "Thank God I have real friends to help me out in my time of need."

"Ouch. Skewered. You got me," Will said. "I did call the hospital this afternoon."

"Sure you did."

"Honest. They said the doctor was seeing you and to call back later."

"And did you?"

"I was going to drive over and see you after I showered."

Laurie turned to Ray. "I don't know. What do *you* think of his story? Should I believe him?"

Ray cleared his throat. "I guess I'll leave you two alone." He gestured toward a cardboard box sitting on the kitchen table. "Anything else I can bring from the office?"

Laurie considered. "I can't think of anything now. Will's got a scanner, so we should be okay."

"So, I'll report here tomorrow at nine?"

"Nine'll be fine."

After Ray left, Laurie turned to Will. "Come here. I want to try something."

He stood close to her as she reached up with her good arm and threw it around his neck. She slowly raised the other arm, winced, and placed it just above his elbow.

"Wow. I'm impressed."

"Now you can kiss me," she said.

He did so and grabbed her hips tighter to pull her against him.

"Hold on, big fella. I don't feel that good yet."

"When?"

"When I feel that good, that's when. Besides, you haven't answered my question. Where have you been? You weren't at school."

Will released his hold and looked at her. "You called the school looking for me?" He frowned.

"Well, sure I did. I was concerned." She studied his face. "Something's happened."

"Ray didn't tell you about Nelson Carpenter paying me a visit last night?"

"Of course he did. But there's something else, isn't there?"

"Let's talk."

Will sat at the kitchen table, moved aside the cardboard box Ray had left, and went through what he had discovered in the rear of the old hunting camp.

When he finished, Laurie just stared at him a few moments in disbelief. "You actually found Samantha Rayley's car?"

"And what's even more amazing is that I didn't touch anything until I called Macomber. What do you think of that, eh?"

"Perhaps you're learning after all." She turned, thoughtful. "But her car . . ."

"And something else." He pulled the cardboard box on the table toward him and looked inside. "What's in here?"

"Case files."

"And Samantha's pictures?"

"Yes. I think so. Let me see."

Will shoved the box her way across the table, and she pawed through until she retrieved the familiar-looking envelope with the old photos in it. She handed it to Will.

It took just a few moments for Will to find the shot he was looking for. Studying it again confirmed the tree in the photo a match for the odd-looking oak. He showed the photo to her and explained where the tree was located along Carter Notch Road.

The implications began to build for Laurie. "So, this is the area where all these shots were taken?"

"I'm guessing that's the case. I'll know better when I see the others."

"Others? What are you talking about?"

Will explained about the pictures in Samantha's trunk and

how Macomber was being coy about them. "But he said he'd show them to me."

"When?"

"Now *that* he didn't say."

"I'll get on the horn to him. I'll see if he can stop by sometime tomorrow after you get out of school. All three of us need to look at them together."

The next afternoon at a little after four-thirty, Macomber spread the old photos out on the kitchen table like a Vegas blackjack dealer. Will stood to the side as Laurie, next to Macomber, sat transfixed.

"These are unenhanced digitized prints," Macomber said, reaching inside another manila envelope. "I want the lab to go over both original sets to see if they might have been taken around the same time." Macomber glanced quickly at Will, then Laurie. "How do you want to do this?"

Laurie leaned forward for a better look with a magnifying glass. "Let's add the new ones one at a time and see if we can find a way for them to integrate with the photos found in her studio." She turned to Will. "What do you think?"

"Sounds good to me." Will appreciated Laurie asking his opinion.

The new photographs, which Macomber slowly laid out, were grainy, some out of focus. A cursory survey suggested they were similar outdoor shots taken from the same area as the orginal ones.

Some seemed to be shot from Carter Notch Road, but the majority indicated low-lying areas with ferns as undergrowth.

One photo featured a large moss-covered boulder. If the digitized copies were accurate representations, they indicated photos in worse shape than those found underneath Samantha's drawer—not surprising considering where they had been.

As Will watched Macomber lay out the photos, his hoped-for revelation never came.

After fifteen minutes or so, Macomber said, "We're not seeing something."

Laurie said, "I think you've tried every possible combination I can imagine."

Macomber stood up and arched his back. "Will?"

"I don't know. I keep coming back to that boulder." He tapped the photo that showed the boulder nestled in the woods with moss growing on top.

"Why?"

"There's something about it that looks familiar."

"Come on, Will," Laurie said. "How many boulders are there in the Whites? How could one of them stick out?"

"Well, it does. Give me the glass a sec, will you?" Will leaned forward across the table and took a magnified look. "And right here—you see that? That faint streak. It might be a trail running close to it." He stood up.

"So, where is this boulder?" Macomber asked.

Will shook his head. "Buried in my brain somewhere."

It took a long time for Laurie to get comfortable in bed that night, no doubt due to her only taking half the dosage of Percocet because she didn't want to wake up groggy.

Her shifting about added up to an uneasy sleep for Will. He dreamed in short bursts, the photos often taking center stage, and one vivid REM job had him hiking on a trail approaching the moss-covered rock, looking down at what appeared to be a depression in the soil, sensing a presence behind him, and wheeling around just in time to see a ghostly figure slash down with the sharp edge of a shovel.

Will woke, sweating. He threw off the covers and sat on the side of the bed. Then he remembered Laurie was there beside him. He quickly checked on her, grateful she hadn't awakened with his abrupt movements.

He grabbed his robe from off the corner chair and stumbled into the living room. At first he thought he would just sit in a chair in the dark to recover, but he was increasingly drawn back into the kitchen.

He got up out of his chair and headed in that direction. He switched on the light. The photographs were still on the table where Macomber had left them. He stood in front of the table.

Maybe he was looking at the photos the wrong way.

On a whim, he arranged them in a circle. He went from one to the next, first clockwise, then in reverse. Nothing. But his eye kept falling to the shot with the boulder. He had been there before. The tiny bell of recognition was dinging.

Then he looked at a print that had similar terrain to that surrounding the boulder and noticed something in the right-hand corner. He grabbed the magnifying glass. It was a half-moon of some gray mass tickling the edge of the photograph. He did a quick search of all the photos and found two more with a similar feature, except that the same image appeared in one on the opposite side, and in the other, on the top edge of the photo.

Excited now, he pushed all the other photos aside, except for those three and the one showing the moss-covered boulder. He played with the four shots, arranging them in different combinations, and it was when he placed the boulder photo in the center and matched up the half-moons that he realized what he hadn't been seeing before. Three photos pointed to the key one in the middle.

Will pondered his discovery. Whether Samantha Rayley consciously created this puzzle was something he would never know. It was more likely that she just snapped these pictures at random and by happenstance picked up the edges of the rock in each shot. She clearly was concentrating on this boulder and also wanted to make sure she captured the terrain surrounding it. The fact that some of the new pictures were blurry also suggested that she was in a hurry. It didn't make sense that a professional photographer would settle for out-of-focus shots.

Will got up to retrieve his topo map from a bottom kitchen cabinet drawer. He returned to the table, pushed the photos aside, and spread out the map.

He went over the area he had investigated earlier in the day, noting the approximate location of the abandoned hunting camp. Of the four trails that met up with Carter Notch Road, he could remember hiking only two of them: Hall's Ledge Trail to the northwest and Bog Brook Trail to the northeast. He closed his eyes for a moment, trying to recall when he had hiked that area, but nothing came to him. It had to be at least five years ago.

He suddenly felt tired, but he shook himself awake. Should he tell Laurie and Macomber about these hunches?

Ever since his fall at Cathedral Ledge, he had been second-guessing himself, and he didn't want to tip his hand just yet, not until he had a chance to scout the area himself.

He would call headmaster Perry Knowlton in the morning

and explain that he needed at least one more personal day because Laurie had just come home and required care. Not too much of a white lie. Besides, tomorrow was Friday, and with no Saturday classes, he wouldn't be missing that much school.

But he wouldn't tell Laurie where he was going.

Friday morning dawned with the threat of rain. Will hadn't had time to check the Weather Channel before he left, but the car radio informed him, on his trek up Carter Notch Road, that a front was coming in with heavy rain expected, and the temperature would be dropping throughout the day.

He parked his truck in the lot where Carter Notch Road dead-ended and pulled his pack out of the utility chest in the bed.

He felt his face flush when he realized he hadn't turned on his pager. In fact, he didn't even have it with him. He would have to make a decision soon about sticking with the search and rescue team or abandoning it altogether. This business of ignoring calls wasn't fair to others who might be expecting him.

Will spread his topo map out on the hood of the truck. Off to the northwest, Hall's Ledge Trail gradually ascended to a rock ledge bearing the trail's namesake. He recalled some hiker getting in trouble up there once—a broken foot or something—and they had to litter him out. But that had happened on the other side of the ledge, and the rescue team had come in off Route 16. It had occurred long enough ago when groups of volunteers were hastily and haphazardly formed to respond, before Dr. Thomas Singleton organized Backcountry Search and Rescue.

But as he studied the map further, he was sure he had been

on this side of the ledge before, perhaps on a recreational hike, and he had most likely used it as a way out coming down from Perkins Notch Shelter, via the Bog Brook Trail that hooked up with Hall's Ledge and finally Route 16. He remembered the shelter serving as a port in a sudden and severe windstorm.

It was 1.7 miles to the ledge summit. Will decided to hike that leg first and, if he had no luck, reverse his route and cover the area to the northeast that led along the Bog Brook Trail to Perkins Notch Shelter.

Will looked up from the map and reviewed his tactics before taking off. Why exactly was he out searching? He mentally ticked off the points: It was most likely the area Samantha Rayley had been photographing. It was near the hunting camp that Carpenter had probably been using and where Samantha's car was found. The moss-covered boulder was familiar, which meant that somewhere and at some time it had registered in his consciousness. Or was he just imagining that he had seen the boulder before? He recalled Laurie's doubts that he could remember one boulder in the vast terrain of the White Mountains. Was he just wishing that he recognized it?

A raindrop splatted on his map, leaving a fat blot that spread and slithered off the map onto the hood. Will folded the map quickly and stuck it in his pack. He checked for water bottles and food, polypro and fleece layers, and threw on his rain gear. The pictures Samantha had taken were safely stowed in a travel wallet he wore suspended around his neck—the shot of the boulder and the three he had triangulated in a separate compartment—and he let it dangle outside his rain jacket at the ready.

He started walking up the road a few more yards to reach the

Hall's Ledge trailhead, and when he passed the iron gate that barred the trail from vehicles, he hit his stride.

Fifteen minutes into his hike, he stopped. He was sweating and decided to save the rain gear for when it began to pour and just hike in his long-sleeved light polypro.

The trail so far wasn't familiar, and when it began to rise in switchbacks, he suspected it probably wasn't the area he was looking for. The higher the elevation, the fewer the moss-covered rocks. He turned around as soon as the trail began its acute ascent up to the summit. He checked his watch. He had been on the trail for a little over an hour.

He wasted little time retracing his steps, mindful of his foot placement but determined in his pace. He felt the air damp and heavy on his face. As he made his way back, leaves that had clung on branches through peak season, ponderous with moisture, lost their grip and fell as lazily as snowflakes.

It always amazed Will how different trails looked when you were hiking from the opposite direction, and he told himself to concentrate on the boggy areas as he passed. He thought he struck pay dirt when he rounded a bend and spotted a moss-covered boulder off trail to his left.

He immediately bushwhacked and stood in front of it. He pulled out the four pictures and referenced them. The boulder looked too small, and the trail skirted away from it. In front, a marshy area puddled up now, even with the small amount of rain that had fallen. This was not the place.

He pushed his way back through the boggy section and made it to the trail. No other areas jumped out at him as he continued along the route, and he began to second-guess himself all the way back to the parking lot.

He started the truck, turned the heater on, blew into his hands, and rubbed them together. He pulled out his map and shifted sideways on the seat to have room enough to unfold it. He rechecked the route that led northeast to the Bog Brook Trail. It was less than a mile up to where the trail split and the Wildcat River Trail came in on the left.

Will's gut sense told him that if the pictures depicted an area where something or someone was buried, then it really couldn't be too deep into the woods. If Macomber was right and there was another body out there, how far, after all, could Carpenter have possibly carried it? For a brief moment, this thought buoyed Will's spirits. Then he remembered where Samantha Rayley's body had been discovered and realized that Carpenter could have carried it pretty far in.

Will chewed on an energy bar and sipped water. The rain had picked up and drummed a steady tattoo on the roof. He was alone in the parking lot. Given the weather, his being by himself in these woods didn't surprise him, and he doubted he would see anyone else on the trail.

When he had finished eating, undaunted by the weather or the nagging sense that his quest was folly, he set out again to explore in the opposite direction along Bog Brook Trail.

He pulled the hood of his rain jacket over his head and shoved his hands into the slash pockets. He wore well-broken-in, midweight leather hiking boots that had recently been treated with waterproofing, so he had few qualms about striding through the mud and pools of brackish water that he ran into along the trail.

Less than a half mile in, he stopped, suddenly arrested by an overwhelming sense of paramnesia. Yes, he had been here before. But it was long ago, and the memory felt stronger then it should be. Then he realized it was because of the photographs.

He quickly removed the shots from his travel wallet and shuffled through them until he found two that depicted the woods in front of him, the overarching branch, the deadfall to the right, its raw roots exposed, the stepping-stones around a depression of trail.

Will slowed his pace. He was close. He could feel it. In a few more yards, he zeroed in on a side trail off to his left that wasn't on the map. He instinctively followed it in.

The path was overgrown, but it went deep into the woods before it ended in a clearing at what looked like a camping spot, with blackened rocks scattered about from an abandoned fire pit. He felt a distant familiarity, as if he had camped here a long time ago.

Will turned to his left, and there in front of him was the moss-covered rock, as recognizable to him now that it might as well have been a national monument. He stared at it without moving—for how long he didn't know—as if he were on sacred ground.

He took out the four photos and checked them against what he was seeing. Yes, there was no doubt.

There was no sign of recent activity, no disturbance of the soil and detritus around the boulder, and, as far as Will could tell, no footprints. He took a few tentative steps toward the rock, his eyes glued to the ground.

He silently cursed the rain and knew, despite an overwhelming urge to start digging, he had better leave it as he had found it. If it was a crime scene, he would honor it.

A flush of vindication enveloped him. He headed back up

trail, feeling a few pounds lighter. He had been right. He suddenly felt a strong connection with Samantha Rayley, as if she had been shouting at him for over a month and he had finally heard her. *We'll get him, Samantha.*

When he had almost reached the trailhead again, his eyes were drawn to a depression in the mud on the side of the trail. He knelt and found a footprint. A lug sole. And it looked fresh.

He wheeled around instinctively. Was it a casual hiker or had someone deliberately followed him in? Carpenter?

A chill shuddered through Will when it flashed through his mind that he was out by himself, no one knew he was here, and he was unarmed.

He followed the prints where they led back up trail, but whoever it was had chosen to walk along the side of the path in an attempt to disguise his presence.

When the footprints came to a stop and clearly doublebacked where the side trail went into the woods, Will knew he had been followed and that Carpenter must still be close by, no doubt desperate because of Will's discovery. Though Carpenter hadn't shot him in his house, he surely wouldn't hesitate now that he knew Will was on to something. But what had he really found?

At first Will thought he might try to follow the footprints and perhaps catch Carpenter by surprise, but when he realized Carpenter probably was watching him, he just stood still and listened.

The rain patted his jacket in an irregular rhythm, tricking him to imagine, he was sure, other sounds that weren't really there. He scanned the woods. No bright colors stood out that might suggest a rain jacket or hat.

But he couldn't shake the feeling he was being watched.

If he was in someone's crosshairs, there was no sense running. He had nothing to do but walk out, sticking close to the
edge of the trail for cover.

It took less than fifteen minutes to get back to the parking
lot. Before getting into his truck, he took one parting look at an
especially well-defined boot print, and it struck him immediately that something was wrong.

He knelt to examine the impression and used the palm of his
hand as a measuring tool. It registered what was bothering him:
The print was at least two sizes bigger than the one he had found
behind the mini-mart after Laurie was shot.

Chapter 15

On his way back home that afternoon, Will pondered the discrepancy in boot size. Carpenter may have had to commandeer boots from somewhere to replace the ones found in his house, and being forced now to wear two sizes bigger wouldn't cause too many walking problems. It wasn't like Carpenter was wearing clown shoes, after all. But still, the discovery of the footprints bothered Will as he drove. Could it be that Carpenter had been telling the truth?

When Will turned in to his driveway, he found Laurie, sporting a bright yellow poncho, outside on the lawn. She approached his truck as soon as she saw him.

He rolled down his window. "What the hell are you doing?"

"Laps. Around the house."

"What for?"

"I'm in training."

"The doctor say it was okay?"

"What doctor?"

Will shook his head. "I should have known."

"I did ten laps this morning and finished ten more just as you got here." She was breathing heavily. Her hair fell in wet strands and clung to the sides of her face.

"How did it feel?"

"Great!" She beamed at him.

"Only great?"

"Stupendous!"

Inside the house, in the kitchen, she said, "So, how was your day?"

Will didn't hesitate. "I found the moss-covered boulder."

"You what?"

"I played hooky and did some poking around."

It was her turn to shake her head. "God, Will. You never learn, do you? It's like you're this big kid who can't behave himself. You just think it's okay to go off on your own, to—"

Will placed his finger over her lips. "That's enough of that. Seems to me you're in no position to criticize me for being a bad boy when you've been out cruising around the house."

She took a moment before protesting. "The doctor said I should walk if I felt like it."

"Twenty laps in the rain?"

"Okay. So, we're both bad." She stepped closer. "Tell me about what you found."

Will related his experience last night of separating out the four photographs and unfolded the process of discovering the boulder this afternoon. He included his suspicion that Carpenter had followed him, but he didn't mention the oversize boot-prints for fear it would confuse the issue. While he was still convinced they could be easily explained away, the discrepancy nagged at him.

"I think I know exactly where the Bog Brook Trail is," she said.

"It's pretty close to the parking lot at the end of Carter Notch Road."

She chucked him on the arm. "Let's go."

"You mean now?"

"Why not?"

"Because it's getting dark and it's raining like hell."

"Tomorrow then."

Will hesitated. "I don't think that's such a good idea, either. We've got to wait until this weather clears before we start digging around. We need to bring Macomber in on this as well."

"All I want you to do is take me there. Besides, you need someone to check to see if you haven't really lost your mind, that this boulder is really the right one."

"Good point. But you're in no shape to go gallavanting through the woods."

"It doesn't sound too demanding, Will."

Will was losing patience. She could really be aggravating without really trying. "Laurie, do I have to remind you again that you've been shot and you're still recovering?"

"I can take care of myself."

"And as long as we're talking about your health, with Carpenter on the loose, I don't think it's a good idea to be doing laps around the house dressed up like a big yellow target."

"He's not going to shoot me."

"What makes you so sure?"

Laurie grew pensive. "Because . . ." She met Will's eyes. "Don't you think it's odd that he didn't shoot you today?"

Will thought about that. Odd also that he didn't kill him the other night. He remembered Carpenter denying he shot Laurie. *I couldn't shoot anyone.*

She ran her good arm around his waist. "Kiss me," she said.

Will shrugged. "Sure." He held her in a gentle embrace.

In a few seconds, she broke away. "I've got a proposition for you."

"I'm all ears."

"Suppose we go in the bedroom now and I prove to you what shape I'm in. Then will you take me there tomorrow?"

Will raised an eyebrow. "Isn't that, like, a bribe?"

"Yes."

Will nodded. "Just checking."

All that evening, the wind howled through the eaves and rain pelted the windows. By morning the rain had turned to sleet, and Will slept in, staying in bed past eight o'clock. When he finally mustered the energy to make it to the kitchen, Laurie was sitting at the table having coffee and reading the morning paper.

"Man, it's been a while since I slept like that," he said.

Laurie put down the sports section and took his hand. "You needed it."

"I still feel groggy."

She squeezed his hand and let go. "There's plenty of coffee."

Will nodded. "Nice to see you sitting up."

"I'm in good shape, I tell you."

He smiled. "Well, if last night was any indication . . ." He went to the kitchen counter, and as he grabbed the carafe handle, the LEDs on the scanner suddenly lit up. He stood listening to the call. A hiker lost on Mount Washington.

Laurie stared at him. "You going?"

Will poured his coffee and sat across from Laurie. "I don't know. Let me have some coffee and think about it."

She put the paper down. "What's wrong, Will?"

"Nothing."

"A few months ago you would have been out the door by now."

"I thought you wanted me to show you that rock."

"I do. But we can always go when you come back. If someone's in trouble . . ."

"I hear you. I said I'd think about it."

"You don't have to yell, Will. I'm right here."

"Was I yelling?"

She reached across the table and took his hand again. "I think you need to talk."

"About what?"

"About your feelings. I mean, you're always wanting us to talk things through. You're always big on talk. Talk, talk, talk."

He let go of her hand. "All right. You made your point."

"I don't think so. You still haven't said anything."

"What do you want me to say?"

"I'll start. I think you're scared."

Will reacted immediately. "About what?"

"About going out on calls. Ever since your accident on Cathedral, you've been avoiding them. I think you're afraid something else is going to happen out there."

"I think I've been a little preoccupied lately. There have been a few other distractions in my life."

"That sounds defensive to me."

"What are you, a shrink?"

She shrugged. "It's just psych 101."

Will took a sip of his coffee. He set the mug back down and stared at the faint swirls of black coffee. "I don't think I'm scared of anything except being embarrassed again."

"Embarrassed? Because you fell?"

"It was a 5.6 traverse, for God's sake. I should have been able to free climb it."

"But you slipped. So what?"

"I'm not supposed to have accidents. I'm supposed to respond to them."

Laurie sat back in her chair. She winced when her shoulder hit the slat of the ladder-back chair. "Wow. That's a lot of pressure to put on yourself. You're not perfect, Will."

"Don't I know it."

Before Laurie could reply, the phone rang. They both stared at it a moment before Will picked up. It was Lieutenant Randall Cody of New Hampshire Fish and Game.

"Yes, sir," Will said into the phone. "We just heard it on the scanner."

Cody said, "I think you might want to come along on this one. We could use your help. I just wanted to make sure you knew about it because of who's missing."

"So who is it?"

"Dr. Thomas Singleton."

Will reported to the Trading Post at the Pinkham Notch Visitor Center, the same staging area used for the lost nine-year-old kid call over a month ago. Lieutenant Randall Cody was upstairs in a small office at a steel desk, hunched over his laptop, looking over the top of his reading glasses at the screen.

Cody's head snapped up at Will's approach. "Glad you could make it, Will." Cody stood up to shake his hand.

Will smiled at him and quickly scanned the room for others, and he wasn't surprised, given the stature of the missing climber, with the turnout at this early stage of the search. Without Dr. Thomas Singleton, there never would have been such an experienced group assembled so quickly to search for him, and the irony of their founder needing to be rescued wasn't lost on Will.

Toby Winston glad-handed Will. "Mr. Buchanan, it's good to see you again." Behind Toby, grinning like a toothless badger was "Mr. Smith," aka Skanky, who saluted Will. René Levesque, along with his brother Philip, Celine Mayor, one of the three women on the crew, Brian Hatcher, and Roland LaPierre rounded out the group that had responded so far.

"Okay, here's the scoop." Cody hiked up his pants. He had a paunch, but it was tight and muscular. "Dr. Singleton, as some of you might know, had hip surgery a little while ago, and now he's got this new titanium one that I guess he wanted to try out by going on a challenging hike, and he's got himself lost somewhere between the Alpine Garden and the auto road."

Will could imagine Singleton doing just that, testing himself by going to extremes, and it pointed out to Will the capacity for experienced climbers, no matter what their age, to deliberately put themselves in danger for the thrill of it. It wasn't only the neophytes who got into trouble on this mountain.

"Who reported him missing?" LaPierre asked.

"He called in his own rescue on his cell phone."

"How long ago was that?" Toby asked.

"Two hours." Cody twirled his glasses in his beefy fingers. "Look, let me explain everything; then you can ask the questions."

"Sorry, sir," Toby said.

"So, you've got to know that the weather up there's blowing like hell. We figure the snow line is something like three thousand feet, but it's whiteout conditions above that and extremely dangerous. What we got going for us is that Dr. Singleton has a lot of experience. Before his cell phone died, he reported he was in his sleeping bag inside a bivy sack." Cody paused. "But I'm concerned because of his age."

Singleton's age was something no one really knew, but he was old enough to have served as a medic in the Big One, and Will guessed he was pushing eighty, if not beyond that milestone.

Will thought about his own winter solo on Mount Washington to qualify for search and rescue. He had run into a horrific squall, and if he hadn't been able to burrow into a snow cave he'd probably have turned into a popsicle. Given the extreme conditions toward the summit, there was little doubt Singleton was in trouble.

"Come on. Let's have a look." Cody went back to his small desk, put his glasses on, and stared at the computer screen again. The group slowly closed in around him in a semicircle.

From where he was standing, Will could see a map of the Mount Washington terrain open on the screen and realized Cody was using a piece of software called Terrain Navigator Pro, set up with UTMs (Universal Transverse Mercators), which were important in sifting through the data fed by the GPSs his searchers carried.

"Now, here's my thinking," Cody said. "His PLS was about

here. He was seen by a husband and wife coming from the opposite direction." He tapped his screen with the tip of his ballpoint. "Now, we need to have a group go up the auto road, then one—"

"Excuse me, sir," Celine Mayor said. "I'm really having trouble seeing your computer."

Cody stood up. "Okay. We'll do it the old-fashioned way." He walked to a huge topo map attached to the wall near the entrance. The overhead fluorescent lighting wasn't that strong, and parts of the map were in shadow. "Someone get me that flashlight from my drawer."

Toby Winston retrieved it quickly and handed it to him.

Cody flicked it on and pointed it to the right-hand side of the map. "So, like I was saying, the auto road. Let's have Celine, René, and Brian take it up to the Nelson Crag Trail."

"Was that Singleton's original route?" Hatcher asked.

"No. But we think he called in somewhere around Nelson Crag. He started off going up Lion Head, then across the Alpine Garden Trail, and finally, his plan was to complete the loop down the auto road." He traced the route with a light beam as he spoke. "So, why don't we have Skanky, Roland, and Philip retrace his original route."

"That husband and wife okay?" Skanky asked.

"A little frostbite on the toes." Cody looked over the room. "That leaves Will and Toby to go up the Huntington Ravine Trail."

Will felt his stomach drop. The Huntington Ravine Trail was considered on the short list of the most dangerous in the White Mountains. The guidebook was full of caveats, especially about down climbing in the winter. He remembered visiting a

Web site established in honor of victims of avalanches and falls and having to scroll through a long list.

"Lieutenant, sorry to interrupt."

"Yes, Brian."

"I don't want to challenge your plan or anything, but since there's only two of us left for Huntington Ravine, it might be better to put the most experienced on it. I think you should pair me with Will."

Cody didn't respond at first and an awkward silence settled on the room.

Will studied Hatcher and wondered, because it seemed such a direct move, if Hatcher was doing this to show publicly that he still believed in Will's abilities despite having had to rescue him on Cathedral Ledge. If so, Will appreciated the gesture.

"Not that Toby isn't qualified," Hatcher continued. "It's just that I think Will and I probably know that trail best."

Cody nodded. "It doesn't matter to me." He looked directly at Toby. "That okay with you?"

"Sure."

"Okay," Cody said. "Let's get going."

Chapter 16

On the porch of the Trading Post, Will and Hatcher checked through their packs, making sure a fiberfill bag, bivy sack, and crampons were included before setting off.

"I think each of us should carry fifty feet of 9mm rope," Hatcher said. "You know what it's like up there. We might have to haul Singleton out of a ravine."

Will nodded. As ropes go, a 9mm was pretty lightweight. In addition to the layers of fleece and polypro, Will also carried a lightweight Primus stove, an aluminum cook pot, freeze-dried meals, and energy bars.

Hatcher snapped shut the buckles on his pack and looked over at Will. "I hope you don't mind what I did in there. I wasn't trying to pull rank or anything."

"I don't think anybody thought you were. What you said made sense." He attached an ice ax through a loop on his pack.

"It's just that, well, you know what this trail is like. And I didn't think having a rookie along would help matters."

"It's okay, Brian. I wouldn't worry about it."

Hatcher shook his head. "Sometimes I don't think Cody thinks things through enough. You know what I mean?"

Will considered. "It's been my experience that Cody usually makes the right moves."

"I mean about personnel."

"He could have wanted to pair Toby with me to test the kid under these conditions."

Hatcher hesitated. "I thought about that. Maybe I should have kept my mouth shut."

"Not at all. I'm just glad you wanted me to go with you."

"Are you kidding? Why wouldn't I?"

"Because of last time."

Hatcher sent a puzzled look.

"You know. On Cathedral."

A trace of a smile played on Hatcher's lips. "You're not still thinking about that, are you? Come on, Will. It's like I told you in the bar. Shit like that just happens. There isn't anybody I'd rather be partnered up with." He paused. "Come to think of it, that's probably where I was coming from when I suggested we go together. I was being selfish."

Will basked in the warm glow of Hatcher's words. "Then I guess we should get going."

Hatcher took a moment for last-minute adjustments on his pack. "But I admit I did want to talk to you anyway. I mean, the last time we saw each other, I wasn't in very good shape. I think I need to explain a few things."

Will recalled that night at the court when Hatcher wasn't "in very good shape" and suddenly thought of Celia. It had been just a few days since he was last at school, but it felt like years. "Well, let's walk and talk."

The two men pushed against the wind that whipped across

the Pinkham Notch parking lot, and it was only after entering the woods and making their ascent via the Tuckerman Ravine Trail that they found, with the relative shelter of the canopy of trees, they could talk easily again.

Will pulled his hands inside the cuffs of his guide jacket to keep them warm as he hiked. He didn't want to put on his gloves until absolutely necessary to keep them as dry as possible.

"So, I must have scared the shit out of you in that practice room at school," Hatcher said. "I don't know what the hell comes over me when it happens. I just know I can't control it."

"It must be a terrible feeling."

"Yeah. I think it started when I was a kid. I got stuck in a drainage pipe and thought I was going to die. I didn't think much of it for years until I went on this spelunking trip with a bunch of guys in high school. They had to helicopter me out. They thought I was having a heart attack or something, my pulse rate was so high."

"You seen anyone about it?"

"Like a shrink?"

"I guess so. Who else do you see for something like that?"

Hatcher stopped walking and placed his hands on his hips as he caught his breath. "I saw a few witch doctors, but they all said the same thing. I've got a phobia and the best thing to do is meet it head-on—you know, acclimate myself to closed-in places. Could never do it." He pushed his wool hat back off his forehead and wiped rain and sweat off his brow. "Wish I could take a pill or something."

They hiked in silence for a few more yards. Will thought he understood better Hatcher's forgiving attitude toward him and his fall at Cathedral. At least Will hadn't had to be helicoptered out.

In a little over a mile, they came to the junction where the Huntington Ravine Trail veered off to the right.

Will radioed in their location. He imagined Laurie sitting next to the scanner, trying to pick up any news of what might be happening, but Will was sure Cody had switched by now to a more localized frequency, far out of earshot of curious locals.

They soon crossed the Cutler River, a healthy brook actually, which drains Huntington Ravine. On a clear day, Raymond Cataract, which splits Huntington from Tuckerman's is usually visible off to the left, but now much of the terrain above was roiling in wind-whipped clouds, and where they were hiking now the wind howled and whistled discordantly through the tops of the trees.

Will flipped the hood of his jacket over his head, pulled on the drawstrings, and tied them tight under his chin. He tried not to think of what the weather was like on elevation. He looked over at Hatcher, who had just completed fastening his own hood.

The look in Hatcher's eyes as he stared at him silently was all the communication Will needed. Both had enough experience in the woods to understand that what they were walking into could kill them, and Will wouldn't be surprised if once again he would have to call upon his partner to save his life, or perhaps return the favor to Hatcher. Now that they were walking into the teeth of this thing, Will was grateful that Hatcher had suggested the change in partners.

Even though they were still in the shelter of the trees, at times the trail acted as a wind tunnel and gusts pushed against them as they struggled to make their way. It was a little after eleven o'clock when they came upon the Harvard Cabin, built as an emergency station and jumping-off place for ice climbers.

The cabin was shuttered up.

Hatcher shouted over the wind, "Can't we just stay here?"

Will smiled weakly. It was tempting to think about busting down the door and crawling in out of the elements, but his thoughts immediately shifted to Singleton, who was lost at a higher elevation, facing much more dangerous conditions. "Let's get going," Will said.

They soldiered on, first across the Raymond Path, then the Huntington Ravine fire road. The trail took them back and forth across the fire road until it emptied out at a first aid cache that served as another landmark, signifying that they had reached the floor of the ravine. Will remembered the guidebook saying that it was 1.3 miles in from the trailhead.

Will radioed in again, but this time the reception was lousy, and he could barely hear Cody through the crackle. What he could make out in response to his request for the latest weather information was that conditions had worsened at the summit, with winds blowing more than seventy miles an hour. Thank God they weren't going to the top.

Before Cody broke up completely, Will could make out, "Use your judgment." He signed off, even though he wasn't sure Cody could hear him.

He said to Hatcher, "Let's keep going until we get to the Fan. We'll take a break there."

"Roger that."

As they walked by the cache, Will touched it as he always did, saying a few words silently, honoring the memory of his good friend who on one cold winter day didn't make it out of the ravine. Attached to the cache, a wooden sign read simply: ALBERT DOW. KILLED BY AVALANCHE DURING RESCUE ATTEMPT ON JANUARY 25, 1982.

Albert was a reminder of all that was dangerous out here, how one misstep, one seemingly innocent confluence of conditions—the weather, fatigue, equipment failure—could bring disaster. To die in the cause of trying to rescue someone else, in Will's thinking, was not heroic. Just unlucky.

They passed a large boulder field where in more salubrious weather Will always liked to scramble on top of the rocks to get a view of the ravine, but this morning was not the time for that. On one of the larger boulders, another plaque was installed: IN MEMORY OF HUGO STADMUELLER. APRIL 4, 1964. DIED IN AVALANCHE.

The grim reminders of the unforgiving, perilous mountain were everywhere, and it always felt to Will, walking this part of the trail that he was on hallowed ground.

Will could feel the temperature dropping as they trudged forward, and the rain began to have a bite to it. He reached the area of scrub growth just before the Fan and dropped his pack. Hatcher followed suit and they both hunkered down out of the wind.

Will pulled out a Nalgene bottle. "Let's get watered up and some food in us before we attack this thing."

Hatcher squinted at him, his eyebrows coated with ice. "You know, I think I prefer snow. We're going to have a hell of a time if this is sleet and freezing rain all the way."

Will chewed on an energy bar. "So, let's not be stupid about this. We'll try it for a while, but if either one of us thinks it's too hairy, we're out of here." He yanked off a big piece of the bar with his teeth. "Agreed?"

"No argument here. I mean, I like Singleton and all, but he was a damn fool to go out in weather like this."

"I'm sure he didn't realize how bad it was going to get."

Hatcher grinned. "And that's always the case, isn't it?"

"We're all fools, Brian. You'd have to be to come out here in weather like this for any reason." Will reached into his pack and put on a pair of goggles.

Hatcher grinned at him. "Now you're talking."

Will put on his gloves. "I think we should get moving again. I'm starting to get cold."

As soon as Will stood up, the wind smacked him in the face, and as they broke out of the scrub growth into the exposed talus field known as the Fan, the gusts muscled them around and they wobbled like drunken ski bums as they fought their way diagonally across the steep slope of broken rock.

Will was mindful of following the yellow blazes that marked the trail, because he understood well that to his left were yawning precipices and one misstep would send them plunging to their deaths.

The path ascended to the left side of the Fan through another area of scrub growth.

Will was breathing heavily by the time they found cover. "Damn. That was hard work."

Hatcher glanced up the trail. "It doesn't look too bad through here."

"Wait until we reach the ledges. That's my main concern. We'll call into headquarters again when we get there. With any luck, they'll have found Singleton by then, and we can go home."

Will kept a sharp eye out for any signs that a climber had been through the area recently. If Singleton had wandered down this far, this scrub growth would be a good place to ride out the weather. But the only signs of humanity were their own footprints.

The path meandered to the right of the main gully, across a brook, and out into the open again to where it ascended sharply more than six hundred feet in a third of a mile.

The rain had turned to hail the size of mothballs, and Hatcher's concern with ice had been realized. The hail pelted them, as if the mountain gods were ganging up on them like schoolboys in a rock fight.

The talus was covered with a glaze, often referred to as bear-glass, and it was banana peels and ball bearings for Will and Hatcher on that section of trail. It took them the good part of an hour to flail their way up.

Will thought several times on his ascent that they should turn around and call it a day, until it occurred to him that going back down was probably more dangerous than continuing on.

When they finally reached the first pitch above the Fan, the hail had turned to driving snow and the wind flapped Will's guide jacket like a limp flag.

"Yahoo!" Hatcher screamed. "It's snowing. Ain't we the lucky ones!"

As silly as it may have sounded, Will understood where Hatcher was coming from. Snow was much easier to deal with than ice, and as the steep ledge opened up to them, it was like stepping into a different world, a winter wonderland. They had obviously reached the rain/snow line, and the depth of snow suggested that it had been all white stuff up here since the front had moved in.

Though he couldn't see it, Will knew that off to his left was Pinnacle Buttress. The trail ahead followed up over rock ledges, arguably the most difficult scramble on the route.

Hatcher yelled at Will over the wind. "Time for crampons?"

They had to backtrack into the scrub a few yards to get out

of the whipping wind, and Will dropped his pack and dug for his crampons. There were many times in snow that these strap-on spikes had saved Will's bacon, but he also knew their limitations.

Once he had attached the crampons, he turned to Hatcher and said, "Have you seen anything?"

"What do you mean?"

"Any trace of Singleton. I mean, it's easy to get focused on ourselves and forget why we're out here."

"No. Nothing. But I hear you, man!"

"You recognize where we are?"

"I think so."

Will knew exactly where he was, and the recognition sparked a newfound sense of confidence. "We should be able to scramble up these ledges with little trouble. From there the trail follows the Central Gully, alternating between rock and scrub growth up past the headwall."

"Right."

"I think in the scrub we should take it slowly and look for places Singleton might have crawled off trail for cover. We're getting pretty high up, closer to where he's supposed to be lost."

Hatcher gave him a thumbs-up.

Before they made their ascent, Will got on the radio again. Cody's voice jumped out at him and startled Will with its clarity. At this elevation there was certainly better reception. Cody told him that the other groups were converging on the area where they supposed Singleton was weathered in. Skanky had called in from the Alpine Garden and Toby from just above Nelson Crag.

"But still no sign of Singleton?"

"Negative that."

Will signed off and adjusted his goggles. He turned to Hatcher. "You want to lead?"

"Sure."

They made their way out into the open again and Hatcher assaulted the ledge. He shoved the pointed end of his ice ax into the snow, lifted his leg deliberately, and carefully planted his foot.

The pace was slow, but just right for Will. He liked the way Hatcher used his ice ax, how in steep places he reached expertly above his head and drove the curved spade-shaped end into the snow with authority, choosing a line of ascent that was both economical and safe. The snow had covered all the painted blazes on the rock, so picking a safe route required attention to detail and sometimes divine inspiration.

Will thought of Toby Winston as he climbed and what this experience would have been like with the weight of leadership falling mostly on Will as senior crew member. For the second time he felt lucky on this steep ledge to have Hatcher as a partner.

When they finally made it to the top of the first scramble, Will breathed easier because he sensed the worst was over. If they had made it this far without incident, chances were good the rest of the way would be relatively simple.

The trail bent to the right into the scrub again but still climbed steeply. When they arrived at a particularly dense section out of the wind, Hatcher said to Will, "Let's break here."

Hatcher was above him on an incline so acute that if he lost his foothold he would effectively land on Will's head.

Will checked his watch.

"How we doing for time?" Hatcher asked.

"A little after two. I figure if we keep at this pace in another couple hours we'll make the Alpine Garden Trail."

"Which should still leave us some light." Will reached for his water bottle, unscrewed the top, and took a long pull.

"You doing okay, partner?" Hatcher asked.

"Holding my own."

"Some fun, huh?"

"That's what you said that last time we were out." Will took another sip.

"I did?"

"On Cathedral. You trying to jinx us?"

Hatcher shook his head. "You're not superstitious, are you, Will?"

Will shrugged. "I think sometimes I am."

Hatcher grinned at him but didn't say anything.

There was something about the grin that bothered Will, but he couldn't place it. He had seen it before, an impish little smile that suggested Hatcher was experiencing a private joke.

"How's that girlfriend of yours doing?"

"A lot better."

"Still no closer to catching Carpenter?"

"Closer, I think."

"I understand that bastard paid you a visit."

Will almost asked him how he knew but then remembered the press had gotten hold of the story. But he wasn't in the mood for talking about it now. "Let's can the chitchat and get the hell off this thing."

"Oooh. Touchy."

"It's not that, Brian. It's just that we've got a job to do."

"I hear you, buddy." Hatcher got to his feet. "Want to lead?"

"I'm happy just dubbing along in the back."

"Come on. You can cut the wind for me for a while."

When they worked their way out of the scrub and stepped

out onto another, shorter ledge, Will and Hatcher switched places.

It was tough going for Will, and the closer they got to a promontory that loomed over the ravine, the more the wind picked up. It was blowing gale force now, the snow stinging Will's face. He kept his head down and focused on his foot placement. On occasion, he glanced behind and could barely see Hatcher only a few feet away from him, looking like a walking phantom.

They made it to where the Diagonal Gully intersected the trail, and Will knew now they were getting close to the ridge line and the Alpine Garden Trail. As its name suggested, the Diagonal Gully cut across the Central Gully at a sharp angle and dropped off the edge of the trail into a steep ravine.

Will stopped in front of a large boulder that fronted the trail. The ascent from here was trickier because it meant scrambling over exposed rock, the heads of huge boulders where the snow refused to stick. He waited for Hatcher to catch up with him. "How do you want to do this?" he shouted.

Hatcher tapped the boulder with his hand. "The trail goes up and over, right?"

Will nodded quickly. The wind almost knocked him down, and he caught himself by leaning against the rock.

"No crampons then."

Will considered. "You're probably right."

"Sure I am. The tops of these things are covered with rime ice. You use crampons and you'll be doing pirouettes off this mountain."

Will sat down in the deep snow. He pulled hard on the leather strap but the buckle was iced. He used the end of his ax to tap it, and the ice flaked off. He had to take off his gloves to unleash the buckle, and by the time he finished getting both crampons off and stowed again in his pack, his hands were numb. He said to Hatcher, "Why don't you go ahead."

Hatcher made an "after you" gesture with the sweep of his arm. "Carry on, Macduff."

Will hesitated. "You sure?"

"It's just bouldering, Will. Remember not to rely on your arms and hands. Just use your feet."

Will studied him a moment. *Why was he addressing him like a rank beginner?* Hatcher was grinning again.

"Shouldn't we rope into each other?"

"Not necessary."

"But if one of us slips—"

"Will, you've got to trust your abilities."

Hatcher's last remark told Will much about how he was sizing up the situation. He was obviously thinking of Will's fall on Cathedral the last time they were out together, playing armchair psychologist and pushing Will to test his limits in order to gain confidence. Ordinarily Will would appreciate the gesture, but Hatcher's sly grin suggested he was enjoying it too much. "I'm taking my time," Will said. "I'm only trying to be safe." The explanation seemed to fall flat.

"Whenever you're ready. I'll spot you."

Will turned slowly toward the boulder. He tried to feel for handholds through his gloves but it was a futile effort. He tore his gloves off and shoved them into the slash pocket of his guide jacket. He could barely feel the rock beneath his fingers, but looking up, he was encouraged that it would take just a few moves to get up and over the boulder.

He hoisted himself up and scraped his left foot along the face of the rock until he found a small depression that would act as a good anchor. Another move to his right, he was cresting the top of the boulder when a gust of wind suddenly walloped him. He held on, riding it out. He could feel his foot slipping.

He scrambled frantically for another handhold, but there seemed to be some force pulling him backward.

He heard Hatcher's voice. "Will, Oh my God! No!"

And Will was suddenly airborne, tumbling backward off the ledge, careening down into the Diagonal Gully.

Chapter 17

Will plummeted down the ravine, grasping desperately for a handhold, his legs flailing and thrashing about as he tried to stop himself. His body went limp as he clipped rocks that spun him first against the north side of the ravine, then down a chute that launched him on a three-second midair flight off a pinnacle, only to land hard and shoot off again past yawning chasms to finally come to rest on the scoop lip of a promontory.

Will had no idea how long he lay there, but when he finally came to, he couldn't see anything. He thought somehow the complete darkness meant he was dead, buried in his own frozen coffin, and he fought against it, swinging wildly, emerging finally to realize that all along he had been covered in a large snowdrift. But as he sat up, he faced more darkness and felt the unforgiving wind-driven snow sting his face.

He lay back, struggling to regain his senses, checking his extremities by wiggling his toes and fingers. He could still feel his toes—a good sign—but his hands were numb. When it finally came to him that he had no gloves on, he recalled, distantly, having shoved the gloves into his slash pockets. He patted the sides of his jacket and found the reassuring bulge on either side. They hadn't fallen out. They were still there.

It seemed to take forever to get them on, though. He managed the right one okay, but his stone fingers inside the gloved hand wouldn't behave. When he finally wriggled the glove onto his left hand, the effort had left him exhausted.

He had no idea what time it was, and it seemed too much of a bother to look at his watch. It didn't matter anyway. It was dark. The weather was lousy. And who cared? He just wanted to sleep.

But somewhere in the distant, primal part of his brain, a nagging voice told him to wake up. He had to get moving. He groaned and fought against it, but the voice was insistent.

A macabre vision of himself found dead with icicles bearding his face soon brought him to a sitting position again. He felt groggy, like he'd been on a bender. He tried to get up, but his legs didn't want to work. He pondered the situation coldly from a distance, as if he were watching himself, an intellectual curiosity.

He rolled over and got to his knees. This seemed to work better. Now all he had to do was figure out how to stand. He knelt in that manner, like some penitent to Our Lady of the Ravines, until he figured out finally how to bring his right leg forward, considering it nothing short of miraculous when the left one followed.

Staying upright was not an easy task, either, for the wind bullied him, daring Will to fight back. But the act of standing had the effect of sharpening the sense of his own lurid condition and what trouble he was in. The one thing he was sure of, as his medical training began to rush back to him, was that he had to get the blood flowing back into his legs. He was shivering, dangerously hypothermic.

He took a few small steps, but the acute angle of the slope almost made him lose his balance, and he had no clue where he was headed. He could see nothing in front of him. He decided to stay in place for a while and stamp his feet, like a soldier marking time. The effort began to take its toll in using up his energy, and Will had to fight once more against the urge to just drop down into the snow.

He rested, standing still, then began stamping his feet again, and, to take his mind off the repetitive marching, he pushed up his sleeve and glanced at his field watch. The luminous hands told him it was after ten o'clock. He reckoned that he had been lying in the snow for over five hours and saw it as a good sign that he could make these calculations.

The tramping in place gradually began to get the blood rushing and his mind began to clear. He thought about his pack and wondered what had happened to it. He remembered he was wearing it when he tumbled off the rock, but the force of the fall and subsequent wild ride down the ravine must have ripped it off his back. It was somewhere. But how far away was it?

He was sure the pack had cushioned his fall at the top when he had jettisoned off the boulder, and he must have ridden on it at least for part of the way down. But finding it now in the dark in these whiteout conditions was an unlikely option. He remembered all the gear he had stowed in it—including the radio he had stashed to keep out of the elements—and he realized, soberly, that if he was ever going to survive, he would have to locate the pack. That is, if he made it through the night.

His thoughts drifted back to his solo experience on the mountain a few years ago, when the temperature had dropped below zero and the windchill had blown a skin of ice over his morning cup of coffee. He told himself he'd been through this before and how he had survived that night by staying awake in his fiberfill bag inside his bivy sack, burrowed into a snow cave. It had been a long ordeal, and that was with appropriate gear. What would he do now with just the clothes on his back?

Could he keep moving all night long? He doubted it. But he couldn't just lie in the snow, for he truly would freeze. He had to find a way to get out of the wind. And that meant moving. Exploring.

But he couldn't see where he was going, and if he went blindly searching he might find himself falling off the edge of some cliff or down a hole he would never get out of. There was really no other option, though. He had only two choices: up or down. He picked going up because he reckoned that if he got himself into trouble, at least he wouldn't have the additional danger of gravity working against him.

Will turned into the wind and started walking slowly. He put his hands out in front of him, like some mystical seeker, to keep from knocking into a rock. He had to struggle hard to keep his balance and was surprised with the severity of the pitch. It was no wonder he had catapulted so far down the ravine.

As he worked his way uphill, the wind and snow blew against him in unrelenting fury, and his mind began to play tricks on him. At one point, he thought that it would take little effort to just climb right out of the ravine, for he swore that ahead of him he could see the dark outline of Pinnacle Buttress. But that was impossible. What he saw was nothing, only what he wished into being, and while he understood this on some level, it was still pleasant to think about. He wondered vaguely if it was possible to see mirages in snowstorms like you could in the desert.

Will stumbled forward into the darkness, but his steps were more plodding and painful as he proceeded, and he began to realize that fatigue was most likely responsible for spurring thoughts as bizarre as the Sahara. He wondered if he would ever be warm again and laughed out loud when he realized he had to be careful what he wished for, with hellfire licking at his heels. He fought to stay focused, to concentrate on what was real, but felt his consciousness slipping away.

In a few more yards, his hands found a rock outcropping, and he worked around it, feeling his way like a blind man, until he became aware, when the rock led him around a corner to the leeward side, that the wind had dropped.

Off to his right, his foot hit something hard, and he proceeded farther in, feeling with his toe, until his progress was blocked. He bent down and touched whatever it was with his glove and found a bush of some kind that grew to about knee level. Further investigation revealed more bushes growing close together. A word formed on Will's lips, and he spoke it aloud: "Krummholz!" The super-dense vegetation that grew in clumps in these ravines.

Will knelt down. If he could find a space to crawl into, then this might serve as the shelter he had been looking for.

He felt his way for an opening in the bushes, and on his hands and knees ducked his head through a small space. There was snow at the roots, but certainly not as deep as in the open. He tunneled in, scraping handfuls of snow aside as he went, and because the fit was so tight, he had to stretch out on his side, cradled between the root systems of two large bushes.

He pulled his hood tight to his chin and drew his arms close to his body. He told himself to stay awake as long as he could. Soon his shivering stopped. He listened for a moment to the distant moaning of the wind, closed his eyes, and went to sleep.

With the faint shimmer of dawn light, Will stirred. He sensed before he opened his eyes that the wind had blown itself out and the storm had moved on. He lay for a long time, taking stock. He was stiff and sore, but as far as he could tell, nothing was broken. He finally backed slowly out of the krummholz, stood, and stretched his arms tentatively to the sky.

To the east, the weather had cleared enough for Will to see the sun rising over Wildcat Mountain, its rosy light diffused by a thin cloud layer. As furiously as the storm had blown through last night, the calm that now settled into the ravine felt strangely unnerving by contrast. But considering all that could have happened, Will felt lucky just to be standing.

He flapped his arms against his body, then suddenly winced and grabbed his shoulder, discovering parts of his body bruised from the battering he suffered clipping rocks on his descent.

Hunger suddenly gnawed at him, and he thought longingly about the food in his pack. He reached down, grabbed some snow, and stuffed it into his mouth. The snow felt cold and soothing against his raw throat, and he ate some more.

He ran through his options. Now that the storm had passed, if he got lucky, the overcast would burn off, leaving the sun to warm him, and no doubt with the improving weather, searchers would be out looking for him—probably a helicopter as well.

Will trudged up the ravine, but he found it tough going. The snow had drifted, sculpted by the wind, disguising terrain so much that on one occasion what Will thought was solid ground turned out to be a crevasse that he postholed, his leg sinking up to his crotch. He struggled hard to free himself, and it took a great deal of digging with his hands to pull himself out.

He looked up ahead and watched the sun hit the headwall above him. From his location, he stared up the long fall line of the Diagonal Gully, which because of its depth and angle afforded just a glimpse of the tip of Pinnacle Buttress directly ahead. But to the northeast, Will had a good view of Damnation Gully, a long slash that emptied out at the opposite side of the Fan from where he and Hatcher had first gone in. Getting his bearings made him reassess his strategy.

What were the odds of finding his pack? The way the snow had been blown in sinuous rills, the wind smoothing it in swirls like meringue, the likelihood the pack was buried was great.

As much as he wanted to eat real food, he knew that he couldn't let his decision making be clouded by his hunger. Searching for the pack by retracing uphill the line of his fall—if his progress so far was any indication—would sap his strength quickly, and he knew he had to conserve whatever he had left.

Two options then. Sit still or head down Diagonal Gully.

The idea of waiting to be rescued was against Will's nature, even though he understood the first rule of survival was to stay put. In this case, though, and with his experience, if he could find a way out of this himself, it was all for the better. For the first time since he had pitched off that boulder, he suddenly thought of Hatcher. What had happened to him?

Will replayed his fall and the memory made his face feel hot. Since his tumble, he had been so focused on his survival that the idea he might have screwed up again hadn't even entered into his thinking. But here he was. Another slipup. What the hell was wrong with him anyway?

Will let himself sink slowly into the snow. He sat facing downhill, holding his head in his hands, imagining headlines: RESCUER RESCUED AGAIN. The intrepid hero, out to save his mentor, Dr. Thomas Singleton, making another boneheaded move that most likely, and yet one more time, put his partner in danger. What *had* happened to Hatcher, anyway? Will strained to remember. He recalled hearing Hatcher yell, but did Will bring him down with him? Will recalled his suggestion that they tie in together and silently thanked the snow gods that Hatcher had the sense not to do it.

No. He would not go through the humiliation of having to be rescued again.

Without thinking much about what he was doing, Will got to his feet and set off striding downhill at a fast and foolish pace. It didn't take long for his momentum to pitch him forward, and he fell, tucked and rolled, slid a few hundred feet, and came to an abrupt stop at the bottom of another ravine.

He didn't move but lay silently cursing himself for his stupidity. He had to keep his head, recapture the same reasoning that made him reconsider going uphill as a way out. If he took his time, kept his wits, he was sure he could make it, but he told himself not to do anything until he had thought through his next move. Just as hunger shouldn't rule his thinking, he had to let go of his anger and self-pity.

The downside of his plan to evacuate out of Diagonal Gully was that he knew little about the area, to say nothing of where the rain/snow line was. As long as he had snow to work with, he figured it could always soften his missteps, but how difficult the terrain was at the bottom was a big unknown.

It was actually pleasant lying in the snow, the sun struggling through the cloud layer, beaming off the sheer expanse of whiteness and warming his body with ambient heat. If he kept his eyes closed long enough, he could almost imagine he was sunning himself on the deck of a ski resort in St. Moritz.

His momentary reverie was broken by the scream of an eagle above his head. He forced himself to his feet and glanced down the gully. Suddenly he thought he saw his pack off to his right. He trudged toward it, but a closer examination revealed it was a wide, flat piece of wood that must have sailed a long way in a powerful wind only to end up wedged between two rocks.

Will began to worry about his beginning to see things, but thoughts about the pack also began to produce a nagging sense that something had gone terribly wrong on top of that boulder that had little to do with Will's ineptness. As he replayed the moment, he couldn't get past the tug he had felt on the back of his pack.

Sure, he had just made a scramble move over the rock and the wind had caught him, but all of that didn't explain away the feeling that Hatcher had deliberately yanked on his pack and sent him flying down the ravine.

Will stopped. He must be imagining things. His head was playing tricks on him again. He told himself to get going.

He began deliberately working his way down the ravine, calculating his steps as he went, choosing lines of least resistance, and even taking the opportunity, in places, to glissade down on his rear end.

At about ten-thirty, he heard a distant thudding in the air. He couldn't see the helicopter, but the sound seemed to come from up ridge close to the flat area on top of the Alpine Garden Trail known as the cow pasture. Had they found Singleton?

Will stood still, listening, to see if the helicopter would circle over the ravine, but the noise soon faded out of range of his hearing. The disappearance of the helicopter was disappointing, but Will was far from crestfallen because he understood, as he surveyed the ravine, that the snow wasn't as deep here and he must be getting close to the bottom.

In a few more yards, though, his line of travel funneled him directly down a gully to the edge of another steep promontory. Will looked over the ledge and quickly surmised, because of the old rusty pitons driven into the rock face directly below him, that this must have been used as a climbing area in the early days of the sport. The dizzying height of the headwall, the exposed rock of the talus floor below confirmed that he had not only found the rain/snow line, but that it would be impossible to down climb without technical gear. He was trapped.

He calmly traversed the edge of the promontory to his right and struggled up an incline but was soon blocked by the nose of a pinnacle that rose sharply. There didn't seem to be any way to get up and over it unless he free climbed. His instincts told him that his options wouldn't be any better on the other side of the pinnacle, so he crabbed his way down to his original position and concentrated on the rock formations to his left.

He struggled up out of the dip in the opposite direction and glanced down at another precipitous drop. What drew Will's attention, at what he estimated to be about twenty feet, was a small rock shelf that stuck out from the sidewall, looking wide enough to stand on comfortably. It had collected quite a bit of snow.

If he could get down that far, the sidewall looked craggy

enough below the shelf to provide plenty of holds for down climbing. He lay on his belly and poked his head over the edge, eyeing the granite wall for fissures. The absence of rusty pitons caused some initial alarm, but Will thought he understood that the challenging route in the middle, just below the gully, was preferable and that climbers wouldn't have even bothered with a route near the sidewall, no doubt because the existence of the shelf reduced the degree of difficulty and hence the appeal.

Will made up his mind. He dug out snow from the ledge until he reached rock, shoved his gloves into his slash pockets, and zipped them shut. He carefully shifted his body and dangled his legs off the edge, his toes searching for purchase until he found a small crack for his right foot. He let his left leg fall, swept it slowly back and forth, searching for his next move, and found a small nub. From there, he let go his left hand, his fingers crawling furiously, spiderlike, across the rock for another hand-hold; then he dropped his right leg again and simultaneously his left hand.

Will knew the hard part was past him, for the secret of down climbing was getting started. He wondered absently, though—his focus intent on his work—how long he would continue to have feeling in his fingers, and he felt dead from the waist down, his legs and feet numb as mallets. Rock climbing in mountaineering boots was difficult to begin with, but the addition of cold temperatures and his mounting fatigue was a recipe for disaster.

He told himself to concentrate on handholds in front of him, and he could see tiny rills and cracks coming more readily into his ken as he descended. He refused to look down, remembering especially what had happened that day on Cathedral Ledge, and with a few more moves he estimated he had made it about halfway down to the shelf.

It was on the next reach, though—one where he swore he had a strong handhold—that his left foot gave way and he felt himself falling. He braced for impact, but it seemed to take forever before he finally landed.

When he looked up, amazed at first that he felt no pain, he found that his drop had been less than ten feet. He smiled wryly. His mind was playing tricks on him again. Right now he wasn't certain about anything.

He glanced down off the shelf and saw below him where Damnation Gully emptied out onto the talus floor that was the Fan. From here, it was just a matter of continuing his down climb over boulders to a snowfield, then working his way through the broken rocks, beyond the rain/snow line, to connect again to the trail where, having effectively completed a giant loop through two ravines, he would find the emergency cache with the dedication to Albert Dow.

It took Will almost an hour to work his way across the boulder field, but it felt good just to stretch his legs and walk on solid ground. The rocks were still slick with bearglass, but the ice coating broke up easily when he stepped on them, having melted gradually with the late morning sun.

As Will made his way, he began to discover more feeling in his feet, and by the time he reached the trail that led back through the scrub, there was a spring in his step. He came upon the Dow emergency cache, touched it, paused to say his few words, but he didn't stay long, driven more by his hunger to continue on.

He did stop, though, for a brief moment when he noticed his and Hatcher's footprints on the trail, still preserved in the mud from yesterday's ascent. He was curious to see if other rescuers had followed them in, but he could find only theirs. He again wondered what had happened to Hatcher.

He took off at a steady pace, and when he followed a bend in the trail he was arrested by the smell of wood smoke. In a few more yards, he came upon the Harvard Cabin, door wide open, smoke pumping out of the tin chimney. He approached the cabin and stuck his head through the open door. "Hello?"

A lean figure, sweeping the floor, wheeled around. "Well, hello, yourself."

When the sweeper stepped toward him, Will recognized him from having seen him around—perhaps at an EMT recertification session—but he didn't recall his name.

It took only a second, though, for the sweeper to recognize him. "Christ. You're Will Buchanan." He dropped the broom and came to the door. "Are you all right?" He grabbed Will's hand and practically pulled him through the door. "They've been looking all over for you."

"Well, I'm here." Will studied him a moment. He looked like a kid fresh out of college, his brown hair combed neatly and parted on the side, and he smelled of aftershave. "I'm sorry. Your name?"

Still holding Will's hand, he shook it enthusiastically and said, "Jasper. Jasper Godfrey. It's a pleasure meeting you, sir."

Not another Toby Winston.

Godfrey seemed to remember himself and led Will to a bunk in the far corner. "Sit down here. Let me check you out."

Will complied. "What's that smell? You cooking something?"

Godfrey nodded. "Just some stew." It took a few moments

for Will's intent to finally register. "Oh, my God. You must be hungry."

Will nodded furiously.

Godfrey immediately strode to the front of the cabin and closed the door. He went to the stove, took off the lid of a cast-iron pot, and with a ladle scooped out meat and potatoes into a plastic bowl. He handed the bowl to Will along with a large metal spoon.

Will held the bowl a few seconds, relishing the warmth on his hands, then tentatively scooped a potato and let it slide into his mouth. He savored it a moment, but as he swallowed his stomach convulsed and he had to fight the spasm. It took a few more slow mouthfuls before his gut settled and he could finish the bowl.

"How 'bout a Coke?" Godfrey asked. "I bet you could really go for one."

A Coke? That was the furthest thing from Will's mind. "Water is fine. Maybe some tea."

With the door closed, the one-room cabin took little time to warm up, and with Godfrey's help Will shed his guide jacket. When Will had finished his stew, Godfrey told him to lie back on the bunk so he could check him out.

A head-to-toe exam revealed nothing broken, but when he lifted Will's polypro shirt, he found a large welt near his shoulder and his stomach and chest splotched with bruises.

"Now let's look at those feet," Godfrey said, reaching to untie Will's shoelaces.

Will grabbed his arm. "Hold off on that."

"But what about frostbite?"

"I'll check the feet after I walk out of here. You take my boots off now, and I might not be able to get them back on."

Godfrey shook his head. "I think you should stay where you are. We can get a litter up here in no time."

"No. No litter."

Godfrey drew back at the force of Will's insistence. "Sure. Whatever you think."

"You do have a radio, right? You can connect to Pinkham?"

"Yes, sir."

"Is Cody still there?"

"I don't know. I haven't called in at all. I just came to the cabin this morning to repair the roof before the season got going. I'm the caretaker, you see."

Will sat up. "You say that people have been out looking for me?"

"That's right."

"So, how much do you know about what happened yesterday?"

"I know you and your partner disappeared on a rescue call."

"Hatcher's missing?"

"Well, yeah. I think so. That's what the talk was at the lodge this morning."

Will took a moment to consider. So, Hatcher must have tumbled off the ledge with him, and he still must be up there somewhere. But the more he thought about it, the more it didn't make sense. He once more recalled the moment on the rock and Hatcher calling out Will's name, suggesting he wasn't the one falling. So, if Hatcher hadn't plunged down with him, where was he?

"Anyway, I'm glad you made it out. I'd hate to see two gone at the expense of saving one."

"Wait a minute. You mean they found Singleton?"

"That's right. Sometime last night."

So, the helicopter Will had heard from the Diagonal Gully must have been searching for Hatcher, or him. "And Singleton's okay?"

"Far as I know." Godfrey walked over to a desk at the opposite wall of the cabin. He pointed to the two-way. "Should I call in and let them know you made it out?"

Will put up his hand. "Hold off on that, too. I need to think."

Godfrey looked at him, puzzled, most likely trying to make a connection between calling in and Will's thinking.

Something was eating at Will he couldn't identify, an unknown that made him hesitate about announcing to the world he had made it out.

He lay back and closed his eyes. Whatever it was had to do with knowing that Hatcher had gone missing for no apparent reason. He had this growing feeling that there was something else he wasn't seeing.

Godfrey held the mike in his hand. "I really think you should let them know, Mr. Buchanan. I mean, people are out looking for you."

Will sat up. "You're right, Jasper. Go ahead." He gripped the edge of the bunk, staring off into space. He was vaguely aware of Godfrey's call into base, but the connection he had been seeking finally flashed in his head.

Without saying anything to Godfrey, Will shoved an arm through his jacket sleeve, stormed out the door, and trudged back up the trail, his eyes glued to the ground. It took only a few yards for him to find the prints. He knelt and studied the impression made by Hatcher's sole. What had been nagging at him must have been his distant recall of the boot prints in the mud just below the Dow cache two hours previous and his hunch that he had seen the print before somewhere.

He measured the print with his hand. There was little doubt it was the same size and sole pattern as the one he had found two days ago near the parking lot off Carter Notch Road.

He stood, shocked by his discovery. It wasn't Carpenter who had followed him in on the Bog Brook Trail. It was Hatcher.

Chapter 18

Will took off back down the trail and met up with Jasper Godfrey just as he was coming out of the cabin.

"Everything okay?" Jasper asked.

"I had to check on something."

"Thought I'd let you know they're sending in a crew with a litter to pick you up."

"What? I told you I didn't need to be evacuated!"

Godfrey recoiled. "Hey, it wasn't my call," he said defensively. "It was Lieutenant Cody's."

Will put a hand on Godfrey's shoulder. "Look, I didn't mean to yell at you, but I don't have time to wait around here."

Godfrey looked warily at Will but said nothing.

"So, I'd appreciate it if you'd just call in again and tell them I'm on my way out." Will smiled at him. "You can say you tried to stop me, but I wouldn't listen. Cody will sure be able to understand *that*."

"Okay. I'm just trying to do the right thing, that's all."

"Listen, did Cody say anything about Hatcher?"

"He asked me if Hatcher was with you."

"So, I guess he's still missing."

"I guess so."

Will let go of his shoulder. "I appreciate your help, Jasper, but I'm feeling fine now. That stew was just the ticket."

Godfrey brightened and started to say something, but Will had already turned to leave.

The implications of the footprints in the mud began to multiply for Will as he set a brisk pace down the Huntington Ravine Trail back to Pinkham.

He was sure now that Hatcher had deliberately yanked on his pack and pitched him off that boulder. He hadn't imagined anything. But why? The only explanation was that Hatcher wanted to get him out of the way, to kill him because he was getting too close to discovering whatever was buried just off the Bog Brook Trail. That had to be it. There was just no other connection between the footprints at both locations that Will could come up with.

And did that also mean that Will had been dead wrong about Carpenter? Will doubted it, and it was possible both men were working in collusion. Was Hatcher trying to rat out his partner that day in the Burger and Brew? Will wondered about that, and also how much he could trust his brain after his recent ordeal on the mountain.

And if Godfrey was right and Hatcher was still missing, the question remained: Where was he? If he tried to get rid of Will once, there was little doubt he would go after him again, and if Hatcher was still in the woods, he might be following him right now. Will stopped and listened. The only sound came from a light stirring of the wind through the trees. He glanced nervously over his shoulder, then trudged on.

It was just after two o'clock when he reached the junction of the Tuckerman Ravine Trail, and without stopping he turned down on his final leg to Pinkham. What drove him on, despite his growing exhaustion, was the realization that he wasn't the only one in danger. If Hatcher had tried to kill him, he most likely wouldn't hesitate getting rid of Laurie for what he thought she knew. The idea hit Will hard.

Did that mean it was Hatcher and not Carpenter who shot Laurie? Will shook his head. It couldn't have happened that way because they found Carpenter's muddy boots in his own house, and the soil matched what was behind the mini-mart. *Come to think of it, just about everything was found in Carpenter's house.* How convenient it all sounded.

Will told himself to keep his focus. He had to stop all this speculating and get down to his truck at the parking lot. There wouldn't be any time to check in with Cody. Will had to get to Laurie as fast as he could to warn her about Hatcher.

It took less than a half hour to make it down. He immediately scanned the lot for Hatcher's Tundra, but it was nowhere to be found.

Will ripped open the door of his truck, grabbed his keys from under the mat, and hopped into the cab.

He twisted the key in the ignition and ground the starter. The engine labored, whirred, but wouldn't turn over. With all the rain and buildup of condensation, he was sure the coil and plugs were wet. He cranked it again, and the engine caught, sputtered, and died.

"Come on!" He smacked the steering wheel. Then he leaned forward, depressed the accelerator halfway, and gently, coaxingly, turned the key. This time the pistons fired and Will pumped the pedal until the engine stuttered into a halting rhythm.

He threw it into reverse and almost stalled out again when he tried to back up, but he caught it just in time to reclutch before it gave out. "That's it, come on." He dropped it into second, twisted the wheel, and lurched toward the entrance of the parking lot, and seeing the way clear, gunned it and tore off south down Route 16.

He reached for the cell phone on the seat and flipped it open, only to discover that in his haste to respond to the Singleton call he had inadvertently neglected to turn it off. The phone was dead.

As he drove, Will couldn't stop thinking about Hatcher's truck not being in the lot. Did that mean he had come out on his own and not reported in? Or was it that he had ridden to the rescue call with someone else? Will tried to think if Hatcher had said anything about how he had gotten there, but he came up with nothing. It was clear to Will that either Hatcher had responded with someone else and was still missing on the mountain or he had self-evacuated and had driven away without telling anyone.

Will accelerated down the highway, the speedometer pushing sixty. When he shot past Glen Ellis Falls and hit the dangerous turn known as Windy Corners, he felt the rear end spin out, and he had to oversteer into the oncoming lane before he could correct it.

The realization that if a car had been on the other side he wouldn't have been able to bail out sobered Will, and he drove more in control through Saxton Mills and finally to the driveway of his house.

As soon as he entered through the kitchen door, he shouted out Laurie's name, but there was no answer. He quickly checked through all the rooms and was heartened that there were no signs of a struggle. What he found in the bedroom, though,

were Laurie's jeans thrown casually over a chair. Her police uniform was missing.

Will picked up the phone and punched in the speed dial for
Laurie's office at the police station.

Ray picked up.

"Laurie there?"

"Not anymore. She was this morning, though."

"What the hell is she doing at work?"

Ray paused. "Look, Will. You don't have to get mad at *me*.
She said she just wanted to get a few hours in—you know,
gradually work herself back into a schedule."

"So, where is she now?"

"She said she had to run a few errands; then she was going
home."

"When was that?"

"I don't know. Late morning. She left before I went to
lunch."

Will glanced at his watch. Three-fifteen. "Did she say what
kind of errands?"

"Nope."

"And you let her use your car?"

"Nope."

Talking to Ray was like dragging information out of a cold
war spy. "Ray, whose car is she using?"

"Her own. The Cherokee's finally all fixed. She called me
this morning and asked if I wouldn't mind driving her to pick
it up."

"Great. And you let her do it?"

"I'm going to tell her no? She's my boss."

"She's also driving one-handed."

Ray didn't respond.

In the silence that followed, it suddenly dawned on Will exactly where she had gone.

"Look, Ray. Did either of you hear I was missing on Mount Washington last night?"

"What?"

"You didn't have the scanner on?"

"Of course I had the scanner on. All I heard was that there was a search on the mountain for Dr. Singleton and that they found him last night. Nothing about you."

Cody probably had kept the chatter down before sounding the alarm, guessing that his two most experienced crew members would eventually make it out.

"Ray, you've got to listen to me and do exactly what I say."

"What the hell's going on, Will?"

"I think Laurie is in trouble. She's not doing errands. Knowing her, I think she's up at the Bog Brook Trail."

Ray took a few moments to process. "I don't get it."

"Just meet me up there at the parking lot below the trail."

"You mean now? I just can't up and leave—"

"Damn it, Ray. Just do it!"

On his way up Carter Notch Road, Will was hoping he was wrong about Laurie being up here, and he kicked himself for revealing the location to her in the first place. But how was he to know the rescue call for Singleton would screw up the works?

He imagined Laurie going to bed early last night, turning the scanner off so that she would be rested enough for Will to take her out as they had planned when he returned from the rescue call. But when Will didn't show, he knew she wouldn't hesitate to go it alone.

Will gunned the truck past the one-armed oak tree and headed uphill. He eyed the hunting camp to his right, but it looked just as abandoned as it had the other day.

As he drove closer to the parking lot, he slowed the truck, tentative about what he might find, trying to convince himself not to worry. Laurie really could be out doing errands. And wouldn't he feel silly when Ray showed up. He'd have to make it up to him, take him out to dinner or something.

But as soon as he reached the entrance to the lot he saw a flash of red off to his right and immediately recognized Laurie's Cherokee parked at the far end.

He drove slowly toward it, not sure of what else he was going to find. He pulled his truck in right next to her Jeep. He got out of the cab and tried her driver's-side door, and it opened.

On the front seat, some of Samantha Rayley's photos were scattered about, but the car looked clean and smelled of vinyl conditioner.

Will shut the door and looked back across the lot in the direction of the Bog Brook trailhead. He considered not waiting for Ray before heading in, but knowing the only vehicle in the lot belonged to Laurie helped quell the desperate urgency Will had felt coming in. He could wait for Ray. He owed him that much at least.

Will suddenly hit upon another theory that explained why Hatcher's truck wasn't found at Pinkham or at the Bog Brook lot, and it served, momentarily, to calm his fears even more.

Perhaps Hatcher had sent him careening down the Diagonal Gully because he wanted to make it look like an accident, which effectively left Hatcher alone to create the ruse that he, too, had become a victim who had succumbed to the fury of the storm. Then Hatcher would drop some of his gear off a precipice to make it look good, betting that everyone would believe he had gotten disoriented and had fallen out of sight into a deep chasm. That way, he could buy time and go just about anywhere he wanted to begin a new life.

But as he thought about it, Will realized that even if someone else had driven Hatcher to the rescue call, his disappearance would still be questioned if his Tundra ended up missing. So much for that theory.

Will looked at his watch. Three-forty. Where the hell was Ray? Will was grateful for the sunny day, but the light wouldn't last too much longer. He walked down to the parking lot entrance and stared down the road.

Still no sign of the cruiser. Will let his eyes drift, and he scanned the edge of the dirt road uphill to where it turned a sharp dogleg to the left. It was then that he noticed a gray mass behind a thick copse just ahead of the bend. He squinted, trying to make out what it was, and as he walked up the road the roofline of Hatcher's Tundra came into view. For a few moments, Will just stood staring at the truck. Of course Hatcher wouldn't have parked it in the lot, right out in the open.

His heart sank as he approached the truck. The doors were locked. He peered through the driver's-side window. Inside the cab looked like a laundry dump and Will recognized the clothes as the ones Hatcher wore on the rescue call. More disturbing, though, was his discovery, peeking out from beneath balled-up layers of polypro, of a half-empty cardboard ammunition box of what looked like hollow points.

Will walked to the front of the truck and placed his hand on the hood. It was still warm. He slowly began to understand what must have happened. Hatcher had been minutes ahead of him when he came in off the trail at Pinkham, and he, like Will, had hopped into his truck without reporting in. It explained why no one at headquarters had reported Hatcher returning. And it was clear Will had just missed him here as he had at Pinkham.

Will tore back down to the lot entrance just as Ray came crawling up the hill in the cruiser. Will waved his arms in a frantic attempt to speed him up, but Ray had only one gear.

As the cruiser finally turned in to the lot, Ray rolled down the window. "It took me a while to find this place."

"You've never been up here?"

"Why the hell would I be up here in these godforsaken boonies. You think I like to hike or something?"

"Why didn't you tell me?"

" 'Cause you didn't give me a chance. You hung up on me, remember?"

For a moment, Will couldn't say anything. "All right. Forget about that. Park the cruiser."

Ray didn't move. "Macomber said to wait for him."

"Macomber? What's he got to do with it?"

"I called him."

Will could feel his blood pulsing at his temples. "You took the time to call him when you knew Laurie was in danger?"

"I've only got your word on that. Macomber told me to let him know anytime I felt you were trying to play cop."

Will almost pulled Ray through the open window. "You park this damn cruiser, Ray, or you're going to be one sorry bastard."

Ray killed the engine, got out, and stood in front of Will

with his thumbs hooked over his belt like he was ready to take him on.

Will calmed himself. "I'm going to say this once. I don't have time to tell you everything, but I'm asking you to trust me. I want you to go in the woods with me because I need your help. There's a good chance Hatcher's going to kill Laurie, if he hasn't already done it."

"Hatcher? You mean Brian Hatcher?"

"That's what I said."

Ray assumed his deer-in-the-headlights look. "What are you talking about?"

"Are you coming with me or not?"

"But I told Macomber—"

It was no use. Ray just didn't get it. Will suddenly snatched Ray's pistol from his holster. "If you're not going in with me, I'm going to need this."

Ray instinctively raised his hands and looked at him, his eyes wide. "Okay, okay. I'll go in with you."

Will handed him back his sidearm. "That shotgun still in the cruiser?"

"Jesus, Will. I can't let you have *that*."

Will ignored him and opened the driver's-side door and slid into the bucket seat. It was an aging Crown Vic about to be replaced, if voted in at the town meeting in March, by a much-needed all-wheel-drive Expedition.

Will reached above his head where a Remington Model 870 police shotgun was housed in a Pro-Gard universal mount attached to the interior of the roof. He pulled out the shotgun, careful not to disturb the computer between the bucket seats. He scrounged for shotshells in the glove compartment and shoved a handful into his jacket pocket.

Ray appeared at the car door. "At least let me get hold of Macomber."

"Be quick about it."

Ray called in over the radio. Macomber responded immediately he was en route and wanted to talk to Will.

"Where exactly on the Bog Brook Trail are you heading?" Macomber asked.

Will keyed the mike and described the area quickly but didn't wait around for any questions. He signed off and grabbed Ray by the arm. "You ready now?"

"We're still not waiting for Macomber?"

"No. You can if you want."

Ray stood frozen in indecision.

Will placed the Remington in the crook of his arm and walked past Ray to the trailhead. He soon heard Ray's voice behind him.

"Damn it, Will. Wait up."

Hatcher may have changed his clothes, but the footprints on the trail told Will he had on the same boots, and there was little doubt he was following Laurie in. Reading Hatcher's and Laurie's footprints in the mud was like playing a child's game of connect the dots, and Will doubted Macomber would have any trouble locating where they were headed.

Ray was all questions. "So, what do you mean Hatcher's going to kill Laurie?"

"For God's sake, Ray. Will you keep your voice down?"

The trail was wide enough for both men to walk shoulder to shoulder, and Ray whispered, "So, what do you mean Hatcher's going to—"

"I told you I can't explain it now."

"Even if we whisper?"

Will's response was to ignore him and accelerate his pace.

In a few more yards, Ray started puffing and soon fell behind. Will walked back to him and found him bent over, his hands on his knees.

"Slow down, will you?" Ray said.

Will looked at Ray's muddy shoes. He hadn't even thought enough ahead to wear boots. "Okay. This is what we're going to do. You keep up with me the best you can. Just follow my prints."

Ray's eyes widened. "You're not going to leave me alone out here, are you?"

"You'll be fine. You're my backup."

"I've been thinking . . . thinking we ought to switch," Ray said between breaths.

"Switch what?"

"Weapons." He pointed to the shotgun. "You ever fire that thing?"

"Not this particular one, no."

"Well, it's got a hell of a kick. It's rigged with a ghost-ring sight and a special Davis speed-feed magazine."

Will blinked at him, not sure he understood what he just heard. As much as he didn't respect Ray for his decision making and sloppy police work, his knowledge of firearms was impressive.

"Here, you can use my Sig." He handed Will the pistol butt end first, and Will gave him the shotgun and the extra shotshells.

Will looked at the pistol. "Your Sig?"

"Sig Sauer P220. It's a .45 caliber. A semiautomatic."

"I know that much."

"It's fully loaded. You've got nine rounds. If I'm going to be your backup, I prefer the shotgun."

"Okay. Thanks, Ray."

Will turned to leave, but Ray grabbed his arm. "And one more thing."

"What's that?"

"I didn't give you the Sig. You took it from me, and I followed you in with the shotgun. That's what happened, right?"

Will nodded. "Whatever works. Just make sure you cover *my* ass."

And with that, Will took off.

He felt lighter without the shotgun and cruised along the trail at a rapid pace. It took less than a half hour before he came upon the faint trail opening to his left that led to the abandoned camping area.

He waited a few minutes for Ray to make up the distance, but there was no sign of him. Will pushed in, his steps measured and quiet, the Sig pointed upward. He kept listening for voices, but the woods were deathly silent, no wind stirring.

He stopped. Above his head, he just caught the glint of the sun off a high-flying jet, its contrail streaming out behind it like cotton. The sky was blue but darkening. He suddenly heard Ray thrashing along to his rear, and he backtracked to meet up with him.

Will put his finger to his lips as soon as he saw him.

Ray stopped.

Will approached and whispered. "I'll take a line on an angle from here, and you just stay on trail until you reach what looks like a camping spot."

Ray nodded. The lack of questions and the concentration in Ray's face suggested he was finally getting it.

"And for God's sake, be quiet about it."

Both men moved in, communicating by hand signals.

Will paralleled the trail and tread through low-lying, wet vegetation that clung to his boots. Sapling branches periodically flicked at his face. As he moved steadily forward, the silence began to wear on him.

Where was Laurie?

Finally they reached the clearing, and Will held up his fist as a sign for Ray to stop.

Will surveyed the area. From his vantage, he could glimpse the fire ring, and farther to the left, the familiar boulder. He waited a full minute, but the only sound was a whispering of leaves when Ray shifted his weight.

Finally Will pointed to Ray, then held up his palm. He pointed to himself and made a walking motion with two fingers. Ray nodded.

In the clearing, Will looked around, but he could see nothing disturbing except lengthening shadows. But it didn't mean that Hatcher wasn't looking at *him*. He focused on the ground and soon came up with Laurie's footprints, followed a few yards back by Hatcher's. It didn't take long to process what they meant.

Laurie had probably heard Hatcher coming in and took off. Hatcher then came in to the clearing, saw her prints, and followed.

Will waved Ray ahead to join him. He explained what he had found.

"So, Laurie's running away from him?"

"Well, just look here." Will knelt and pointed up ahead. "You can see her stride lengthening." Will stood. "Let's stick together now. We don't need to split up."

"Fine with me."

Will led Ray in and followed the footprints to where the trail petered out to nothing, and saw, with horror, where Hatcher had finally caught up with Laurie. The ground was stirred up and branches broken off. It looked as if she had put up a struggle, but it didn't last long because she was so weak.

The footprints up ahead also didn't lie. Hatcher most likely had her around the waist and was forcing her forward. The erratic steps, the one shoe dragging, suggested she was having trouble staying upright.

Will pushed on, Ray dogging his heels, until he came to another small clearing where Laurie's halting footfalls suddenly vanished. *What the hell happened?*

Will surveyed that area and off to the left found Hatcher's again—but only his—and the deep impression in a muddy area offered the only explanation. Hatcher was carrying Laurie.

Why was he carrying her? Will imagined the worst.

Chapter 19

Will headed deeper into the woods with growing dread, puzzled about where Hatcher was leading them. There was nothing out here in this bog, and the footprints were clearly heading uphill to the north.

Will's only consolation was that he hadn't seen any blood where Hatcher and Laurie had struggled. He hoped that Laurie had simply collapsed, her energy spent, leaving Hatcher with no choice but to carry her. Of course, Hatcher could have strangled her or knocked her out, but Will pushed those possibilities to the back of his mind.

The woods grew thicker as Will and Ray made their way out of the low-lying briar and berry bushes and up a small rise, and it occurred to Will that Hatcher probably wasn't heading to any specific place, only seeking somewhere remote to kill Laurie and bury her.

They reached an area that opened up into a stand of mixed hardwoods, the forest floor drier underfoot. It was easier going, but the dropping sun was at such a low angle now that the bright rays blazed a broad band of yellow across the tops of the trees.

With the fading light at ground level, it was getting increasingly difficult to see.

Will put his hand up for Ray to stop.

"What is it?" Ray whispered from behind.

"Thought I heard something."

Both men stood, senses straining. Then, faintly, beyond a stand of poplars: "Put me down!"

Will's heart leaped at the sound of Laurie's voice.

"Shut up!"

Will knew immediately it was Hatcher responding and motioned with his head for them to continue on.

They moved in carefully. Laurie's arguing with Hatcher continued, effectively masking their approaching footfalls.

In a few yards, Will could make out Hatcher standing in another small clearing, but he couldn't see Laurie. By the way Hatcher's head was bent forward as he spoke to her, Will guessed she was sitting on the ground. He turned to Ray and whispered, "I'm going to circle around. You hold your position."

"I should get closer, too."

"You can't get a bead on him from here?"

"I could, but it would take one hell of a shot."

Will glanced up ahead. "Look, you can see Hatcher, right?"

"Right now, yes."

"And that big poplar he's standing in front of?"

"I guess so. I can't tell a poplar from a pine tree."

"It's the biggest tree there, Ray. I'm going to work my way to it, and as soon as you see me there, close in. If you have a clear shot, take him out."

Ray swallowed hard. "Okay."

"Remember—don't move until you see me."

Will sidled to his left, light on his feet, stepping in toe-heel fashion. While he appreciated Ray backing him up, he didn't trust his ability to move efficiently through the woods, and he hoped Ray would do what he was told.

Will chose a wide arc and skirted quickly through an area that afforded little cover, then gradually moved closer to Hatcher and ducked behind an earth berm.

He had a much better view and could see Laurie kneeling in front of Hatcher, her hands tied behind her. Her forced posture of submission wasn't lost on Will, and he had to control the urge to rush in. He could hear them talking. A few yards ahead of his position, he spied the large poplar he had singled out for Ray.

"I should have killed you the first time," Hatcher was saying.

Laurie craned her head upward. "I thought that's what you tried to do."

Hatcher moved closer and stood over her, his knees almost touching her face. "Oh, no. I'm a much better shot than that. If I had wanted to kill you, you'd be dead."

"But why wound me then?"

"You know why. I had to make sure you went after Carpenter. Pretty good plan actually. Until you and that boyfriend of yours screwed everything up."

"Listen, Hatcher," she said. "Let's just talk this out."

"There's nothing to say."

"But what did we screw up?"

"You really don't know, do you."

"Know what? What are you talking about?"

"Nothing. With Will out of the way, and now you—"

"What do you mean, 'Will out of the way?' "

"Let's just say he had a little accident. Like you're going to have." Hatcher suddenly raised his pistol and aimed it at Laurie's head.

Will reacted and sprang forward. He knew his action would immediately give away his position, but there was just no other choice. He hoped Ray was paying enough attention to adjust their original plan.

Laurie cried out, "Will!"

Hatcher whirled and fired in Will's direction. The bullets zipped over his head and one stung the ground near his feet. Will sought shelter behind a rock and returned fire.

The pistol leaped in his hand when he squeezed off one, then two more rounds.

Hatcher hit the ground and rolled toward Laurie.

Before Will could react, Hatcher jammed his pistol to Laurie's head and hauled her to her feet. "Drop the gun, Will."

Will hesitated, then raised his hands. He let the Sig fall to the ground.

"Now walk over here. Slowly."

Before Will moved into the clearing, hands raised, he took note of where he had dropped the pistol.

Hatcher watched Will closely as he approached, then broke into his irksome grin. "That's far enough." He kept his pistol pressed hard against Laurie's temple. "Well, aren't you something, Buchanan? Surviving that terrible fall."

Will didn't grace Hatcher's comment with a response. He faced Hatcher, but he was really looking past him, head-on to Ray's location, watching for any sign of movement. *Keep him talking.* "Look, Brian. You've got to give this up. You don't want to kill us."

"You're right. I don't."

"So, let us go."

"Now that *would* be nice. But I'm afraid both of you are in the way."

"Just like Samantha Rayley?"

"I don't know what you're talking about. Seems you've got me mixed up with Nelson Carpenter."

"That's not going to work anymore, Brian." *Where the hell are you, Ray?* Will imagined Ray had Hatcher zeroed in, just waiting for a moment when he had a clear shot.

Hatcher's eyes suddenly narrowed. "What are you looking at, Buchanan?"

"I'm looking at you, Brian."

"I don't think so." Hatcher's head snapped to the left. He suddenly spun Laurie around and used her as a shield, and as he did, a blast from Ray's shotgun shattered the silence and ripped into a tree just above Hatcher's head.

Hatcher immediately threw Laurie to the ground and let loose with his semiautomatic, firing indiscriminately toward Ray, who cried out. Ray's Remington 870 discharged again, the report echoing through the woods, but the shot sailed above their heads.

Before Hatcher could wheel back around, Will tore across the clearing and tackled him. Hatcher's pistol flew. "Run, Laurie. Get the hell out of here."

Will had no idea if she had heard him, because he was so busy trying to pin Hatcher to the ground. Will sat on him, grabbed him by the throat, and squeezed hard, but he found it difficult to maintain pressure because of the blow he had suffered to his shoulder tumbling down Diagonal Gully.

Hatcher's legs flopped and kicked wildly as he tore at Will's hands; then he managed, with all his manic shifting about, to gain enough leverage to flip Will over.

Will got back on his feet just in time to have Hatcher thrust into him with his shoulder and smash him backward against a tree. The force knocked the wind out of him, and Hatcher threw a punch into his gut for good measure.

Will doubled over and fell to the ground. When he finally got his legs under him again, he found Hatcher desperately searching for his pistol. He knew that if Hatcher found it, he didn't have a chance and suddenly remembered the Sig. He stumbled out to the edge of the clearing just as Hatcher spun around and fired wildly at him.

The bullets buzzed past his head as Will dropped to the ground. He crawled forward, located the Sig with little difficulty, and jerked back, expecting Hatcher to be on top of him, but to his surprise, he wasn't there.

Will hustled back to the clearing.

Hatcher had disappeared.

It was then Will heard Ray moaning, and he immediately surmised Hatcher had gone after Ray to grab his shotgun and finish the kill.

Will tore back through the woods in Ray's direction and found him sitting up leaning against a tree, grasping his thigh. Laurie was beside Ray, trying to calm him, her hands still roped behind her back.

Will dropped to his knees beside Laurie. "You okay?"

"Yes. Untie me."

Will found Laurie's lockback on her police-issue belt and flicked the blade open. It took no time for him to rip through the nylon p-cord that bound her.

"Thanks," she said, and rubbed her wrists. She hugged him tightly.

"Where's Hatcher?" Will asked.

Laurie released her hold and looked up at him. "I don't know. I thought he was after you."

"He must have just taken off."

Ray moaned again.

Will drew his attention to Ray's leg wound. He used Laurie's knife to rip his pant leg from cuff to thigh. He could see where the slug had entered just above the knee, and when he checked the back of Ray's leg, the exit wound was yawning, but it looked clean. "You're going to be okay, Ray."

Ray winced. "Hurts like a bastard."

"I bet. But you got lucky. The bullet missed the femoral artery."

"Yeah, I'm lucky. That's what I am."

Will cut off Ray's pants just below the knee and folded the material into a pad. He turned to Laurie. "Keep pressure on this." He stood up, then headed back to the clearing.

"Where are you going?" Laurie called out after him.

"After Hatcher."

Laurie caught up to him and grabbed his arm. "No. Don't. It isn't worth it."

"I can't just let him walk away."

"Will. For once in your life, just think! Hatcher's not going anywhere. It's getting dark. We've got him trapped."

Will hesitated. "That's not good enough. Not for what he's done to both of us."

She suddenly threw her arms around his waist and again held him tightly.

"Laurie, please."

She shoved him away. "Fine. Go. Get yourself killed."

"I *have* to do this."

"You don't have to, Will. Hatcher's not worth it." She

calmed herself and lowered her voice. "He's finished. Let the cops do their job."

Will started to leave, but she quickly moved in front of him, blocking his way. "I'll go with you then."

"You need to stay with Ray."

"Damn it, Will. I don't want to lose you."

Will smiled. "That's nice to know." He looked at her; then his gaze fell to her empty holster. "Just tell me one thing. What happened to your Smith & Wesson? Does Hatcher have that with him, too?"

"No. He threw it into the woods."

"Good." Will turned on his heels and headed toward the small clearing.

Will easily picked up Hatcher's footprints, but with light falling fast, he had more difficulty tracing them as he moved uphill through the woods. He tried not to think about Laurie, and he knew she was probably right—that he should consider himself lucky just to be alive right now.

But the impact of Hatcher's betrayal compelled Will to act without reason. He'd follow Hatcher to hell if he had to.

Will moved deeper into the woods, having to rely less on Hatcher's footprints because the darkness at ground level was so great. Instead, he concentrated on what he could see ahead of him, especially the snapped-off twigs at shoulder level as he continued to work his way uphill through a stand of pine.

Will picked his way across deadfall and dense growth, and his eyes began to adjust to the darkness, his night vision becoming more acute.

Periodically he would stop and listen. He figured he was still moving northwest, but with the sun gone now he couldn't be sure.

Then, off to his left, he saw a flash of light. It lasted a few seconds, then shut off. It had to be Hatcher.

Will waited. Hatcher's flashlight went on again, this time for a longer duration. Then off. Will doubted Hatcher suspected he was being followed, and that was the main reason he had ignored Laurie's appeal to stay put. He knew surprise would be on his side.

Will headed in the direction of the light, the stillness of the afternoon replaced by the soft whisper of the wind through the trees, helping to disguise his footfalls. He felt for the Sig in his guide jacket and pressed ahead.

The terrain led down through a small depression, sharply uphill, across a shelf, then into a gully. Suddenly the light went on again and stayed on. Will waited. He figured Hatcher felt safer down here out of a clear line of sight.

He slowly worked his way toward the light. He almost reached it when he sensed something wrong. Then, in a few more steps, he could see the flashlight wavering in the wind, suspended by a lanyard to a branch. It was a trap.

Before he could react, he felt something cold on the back of his neck. "Stay where you are," Hatcher said. "Get your hands in the air." He snatched the Sig out of Will's hands and grabbed the flashlight off the branch.

"Okay. You can turn around now." Hatcher aimed the flashlight at Will's eyes. "Like a moth to a flame."

Will didn't say anything.

"Well, I guess this is it, Will."

Will tried to make out Hatcher's face, but the flashlight was blinding him. He found his voice. "Doesn't have to be."

"You think I should just let you bring me in?"

"Why not?"

"I'm holding the gun."

"Why all this killing, Hatcher?"

"Why? Now that *is* a good question. But one you're going to take with you to the grave."

Hatcher's last remark forced a sense of urgency. What were Will's options? He didn't have any. He had to stall him. "Tell me about Samantha. And don't say it was Carpenter who killed her."

"Nothing to tell. She was in the way."

"Like Jeanne Conroy?"

Hatcher smirked. "Yeah. Especially her."

"How did this all start, Brian? What did Samantha know?"

"It's like I told you that day in the bar. Shit just happens."

"But you don't have to kill me, Brian. You don't have to add me to the list. You can still do something right."

"You're not begging, are you, Will?"

"Look. You may get away from me now, you can kill me, but people know where you are. It won't take much to find you out here."

"Which is why you have to shut up and die."

"You don't want to kill me. You said so yourself."

Hatcher wagged his gun at Will. "I kill because I have to."

"You're pathetic, Hatcher."

"Don't push me, Will."

"Pathetic."

Hatcher pointed the gun at Will's forehead. "On your knees."

Will slowly dropped to the ground.

Hatcher moved to his rear and forced his gun to the back of his head. "Final speech, Will?"

Will didn't respond. Not a chance. He closed his eyes, fully believing the last sound he would hear would be a pistol report. Would there be pain? He tried to think of something to say to Hatcher that would keep it from happening, but all he could think of was Laurie warning him not to go after Hatcher. She had been right. If he had listened to her, he could have been in her bed tonight.

Will suddenly felt weary of everything and wanted it to be over with. He felt Hatcher putting more pressure on the back of his skull with the muzzle of the pistol, and he dropped his head in response. Then, unexpectedly, the pressure released. He imagined Hatcher standing back, aiming.

The blast exploded in Will's ears, and he involuntarily fell forward. He lay there, his face on the ground, waiting to lose consciousness, but his senses seemed unusually sharp.

Then he heard, "Stay where you are, Hatcher." It took a moment to process, but he recognized Macomber's voice and understood immediately that the loud report had not come from Hatcher's gun but Macomber's, a warning shot that had torn into the trees above his head.

Will rolled away quickly and was just able to see Hatcher's shadowy figure stumble forward, his pistol drawn, still holding his flashlight in the other hand.

"Drop your weapon," Macomber ordered. He flicked on his Maglite and aimed it at Hatcher's face.

Hatcher raised his pistol, but it trembled in his hand.

Macomber responded with one quick burst, and Hatcher's pistol flew as he grabbed his leg, spun like a rag doll, toppled over, and hit the ground face-first. He rolled over and groaned.

Macomber walked slowly out of the woods, his pistol trained on Hatcher. Then he shined his light in Will's direction. "You okay?"

"Took you long enough."

Macomber shook his head. "You're one crazy bastard."

"I guess you ran into Laurie and Ray."

"Actually, I found them just as you were heading in to get Hatcher. I was right behind you."

"Lucky me."

"You could say that."

Will approached where Hatcher had fallen and retrieved the flashlight. He aimed the light on Hatcher's face. There was blood coming from the corner of his mouth. His eyes were still open and he was trying to say something. Will leaned closer to hear him.

"Finish it," Hatcher said. "Kill me."

Will looked up at Macomber, then back to Hatcher. "I don't think so."

As Will studied Hatcher's wounds, the flashlight caught something glinting on his jacket. Will knelt closer to see what it was and discovered the familiar circular pin, a gold compass rose with the heavy points of a Red Cross sticking out behind. In the center, the profile of the Old Man of the Mountain, and in the foreground, a raised hand holding an ice ax.

"You won't be needing this anymore," Will said, and ripped the pin off Hatcher's jacket.

Chapter 20

It took over three hours for emergency personnel to evacuate Hatcher and Deputy Ray Fleming and deliver them to Conway Memorial. They had lost a lot of blood, but it looked like they were both going to pull through.

Will was dead on his feet, but he knew he had to get to school and locate Celia before she found out secondhand what had happened to her father.

"I need you with me," he said to Laurie as soon as they made it back to the Bog Brook parking lot.

She didn't hesitate. "I'm there."

Will nodded and smiled faintly.

They left Laurie's Cherokee in the lot, and it was after eleven o'clock by the time Will drove his truck through the main gate at Saxton Mills School. They alerted the dorm parent, entered Celia's room, and found her in her nightgown, reading in bed.

Celia immediately sensed trouble. "What's wrong?"

"It's your father," Will said. "I'm sorry. He's been shot." As soon as he said it, he realized he probably could have soft-pedaled the news better, but how else to spin it?

Celia got out of bed. "Is he okay? He's not dead, is he?"

Will walked closer to her. "No. I guess he's in surgery now. It's pretty serious."

Celia suddenly broke down. Will reached out and hugged her as she cried, her head against his chest. Laurie stood close to them and quietly stroked Celia's back.

"I wanted to be the one who told you," Will said.

Celia recovered, released her hold, and looked up at Will. "Can I see him? Will you take me there?"

"I don't think he'll be having visitors right away."

"But how did it happen?"

Laurie and Will exchanged glances; then Laurie said gently, "We have to explain a few things to you, Celia. We think you should go home with us tonight. Let's get you dressed and pack a few things." She glanced up at Will, and he got the message to get out of the room. He waited for them in the hall.

At Will's house, they talked until three o'clock in the morning. Will explained as best he could what they knew, but the news that her father was a man who had killed several times was something Celia just couldn't accept. Will hadn't even mentioned that her father had also tried to kill *him*.

Finally Celia dropped off to sleep on the couch, her head resting on Laurie's shoulder. Laurie whispered to Will, "Go to bed."

Will didn't have to be told twice.

When Will finally woke, the clock read 3:20. For a second he thought he hadn't slept at all, but then it occurred to him, by the light coming through the bedroom window, that it was late afternoon on Monday. He had slept twelve hours.

He lay in bed, staring upward at the ceiling. He wondered absently why his gut ached, and then he realized how hungry he was. He threw his legs over the side of the bed and got to his feet but immediately fell back on the pillows. He'd have to take it slower than that.

He tried it again, and this time sat on the edge of the bed for a few moments and took stock. He checked his toes. There were a few white spots, but he had definitely escaped severe frostbite. He rubbed the back of his neck where Hatcher had so rudely shoved the point of his pistol and once again stood up. His legs felt cramped, and he had to walk stiff-legged to the kitchen.

He put on some coffee, found a carton with eight eggs left, broke them all into a bowl, and scrambled them. He made six pieces of toast. He sat quietly at the kitchen table, relishing each bite, and it was only after he had finished eating that he thought at all about Celia and Laurie. He figured Laurie, despite her ordeal, must be at the station doing paperwork, but where was Celia?

He left the dirty dishes in the sink and headed back upstairs to the bathroom to shower. With the first burst of hot water, his toes stung, but he stayed in a long time, gradually feeling his muscles relax.

When Will finally stepped out, he was startled to find Laurie waiting for him with a towel. "What are you trying to do? Scare me to death?"

She stared at him, still holding the towel. "Look at those bruises on your chest, Will. You sure nothing's broken?"

"Are you going to give me that towel or must I suffer hypothermia right here in the bathroom?"

She threw the towel at him. "Long suffering, Will. You have such a flair for the dramatic."

Will dried his shoulders, then wrapped the towel around his waist. "Where's Celia?"

"At a friend's house."

"Couldn't stand us, eh?"

"There's really no place for her here, Will."

"Who's she staying with?"

"Jennie Franks."

Will nodded. Jennie was a good kid, a day student on Celia's soccer team, and he recalled how well they played together as a defensive pair. Her parents were thoughtful and caring. It would be a good place for Celia.

"She didn't go to school today, did she?"

"No." Laurie paused. "It's going to take a while, Will."

Will toweled off and went back into the bedroom. "School," he said. "I wonder what that is." He put on a clean pair of boxers and crawled back into bed.

"What are you doing?" Laurie asked.

"What do you mean, what am I doing? I'm going back to sleep." He lay his head slowly back on the pillow.

"Oh."

He propped himself up on his elbows. "Okay, what is it, Laurie?"

"Nothing. If you need more sleep, then go ahead."

"Oh, right. I'm really going to be able to sleep now."

Laurie sat on the edge of the bed. "Macomber and the Major Crime Unit found a body buried near that boulder."

Will wasn't surprised. "They know who it is?"

"Not for sure—not yet, anyway. But they figure it's been there for a while." Laurie paused. "It's female. Macomber thinks it's Hatcher's wife."

"What? Wait a minute. Wasn't she supposed to have been kidnapped?"

"That's right."

"And wasn't Hatcher cleared? Didn't he have an alibi?"

"That's right, too."

Will, tired of being on his elbows, sat up next to Laurie on the bed. "So who killed her then?"

"We're hoping Hatcher will tell us."

Will humphed. "Yeah, right. Fat chance."

"No. He says he wants to tell us everything."

"So, go talk to him."

"He has one condition."

"And what's that?"

"He'll only talk to you."

That evening Will identified himself at the nurse's station at Conway Memorial. Hatcher's instructions were for Will to come alone.

He walked down a narrow hallway. Hatcher had a private room isolated from other patients with an armed rent-a-cop sitting in a chair outside his door.

Will greeted him. "How you doing?"

The man, with a full head of silver hair pushed straight back, got up. "Oh, you must be Will Buchanan." He reached out his hand for Will to shake. "I've been expecting you. I'm Ezra Poole."

Will squeezed his hand. "Hatcher awake?"

"He was the last time I looked." Poole studied him. "You're not carrying any weapons, are you?"

"Just this." Will showed him a small digital tape recorder Laurie had insisted he carry.

Poole smiled and winked. "Try not to hurt him with that."

Will hesitated at the door. Now that he was actually here, he wasn't sure he wanted to talk to Hatcher. After all that had happened, he didn't feel up to listening to any flimsy explanations.

When he finally stepped into the room, he found Hatcher sitting up in bed, his injured leg elevated, IV drip pinned into the back of his hand.

Hatcher spoke first. "Grab a chair, Will. I appreciate you coming in."

Will heard the nonchalance in his voice and felt the hairs on his neck stand up. Hatcher was acting as if nothing had happened between them. "It's not my choice to be here."

"And I don't blame you. I'd feel the same way."

Will studied him a moment. Hatcher's color had definitely improved, and if Will hadn't known he'd been shot, he would think he was chatting with him in a bar somewhere. "Before you say anything, I wanted you to know I'm going to tape this." Will pulled out the recorder and placed it on the nightstand.

Hatcher paused. "Then you might as well leave now. What I have to say is between us."

"I don't get it. What's so special that it's only for my ears?"

"Because you were once my friend. If anyone can understand what happened, it's you."

"So, now you want my understanding."

"I just want you to listen to me. You can judge me if you want when I'm finished."

Will took a moment to decide, then pocketed the small recorder. "Okay, talk. But you have to know that I'm going to be reporting whatever you say."

"Fine. Do what you want."

Will thought he understood why Hatcher was so touchy about the recording. He didn't want to leave behind anything permanent that might be used against him in the future. It would be Will's word against his.

"I'll start from the beginning, like you wanted," Hatcher said.

"Like I wanted?"

"You remember yesterday when you asked me what started it all?"

"I do."

"Samantha Rayley started it all."

"Your lover."

Hatcher lay back. He rested the back of his free hand on his forehead. "I had an affair with her. Got her pregnant. She wanted me to leave my wife, Tara. I told her it would never happen."

"And you broke it off."

"I tried to, but Samantha was determined. She was out of control. She told Tara everything. Tara was filing for divorce, and I couldn't let that happen."

"So, you killed her."

Hatcher suddenly sat up. "I had to, don't you see? If it had just been Tara and me, then it would have been different. I could have divorced her and married Samantha. But Celia was just born, and I couldn't lose my child. I just couldn't."

Will tried to put himself in Hatcher's position. Is it possible he could love his little girl so much that he would kill his own wife to keep her?

"Tara and I weren't getting along anyway. In fact, I really started to hate her long before my fling with Samantha. Our marriage was coming apart, and I know for a fact Tara was sleeping around."

Will wondered about that. It sounded too much of a stretch to justify his actions. "How did you do it, Brian?"

"I went off on a fishing trip with a buddy for the weekend. It was at a lake not too far from here. We were drinking pretty heavily—at least I gave him the impression I was pounding them back—but I spiked one of his beers with sleeping pills.

"Then I went back home and strangled Tara in our bed and buried her off the Bog Brook Trail. By the time I got back to my buddy, he was still asleep and had no clue I had left."

Hatcher said this so matter-of-factly that it had the effect of making the crime even more chilling.

"Wait a minute. That was a bit too fast. Where was baby Celia while you were doing all this?"

"She was with me."

"You brought your little child along with you to bury your wife? With her body in the truck?"

"No. Not in the truck. In her car. Tara was up front with me. Celia was sleeping in the back."

Will had difficulty accepting the image Hatcher was painting.

"You see," Hatcher continued, "I had to make it look like there was some kind of foul play, like Tara had been kidnapped. You know, blood on the seats and all that."

"I thought you said you strangled her."

"I did. But I had to knife her a few times to make it look good."

Hatcher's expressionless statement about the knifing made Will's stomach clench and he almost had to leave the room.

Hatcher looked away from him. "And then I just left the car with baby Celia in it on Route 16."

"And you weren't worried about your child?"

"Naw. I knew the car would be found pretty fast." He paused. "But there was one thing I didn't know. Samantha Rayley had seen me carry Tara's body out of the house and followed me."

"What was she doing at your house? Wasn't this late at night?"

"She'd been stalking me. I told you she was out of control. But I had no idea she had seen me do it until this past summer."

"And that's when she showed you the photographs where you had buried your wife."

Hatcher looked off into the distance. "She kept that secret all those years. She told me she had been too scared to say anything at first, but when Ben got ill, she was desperate to save him. The only thing that mattered in her life was our son, Ben."

Hatcher considered Ben *his* son despite everything that had happened? Will couldn't believe what he just heard.

"And you know, I can understand where she was coming from, because of what I feel about Celia." He looked over directly at Will. "But I had no money to give her to pay for Ben's medical expenses. She didn't believe me and threatened to show the cops exactly where I had buried Tara if I didn't give her cash."

Will wasn't sure he believed him, either. "So, you had to kill her."

"Fourteen years, Will. Fourteen years and she shows up on my doorstep demanding hush money."

Will suddenly recalled the day he found Samantha's body.

"What about the other woman, Jeanne Conroy. Did you *have* to kill her, too?"

"Yes, that was unfortunate. She just got in the way."

"She was collateral damage?"

Hatcher studied Will a moment. "I guess you could say that, yes. I mean, it was simply her bad luck coming on me just as I had knifed Samantha." He shook his head. "Sometimes you think you've got it all planned out and some crazy thing happens you don't expect."

It was as if Hatcher were detached from himself, describing so calmly how someone else was responsible. Will couldn't stand listening to him talk so casually about killing any longer and shifted the conversation. "Which leads us to Nelson Carpenter."

Hatcher's impish grin began to play on his lips. "Yes, poor Nelson. I guess I really did a number on him."

"So, he had nothing to do with any of this?"

"That's right. It was actually pretty easy. You see, I knew Samantha had slept with Nelson that summer she first came here and that people in the town would probably remember it. I mean, everyone knew about them. That was the connection I had to make."

"So, it was you who shot Laurie."

"I had to."

"What do you mean you had to? You could have framed Carpenter without shooting her."

Hatcher shook his head. "You just don't understand, do you? Once I figured how to use Carpenter as a scapegoat, I had to drive it home. I mean, I had you going, didn't I?"

Will didn't respond. It was useless trying to reason with Hatcher. Will suddenly thought of Carpenter, how he had been wrong about him. He would have to somehow make it up to him. Then Will remembered something else. "What about the drugs? Nelson's also not the big pusher you made him out to be?"

"Nelson is innocent of everything."

"So, where did the drugs come from?"

This time Hatcher was silent, and Will read his lack of response to mean that *he* was the one who had been the dealer he had purported to hate with a passion. Will thought he understood better how upset Hatcher had been with his discovery of Celia's alleged using, caught as she was in a web of her own father's making.

"So, is it true that Celia was into pot or did you just make that up?"

"No. That was true." Hatcher had a faraway look in his eyes. "I tell you, I never suspected she would get into that stuff, but I guess you never know." He turned toward Will and attempted a smile.

"So, Celia lied to me about her smoking on campus?"

"I don't think so, Will. That night I spoke to you on Family Weekend, I was only trying to plant the idea that Celia had a problem with drugs. When we saw Carpenter at the Burger and Brew after the evacuation at Cathedral Ledge, I really pushed it that he was the dealer."

"Unfortunately, you also set up your daughter in the process."

"She was smoking with those losers over the summer, Will. That part I didn't make up."

"Then what makes you so sure she wasn't smoking at school?"

Hatcher sighed. "Look, I'll tell you what she told me. She

said she was just walking on that path to Rusher Hall when the girls called out to her. She went to talk with them when that teacher ran by. She said she didn't smoke, and I believe her."

Will tried once more to imagine the scene with Martin Brodsky jogging by. He supposed there was a possibility that Brodsky had jumped to conclusions, especially given how far the girls were away from him, and perhaps Celia really was a victim here, caught innocently in the "knowing presence."

Hatcher's smile faded. "Don't be too rough on her, Will. She's a good kid."

Will had no response.

Hatcher looked away from Will again. "You know, I often think that none of this would have happened if I had been your partner that day when that boy went missing. If you hadn't found Samantha's body, then I'd be home free."

"So, this is my fault?"

Hatcher shook his head. "It's nobody's fault. Shit just happens."

Could Hatcher really believe that no one was at fault? It was too much to take. "So, why did you want to tell *me* all this?"

"I thought you should know the truth. I thought maybe you could be the one to explain it all to Celia."

Will shook his head. "I don't know how I'm going to do that."

"Oh, but you can do it. I know you can. You're good with her."

Will suddenly felt very dirty just being in his presence. He stood up. "Are we through?"

"Just one more thing. I want you to know I'm glad you didn't die at Huntington. I'm sorry now I tried to kill you."

Hearing Hatcher's attempt at apology pushed him over the edge. Will shoved the chair back to the wall so hard it punctured the sheetrock.

"I know you probably think what I just said is a bunch of bullshit, Will. But I really do like you and—"

"Shut up, Hatcher."

"I'm only trying to—"

"I said, shut up!"

Will headed out the door.

Seconds later, as Will walked down the hall to visit Ray, he heard a gunshot coming from the direction of Hatcher's room. He raced back and found Hatcher in front of the open doorway to his room, leaning on one crutch, brandishing Ezra's pistol.

Ezra was on his knees, his scrawny hands raised in the air.

Will quickly assessed the scene. Two nurses huddled together behind a counter, and Ezra looked like the only one in immediate danger. But it was clear Ezra hadn't been shot, and Will reasoned the pistol must have discharged when both men struggled. "Don't do this, Brian."

Hatcher looked up and smiled. "You came back, Will. Did you miss me?"

"Put the gun down. It's not worth it."

Hatcher's smile faded. "Better call 911, Will." He grabbed Ezra roughly by the shirt and pulled him to his feet. "This is serious business. We've got a hostage situation here."

"Let him go, Brian."

"I'm not going to hurt him. I just need to borrow him."

"Take me instead."

Hatcher thought about it and shrugged. "I guess it doesn't matter who I get to go with me." Hatcher released his hold on Ezra and patted him on the shoulder. "Thanks for the pistol." He grabbed his crutch and limped toward Will. "Nice of you to volunteer."

Both men made their way slowly down the hall, and out of the corner of his eye Will could see one of the nurses reaching for a phone.

"You'll never get out of here, Hatcher."

"Maybe not. Stranger things have happened, though."

"But even if you escape from the hospital, where will you go?"

"Let's get that far. Then we'll think about it."

Hatcher's eyes suddenly rolled, and he grasped the hall railing to steady himself. Will saw his opportunity and tried to yank the pistol out of his hand, but Hatcher shoved the muzzle into his neck. "Don't." He caught his breath. "Just don't!" He pulled the pistol back. "Walk in front of me."

As they made their way down the hall, Hatcher said, "I meant it about Celia. I want you to tell her everything. She has to know that I loved her so much I couldn't let anyone take her away. Not even her mother."

Will turned away from him.

"Look at me, damn it, Will! I want you to tell Celia I love her!"

There was an odd tremor in Hatcher's voice that made Will involuntarily look back at him, and he was startled to find tears. Will had never seen anything resembling emotion from the man before.

Hatcher grabbed him by the coat sleeve. "Tell her!"

Will looked up at him. "All right, Brian," he said calmly. "I'll tell her."

Hatcher released his hold.

They made it to the front entrance, and Will pushed through the outside door, Hatcher on his heels.

Hatcher stood on the stoop, breathing in the cool, biting air. "Ah, Will. You and I know the beauty of just being out here. You can taste the air."

Will saw him shivering. "Brian, you don't even have a coat on."

"Don't need one." He breathed deeply again.

"So, do you want me to get my car?"

"In a minute, Will. Let's just stay and enjoy the moment."

Soon the first Conway cruiser arrived and came to an abrupt stop in the parking lot, blue lights flickering. As the officer took a position behind the front fender of his vehicle, another car pulled in.

Will watched the force gathering. "Brian, you don't have a chance."

Hatcher didn't respond. He breathed deeply again and exhaled a mist of condensation. When the next cruiser came screeching in, he said, "Okay, I guess there's enough of them now. I'm ready to go."

"Go? Where the hell are you going?" As soon as he said it, Will guessed what Hatcher was up to. "No, Brian. Don't."

"You're going to walk in front of me for a little bit, and if you do what I say, you won't get hurt."

"This is crazy."

Hatcher grabbed him by the shirt again. "Listen to me. Just listen. We've got to make this look good." He leaned close to Will's face and whispered, "You know I can't go to jail. I wouldn't last one day in a cell." He let go of Will's shirt. He pleaded with him, "You've got to help me out here."

Will hesitated, then realized there was no reason to fight him. This would be an act of mercy.

"Put your hands in the air and start walking. I'm right behind you. When I tell you, just drop to the ground."

Will started to say something, but he couldn't find the words. He walked dead ahead, the dancing emergency lights blinding him.

Then a bullhorn squelched. "That's far enough, Hatcher."

Hatcher suddenly shoved Will and said, "Now!"

Will dropped to the ground and placed his hands over his head.

Hatcher fired indiscriminately at the blue lights, and a fusillade of bullets answered.

Will turned his head in time to see Hatcher's body twitch as the bullets ripped into him. His pistol dropped to his side, but he still held on to the weapon as he staggered forward and collapsed.

Will and Laurie lay in bed later that evening, talking. Sleep was impossible.

"I should have known Hatcher would do something like that," Will said. "Suicide by cop."

"How could you know?"

"His claustrophobia. You should have seen him that night at Celia's trial. I should have expected it . . ."

"I don't know why you're beating yourself up about this. Hatcher made his own choices."

"Did he?"

"Of course he did."

"Laurie, listen. You know how a sickness can rule a person's life. Your sister Candace is just now able to get out of the house after years of agoraphobia."

"It doesn't excuse anything."

"I'm not trying to excuse Hatcher's actions. I'm trying to understand them. Hatcher told me in that hospital room I could judge him after I heard his story, but I don't think I can."

"I don't get it, Will. What's to understand? The man was a killer."

"I just think there were reasons. I never realized until tonight how much he loved his daughter."

"But, Will, he killed his own wife to keep her."

"I know. I know. It's really sick. But I'm pretty sure that if Samantha Rayley hadn't come back to demand money, then Hatcher would have gone on with his life without killing anyone else. He didn't want to murder Jeanne Conroy. She got in the way. He didn't want to concoct the scheme to implicate Carpenter. He didn't want to kill me."

"And I suppose he didn't want to shoot me, either?"

"He was driven by his phobia, a force larger than himself. Jail time was never an option. It was self-preservation at all costs."

"I thought he was driven by the love of his daughter."

"It was both." Will turned and faced her. "Look, don't get me wrong. Hatcher deserved what he got. There's no excuse for what he did. All I'm saying is that I think I understand better why he did it. That's all I'm saying."

Laurie took a moment before responding. "How can you be so sympathetic about a man who almost killed you."

"He also saved my life. Remember Cathedral Ledge? I once considered him a friend."

"Are you sure he wasn't trying to kill you then?"

"What? No." But Will thought about it more. Hatcher could have rigged it so that if Will did slip, he would be sure to lose his protection. But it would have been a difficult accident to plan. "I don't think he was out to get me then. In fact, it's more likely he wanted me to think he was my friend to take any suspicion away from him."

"Well, he wasn't so nice to me."

"I asked him about that, you know. Why he shot you."

"And what did he say?"

"He said he had to. I mean, I don't get it. He really didn't have to."

"Oh, I think he did, but not for reasons you might suspect. What you're missing here is that Hatcher was a psychopath. He was not like you or me. He got a tremendous thrill from killing, and I wouldn't be surprised if there were others that we don't know about. He had no remorse, no conscience. He didn't need a reason."

"But didn't he say he was only trying to wound you?"

"And I don't believe him for a minute. He was just explaining away his inability to shoot straight. He was trying to kill me, all right."

"So, I should stop trying to understand him?"

"You can try, but thank God you'll never be able to."

Both lay quietly. Finally Laurie said, "So, what happens with Celia now?"

"I'm hoping she can stay with Jennie Franks for a while. Then college next year, I guess. I really have to be her adviser now. Hatcher wanted me to tell her everything. But I really don't know what to say." He paused. "It's too bad she couldn't live with us."

"Not the way things are."

Will sat up. "How are things, anyway?"

It took a few seconds for Laurie to respond. "I've decided to go back to my place in the morning."

"Why?"

"I think it's better that way."

"You're mad at me about something, aren't you?"

"No. Not mad. Just upset. And I think more realistic."

"About what?"

"Us."

"Come on. Tell me what you're thinking. You can't just lie there and say nothing."

"Okay. You remember in the woods I was practically begging you not to go after Hatcher by yourself?"

"I remember."

"Well, it all suddenly became clear exactly where I stand with you. At that moment, I was holding on to you, literally, desperate to keep you from killing yourself, and you just ignored me, wouldn't even listen."

"I had to go after him, Laurie."

"No, you didn't. You knew Macomber was coming right in behind you. You could have waited for him, but you just had to chase after Hatcher on your own."

Will started to mount a defense, but she cut him off.

"No. Don't say anything. I want to stay mad at you."

So she is mad.

"We'll still see each other, have our 'arrangement' as you like to call it, but I think I need time for myself. It's been great living here with you these past few weeks, and I thought we were really getting along well. I appreciate your taking care of me and all that, but I just . . . damn it, Will. Sometimes you just make me so angry!"

Will knew arguing wouldn't help. He rolled over.

Soon Laurie fell asleep, but Will stayed awake most of the night. He ran over all that she had said and thought he could understand how she felt.

But he couldn't just let her walk out of the house with that being the final word. He had to do something. According to the clock, it was 5:23 when he got out of bed.

Will made coffee and sat at the kitchen table.

Laurie came down about seven o'clock, carrying a day pack full of clothes. "You're still here?" she asked. "I thought you'd have left for school by now."

"I don't have a first-period class. Want some coffee?"

"No. I'm in a hurry."

"Come on, Laurie. You can't be in that much of a hurry. Just have one cup with me."

"I really have to rush."

"You have to rush because you can't wait to run away from here. That's the only reason."

"I have to get to work."

Will singsonged, "Little Liar Laurie."

She placed her hands on her hips. "All right. I'll have one cup of coffee. And I'm not running away from anything."

Will got up from the table, went to the kitchen counter, and poured her a cup. "Are too."

"I told you last night why I think we should live apart."

He handed her the cup. "I remember what you said, Laurie, and I still think you're a little liar."

She stared at him and didn't take the cup at first. "Stop calling me that."

He shoved the cup closer, and she finally took it. "Now sit down, and I'll tell you why."

Laurie hesitated. "Better make it quick."

"I know. You're in a hurry."

At the table, Will looked across at her. "You have to take at least one sip," he said.

"Just say your piece, cowboy."

"You're a little liar because you're using my actions as an excuse to leave me. If it hadn't been my going after Hatcher, it would have been something else. The truth is that commitment scares you to death and you look for any reason to avoid it. That's the truth, and that's why you're a little liar."

"Are you finished?"

"No. I also want you to know something else."

"What's that?"

Will got up from the table and went to her side. He reached his hand out to her.

She looked at it a moment, then reluctantly took it in hers. He pulled her up toward him, threw his arms around her, and kissed her hard on the lips. After a few moments, he released her.

"Are you finished now?" she asked.

"For the time being."

She straightened her blouse. "I'm still mad at you."

"But you still love me."

"I think I should go now."

"Say it."

"All right. I still love you."

Will smiled. "There. Now that wasn't so hard." He walked back and resumed his seat at the kitchen table. "Well, have a good day."

She stared at him a moment. "Okay. You have a good day, too." She headed toward the door. "What's going on, Will?"

"What do you mean?"

"You're up to something. I can tell."

Will lifted his mug. "You'd better get going. You're in a hurry, remember?"

She took tentative steps toward the door, opened it, turned, and shook her head. She finally exited.

Will waited, sipping his coffee.

In a few minutes, Laurie threw open the door again and stormed back into the kitchen. "Will Buchanan, what have you done to my car?"

Will got up from his chair. "What do you mean? What's the matter?"

She approached and smacked him on the arm. "Don't play games with me. You've done something to it."

"How could you say such a thing?"

"Don't lie to me. You . . . you . . . little liar, Willy."

Will reached under the kitchen table. He pulled out her car battery and chunked it on the counter. "This poor thing is dead as a doornail. It'll take at least a day to recharge."

She looked at the battery. "I don't believe you."

Will smiled. "Good." He grabbed her around the waist. "Because I *am* lying."

She fought against his embrace, but Will held on until she stopped squirming. He kissed her again.

It took a few moments for Laurie to push him away. She smiled, wryly. "What gives you the right to monkey with my car like that?"

Will pulled her close again and said softly, "I don't know what you're so upset about, Penelope. You're the one who gave me the idea."